Memphis Mojo

Memphis Mojo

Gerald Duff

LAMAR UNIVERSITY press

This book is a work of fiction. Names, characters, places, and incidents are either products of the author's imagination or are used fictitiously. Any resemblance to actual events or locales or persons, living or dead, is wholly coincidental.

A portion of this novel has appeared earlier in different form in *Sleet Magazine*.

ISBN: 978-0-9911074-2-1
Library of Congress Control Number: 2014932379
Manufactured in the United States of America

Cover Photo: "Beale Street Rain" by Frank Ficalora
Cover Design: Anne Meltzer
Book Design: Amy Morgan

Lamar University Press
Beaumont, Texas

*For Dicia Jane and Jeff Putnam
who should have lived in Memphis*

Books from Lamar University Press

Jean Andrews, *High Tides, Low Tides: the Story of Leroy Colombo*
Alan Berecka, *With Our Baggage*
David Bowles, *Flower, Song, Dance: Aztec and Mayan Poetry*
Jerry Bradley, *Crownfeathers and Effigies*
Robert Murry Davis, *An Academic Life*
Jeffrey DeLotto, *Voices Writ in Sand*
Mimi Ferebee, *Wildfires and Atmospheric Memories*
Ken Hada, *Margaritas and Redfish*
Michelle Hartman, *Disenchanted and Disgruntled*
Gretchen Johnson, *The Joy of Deception and Other Stories*
Lynn Hoggard, *Motherland, Stories and Poems from Louisiana*
Dominique Inge, *A Garden on the Brazos*
Tom Mack and Andrew Geyer, eds, *A Shared Voice*
Janet McCann, *The Crone at the Casino*
Erin Murphy, *Ancilla*
Dave Oliphant, *The Pilgrimage, Selected Poems: 1962-2012*
Harold Raley, *Louisiana Rogue*
Carol Coffee Reposa, *Underground Musicians*
Jan Seale, *Appearances*
Jan Seale, *The Parkinson Poems*

www.LamarUniversityPress.Org

Other books by Gerald Duff

Fiction
Decoration Day and Other Stories
Dirty Rice: A Season in the Evangeline League
Blue Sabine
Fire Ants and Other Stories
Coasters
Snake Song
Memphis Ribs
That's All Right, Mama: The Unauthorized Life of Elvis's Twin
Graveyard Working
Indian Giver
Poetry
Calling Collect
A Ceremony of Light
Nonfiction
Fugitive Days
Home Truths: A Deep East Texas Memory
Letters of William Cobbett
William Cobbett and the Politics of Earth

"I got my mojo working, but it just don't seem to work on you."
—Muddy Waters

1

Memphis, three in the morning in the House of Pancakes on Union Avenue, and all of them wanted to talk about the job, about the home invasion deal with the preacher's house, all but Earl Winston. Earl was complaining again about what had happened to him in his sophomore year in high school, the time he was a starting end for the Memphis Central High Warriors.

Tonto Batiste was looking right at him as Earl talked, but everybody knew you couldn't tell when Tonto was listening to somebody or when he wasn't, no matter how close he might seem to be paying attention. That came from the eyes, the way the pupil merged right into the dark iris surrounding it, and the fact that he hardly ever blinked enough for anybody to notice. He would narrow his lids in broad daylight, though. Not even a full-blooded Cherokee could stare straight into the Memphis sun without flinching a little.

"I wasn't but fifteen years old," Earl Winston said in Tonto's direction and then looked around the table to see if the other two men were meeting his gaze. Neither was, but Coy Bridges did make a grunting sound to show he was hearing something. Bob Ferry kept his head down, tending to his breakfast, eggs scrambled just this side of too dry, so much so that he was having to chew each mouthful longer than he really wanted to. Why couldn't they ever get that right?

"Fifteen, and I didn't weigh no more than a hundred and fifty seven pounds in pads and cleats," Earl Winston said.

Nobody said anything, and in a minute or so, Earl Winston went on. "And you know what?" he said. "You know what else?"

"What?" Bob Ferry said.

"I'll tell you what. No team ever ran but the one play around my end that whole half season I played for Central."

"Why was that?" Bob Ferry said. "What would make them avoid you that way?"

"They felt sorry for him," Coy Bridges said. "The way Earl fell down that first end-run at him and started squalling and all."

"Tell us why," Tonto Batiste said, still looking into Earl Winston's eyes. "Why wouldn't they come at you again there all by yourself?"

"The way I did that ball carrier," Earl Winston said, "first time I got a hold of him. How I'd get my hand down there in his helmet and pull at his face."

"You couldn't do that no more," Tonto said. "Face masks cover everything up these days. They have got away from that single-bar arrangement."

"Another thing," Tonto went on, "I reckon that was all-white teams back then. You try that shit these days, and one of the brothers would show you your liver."

"The coach tried to keep me when I told him the old man was fixing to haul all of us out of school and move the whole damn family to the piney woods."

"Away from Memphis?" Bob Ferry said. "Where to? Mississippi?"

"Linden, Tennessee."

"Never heard of it," Bob Ferry said.

"Exactly," Earl Winston said. "That's why I never got no damn show with my football."

"They got football at Linden," Tonto said. "Eleven-man, too. That places's not that far from Nashville. Why didn't you play football at Linden?"

"I did," Earl Winston said. "Fullback till I quit school. But, hell, they was just in the C classification. Played towns like Bells, Tennessee."

"Never heard of that, either," Bob Ferry said.

"That's the point, Bob," Earl Winston said and pushed his plate of pancakes away from him. "If I could've stayed at Memphis Central I'd been recruited to play in the SEC."

"Your old man said no to the coach, then," Tonto said.

"Yeah, the sorry old drunk," Earl Winston said. "He made me move with the rest of them way out there in them damn woods."

"They let you carry the ball at Linden, though, you said," Bob Ferry said.

"A defensive end at Central in them days was worth a whole truck-load of backs anywhere else," Earl Winston said. "That's back when the

Warriors was the stud horses."

"But you didn't get to stay at Central," Tonto said. "And defend that Warrior line."

"That's right, Tonto," Earl Winston said. "And that's why instead of me going on to play in the SEC and maybe go pro, I'm sitting here in a damn House of Pancakes in Memphis with y'all trying to figure out the best way to get all that rich preacher's money."

"You could've been that rich preacher," Coy Bridges said. "That's what you're telling us. You could've been the one we're fixing to take all that money away from, I suppose you mean, if you'd a been able to stay in Memphis. You'd have been somebody money would come to."

"Yeah," Earl Winston said. "That's what always galls me."

"Money don't come to you," Tonto said. "You go to it."

* * *

Across the House of Pancakes dining area, Detective Sergeant J.W. Ragsdale addressed his plate, knowing his partner was going to ask about the bacon. Tyrone Walker would not miss the chance to remark on what J.W. had ordered as a side to his scrambled eggs and was now contemplating before him.

A wisp of steam arose from the mound of grits situated at two o'clock on J.W.'s plate, but that was nothing to compare visually to the sheen of grease coating the three strips of bacon. The slices shone as though they'd been varnished.

"All right, Tyrone," J.W. Ragsdale said, "let's hear it, so I can get started on my breakfast."

"Hear what?" Tyrone Walker said, "What're you talking about?" He sipped at his cup of tea, rattled a spoon against the bowl of chopped fruit before him, and directed his gaze straight into J.W.'s eyes. "What?"

"Tell me about the bacon," J.W. said. "Let's hear the damn news about Mr. Hog."

"Oh, I suppose you mean about the nitrites," Tyrone said, laughing in the manner of a scientist who'd just made a breakthrough in the understanding of a problem long plaguing mankind. "You're referring to its effect on blood pressure and heart function, not to mention weight

3

control. I bet that's what you're wondering about bacon and its consumption by middle-aged Caucasian males."

"Thanks, Tyrone," J.W. said, reaching for the outside slice of bacon on his plate, the one with a portion of rind still attached, "for getting me going. Hearing you say that is just like listening for the starter's gun right before the low hurdles. Turn me loose and let me catch my foot on something I'm trying to jump over."

"I said Caucasian, J.W.," Tyrone went on, "to distinguish between the effect of bacon on a white man like you and an African-American like myself. Not that there's really such a thing as race to be recognized, of course."

"There's not? Why you look the way you do, then, and me the way I do? Damn, this is good bacon."

"What your mouth enjoys your body despises, J.W. Get that by heart."

"Get back to this race thing," J.W. said, loading grits on his fork. "No such of an animal, you say, as that."

"That is the latest thinking, Sergeant Ragsdale, and I'm surprised you haven't come across that in your research into Memphis social structure."

J.W. could tell by the tone of Tyrone's voice that he was willing to keep up his end of the three a.m. banter in the House of Pancakes on Union Avenue, but that he was doing so out of courtesy. Something else was on his mind.

"What?" J.W. said, breaking off half a slice of hard-fried bacon for transfer from his plate.

"What what? Memphis social structure?"

"No," J.W. said, "not that. What're you really thinking about this morning? Y'all's house deal? Getting that financing set up?"

"No, that's going all right, it seems like. Loan's going to go through. Bank told Marvella yesterday."

Tyrone looked down at his bowl and speared a slice of something orange colored. Maybe cantaloupe, J.W. figured as he averted his eyes.

"Nothing domestic then," he said. "Must be foreign policy."

"Don't look now," Tyrone said, "but over yonder in that booth is somebody I believe I know."

4

"Where?" J.W. said, looking in the direction Tyrone had indicated. "You mean that bunch that looks like a roofing crew dreading daylight?"

"Yeah," Tyrone said. "Don't break your neck, craning it around like that. I believe all four of them have spent good amounts of time in a tightly confined space, but I know for sure that one of them has."

"That Mexican-looking one, you mean. Or Hispanic, I guess I ought to call him. The big guy."

"You are so politically correct, J.W.," Tyrone said. "Yeah, that's the one, but he's not from south of the border. He's an American Indian."

"Native American," J.W. said and ate a forkful of grits, "that's what you meant to say. You misspoke yourself, that's all."

"Yes, officer, I did. I can't call his last name right now, but he's known as Tonto something. I arrested him on suspicion of a killing during an armed robbery on Jackson five or six years ago, but the damned D.A.'s bunch wouldn't act on it."

"You were probably profiling, Tyrone," J.W. said. "You see a dark skin and you assume guilt. It's an attitude built into you like a disease. That's the way I figure it, just like the D.A.'s bunch does. Was it Fran Lever who wouldn't buy your story?"

"No, it was before that fat bitch arrived on the scene. It was some young Republican named Fognin or Coffin or something like that."

"See, there you go again. Your prejudice about racial characteristics and gender and body configuration choices just jumps out at me, Tyrone. Lord, Lord."

"I wonder what he's doing back in Memphis?" Tyrone said. "Tonto whatever his name is."

"Roofing, I expect, like I already said. That bunch is just waiting for the light of day and dreading that hot summer sun."

"It's hot all year around in Memphis," Tyrone said. "Except when it's freezing. You about through poisoning your system with pork grease, J.W.?"

"Yeah, it's time to go," J.W. said. "We got to go maintain some order in the Bluff City. But let's go say hello to your buddy Tonto on the way out the door."

"Yeah," Tyrone said. "You call him by his first name. I want to wait and see if he recognizes me before I say anything."

J.W. Ragsdale let Tyrone Walker lead the way out of the booth toward where the four men were seated, and by the time he had gotten fully unlimbered from where he was sitting he could see that two of them were looking up at Tyrone as he approached. Both of them held forks in their right hands and encircled the plates before them with their left arms as though to protect them. Prison etiquette, J.W. thought. These boys haven't been out in the fresh air that long. Still guarding their grub from misfits.

The Indian was different, though, the one Tyrone called Tonto, sitting up straight with a paper napkin in his lap and his left hand holding it in place. He also wasn't looking up at Tyrone or J.W. as they neared him. He's not about to sweat two men walking toward him at three in the morning in IHOP, even though one of them's a tall well-dressed black with the build of an NFL linebacker and the other one looking like what he is, a failed cotton farmer from the Mississippi Delta come to Memphis to find steady work.

Let's see if I can get him to lose his cool for a second or two, J.W. said to himself as Tyrone drew even with the booth where the men were sitting. Maybe make him drop his napkin on this old nasty IHOP floor.

"Tonto," J.W. said, "how's it going this morning?"

"Do I know you?" the Indian said, laying his fork on the rim of the plate and looking up at J.W. His eyes were so black there seemed to be no distinction between the iris and the pupil.

"I expect not," J.W. said. "I haven't had the great privilege of meeting you personally, Tonto, but I know who you are. You built yourself a solid little reputation here in Memphis not so long ago."

"Oh," the Indian said after staring at J.W. for half a beat too long, "that was a bullshit charge, officer. They dropped it in a day's time. A mistake, you understand."

"Yeah, I know, Tonto. Ain't it a sight how so many times innocent citizens get charged with killing people in the commission of an armed robbery? You'd think the police would be more careful before slinging around all these false accusations."

"You would think so," Tonto said. "But you'd be wrong." He picked up his fork and poked at a sausage on his plate, a Jimmy Dean special it appeared to be to J.W, the one shot through with flecks of something red.

"Is that the hot and spicy or just the regular?" J.W. said.

"Supposed to be spicy, but it's not."

"Yeah, Jimmy Dean lies," J.W. said. "It's like a disease, this damn mendacity. It's floating around everywhere these days."

The other three men in the booth with Tonto still hadn't stirred, all staring into their plates as though they saw something strange crawling around on them.

"Well," J.W. said, "I guess y'all about ready to go out to that roofing job this morning, huh? Get started while it's still a little cool and Mr. Sun's not all cranked up yet."

"Roofing?" Tonto said. "No, officer, we're just passing through town, headed for Oklahoma. Got a long drive ahead of us still today."

"Way down yonder in the Indian Nation," J.W. said.

"I ride my pony on the reservation," Tonto said and showed his teeth, but it didn't look like he was grinning.

"Have a good trip, then," J.W. said. "You and your war party."

Outside in the unmarked Memphis police car instantly recognizable for what it was to any Memphian who saw it, Tyrone Walker looked over at J.W. as he fired up the engine.

"Mendacity," he said. "J.W., where did you hear that word?"

"I read books, that's where. I read widely in hardbacks."

"Yeah," Tyrone said, pulling into the traffic on Union Avenue, headed for the Midtown station, "Captain Marvel and the super heroes."

"Naw, Red Ryder and Little Beaver."

"Mendacity," Tyrone said. "Red Ryder. How old are you anyway, J.W.?"

2

The job interview was going well. It had reached the point where both prospective employer and intrigued candidate knew an offer would be forthcoming and that it would be acceptable. All things being equal, of course. Now was the fun part, the period in which discussion could become more expansive, more jovial and free-ranging, more open to boastfulness on the part of the employer about the enterprise being represented and the position being offered, and on the part of the applicant a chance to show how supportive, how admiring, how capable of commitment, and how thorough and energetic a job of sucking-up he could do, given the chance, please Jesus.

This wide-eyed smile as you talk of the joys of employment is only a sample of what I can do to make you feel that executive juice pump through all your veins and arteries. Just wait'll we really lock up tight, belly to belly. You'll see something then.

It's like the moment, Jimbo Reynolds thought as he launched into an explanation of his mission statement to the candidate before him, when you realize the woman you're putting the move on is going to come across. Her eyes are sparkling, she's holding her head at an angle calculated to let her look up from underneath her eyelashes, you can see nothing but white below her irises, she's leaning in like a confident hitter at bat who's figured out exactly which pitch is coming across the plate and knows he will drive it into the gap, and all you've got to do is not screw up the close.

Keep it simple, keep it tight, keep the pressure up, and in less than fifteen minutes, you're going to be seeing that promised land across the valley as you ride the pony home.

"I didn't just happen on the concept fullblown," Jimbo Reynolds said. "It wasn't like a formula already derived and all I had to do was plug in the values and turn the crank. No sir, not hardly."

The lobby bar in the Peabody Hotel was relatively quiet. Tables on each side of the one where Jimbo Reynolds and the candidate for the public relations job sat were empty, and those within hearing range held a collection of midlevel Memphis management types with the odd attorney or two who were not yet drunk enough to be more boisterous than the average Memphian is by nature habitually.

"Really?" the candidate said. "That's a bit of a surprise, since I know there are other groups parallel to your own. Do none of them pre-date the Big Corral?"

The more I hear him talk the more I think it's going to be a good fit, Jimbo Reynolds said to that part of his brain which stood aside always from the moment and told him how he was doing at any given time. That's what I've got that most of them don't, Jimbo thought, and I owe everything to that little part of my mind that's always cool and uninvolved. It might not ever let me lose myself completely in anything I'm doing, I grant you. Getting drunk, getting high, pouring the prod to some filly, closing the deal or making a conversion, but by God, it saves me time and again from stepping in sticky doo doo. I'll take that separation between doing a thing and knowing I'm doing it, no matter if it does have a dampening effect on my immediate fulfillment. It's worth it. And if I ever lose connection with that part of my brain that holds back and says unh uh, I'm as dead as a thrown horseshoe.

You got to remember that phrase, that part of Jimbo's brain which he celebrated whispered to him as he set himself to respond to Don Condon's question. What I just then thought about the horseshoe. That sucker will preach.

"Let me give you the scenario, Don," Jimbo Reynolds said, lifting his eyes to the ceiling of the Peabody lobby bar to consider where to begin. An elaborately carved and painted cornice provided him the answer. The success of every utterance depends on the way in. Jimbo knew that in his bones. How you start does matter, and it matters strongly. How things are held together, not just that they are. That's the secret to fulfillment.

"I was into divine laugh worship, Don," he said. "And had been for some time. Are you familiar with that approach to soul-saving and the financing of the enterprise?"

"I've heard of the phrase, of course," Don Condon said, "but I don't know it in any detail."

"It was a good way to go for a while there. I picked it up early in the nineties, and it proved to be a winner. It went down very well with the believers of our demographic all during the Clinton years."

"Why was that?" Don Condon said and sipped at his drink, a watered Jack Daniel's the color of weak tea.

"It was celebratory. It fit the times. Picture this, and you'll understand, get some flavor of what I mean and where I was coming from.

"Here I am, up before a congregation of believers of a certain stripe. They've come out of a fundamentalist background, and they're all employed and making some money. Putting some cash by in many cases. Got a mortgage, got a bass boat. But they are our kind of people. Hell, a Southern Baptist among them would pass for an intellectual. He'd be like an Episcopalian is to a congregation in East Memphis. You know, thoughtful.

"Here I am, looking at them, all of them prosperous materially, but broke loose from whatever dispensation they were raised in. You know, apostolic, holy rollers, pentecostals, four-fold overcomers, foot-washers, even some snake caressers of the first water with signs following. And I start to laugh, I start to chuckle, I commence to titter, right there in the pulpit.

"A few of them venture to cackle a little bit, coming back at me, see. Then I say to them that the Lord loves a cheerful giver, our God is a God who looks on what He's made and finds it good. And He laughs in joy at the creation of His hands and wit, and He invites us to join Him in divine laughter.

"Then I get into it for real. I bust loose with a guffaw, I let my voice rise up in my throat, and I laugh loud and hardy, I let my belly loose, I lean over and laugh. I rear back and laugh. I let my backbone slip and I laugh. I cavort and skip and dodge like I'm shucking tacklers on a football field."

"And they join in," Don Condon said. "It's downright infectious."

"Do they join in? Did they join in? Back there in the Clinton administration the people I'm talking about, the ones I'm reading, they would laugh like drunken hyenas. I'd see people all over that audience jump out of their seats to laugh.

"They didn't just wave their hands in the air and chuckle. No, they got down and rolled on the floor. They hugged themselves, they hugged each other, they put their hands on the ones next to them in places they wouldn't be allowed to out on the public streets and roads. Women screamed like they were having their first orgasm in eight months and it was sopping wet good to them, old folks lost their upper plates, the kids laughed until they scared themselves and started to cry about it and wet their pants.

"A good meeting sounded like a goddamn insane asylum at feeding time. Oh, Don, I tell you it was a sight."

"The way you tell about it makes me want to laugh right now," Don Condon said, "sitting here at the Peabody during the cocktail hour."

"It was entertaining, I got to say," Jimbo Reynolds said. "I got to admit, and it paid off like a busted slot machine in Tunica, Mississippi, for a while there."

Jimbo stopped to sip at his drink, rattling the ice in the glass as he sat it back on the table, loud enough that one of the waitresses in the Peabody gray and maroon dress was bending over to take an order in less than a minute, showing him a nice expanse of skin in the process.

"I love freckles," Jimbo Reynolds said as he lifted two fingers and made a little circle with them.

"I've got them, all right," the waitress said, "nothing I can do about it. I used to just slather on the foundation and powder, but I just finally gave up and stopped trying to hide them."

"God bless you, girl," Jimbo said, "for accepting the gifts you've got and letting the world take a good look at them."

After she had left in the direction of the bar, the tail of her skirt twitching like a pendulum, Don Condon asked why Jimbo had decided to segue out of the divine laugh approach to public worship of the risen Christ.

"Was it because it was hard to follow up a session of laughing?" he said. "I can imagine it'd be hard to find words that fit and serve. How can you close the deal after something like that? Not many of the clients would've been ready to listen to a pitch by then, I expect."

"Oh, you'd be surprised, Don," Jimbo Reynolds said, knocking back a first swallow from his fresh drink and letting that good bite of sour mash ease over his palate and down his throat. "You didn't have to say much, really. That was a definite major advantage of the divine laugh approach to worship. They'd all be sitting there wiping their eyes, hiccupping and moaning and groaning like they'd just laid a big wad deep in somebody or had somebody lay one deep in them.

"I wish you could've witnessed one of my strong sessions back then. You'd have seen how it worked them, I flat guarantee you. It was like a dose of salts through a yearling, I'm here to tell you. Yeah, that was the beauty of the divine laugh. They were all so loosened up after a well done session, all you really had to do was just pass the plate and get their credit card information on the forms waiting for them."

"But you moved out of that," Don Condon said, "and you must've had a good reason to leave that behind."

"Oh, yeah. Too damn good a reason. It's simple. The laughing thing stopped working. Went gefizzle on me and everybody else working the divine laugh. All the prosperity preachers, even the really big ones, Lon Anthony down in Florida, Jim 'The Duke' Lanier in Oklahoma City, Dandy Don Llewellyn over in Nashville, all of them had to chunk it in, and all within a few months of each other. The divine laugh was as dead as Bob Dole's nuts in less than a year after that mess in Tallahassee."

"You talking about the 2000 election?" Don Condon said. "All that hanging chad stuff and the Supreme Court scam and so on?'

"Yeah," Jimbo Reynolds said. "Don't get me wrong now. I go along with whatever happens, and I learn to adapt to the times and the situation. What choice do you have? Talking to you, I expect you're of the same philosophy."

Don Condon made a fist with his right hand and pumped it twice into the cooled air of the Peabody lobby bar, not having to say a word to express his wholehearted agreement.

"Yeah," Jimbo Reynolds said, "as soon as Bush took office, hell before that, as soon as Justice Scalia delivered the divine laugh worship gig shut down like you'd welded a faucet shut and dynamited the stream the water come from."

"I think I see where you're going," Don Condon said. "The atmosphere changed, and I bet 9/11 slipped the final knife to it."

"In the whole country, particularly with our demographic. See, with little Bush in charge, it got harder and harder to get our people to bust loose and laugh and loosen up the pocketbook. The ones we depend on are just exactly the bunch likely to be unemployed during an economic downturn, and to get them knuckleheads to laugh when they ain't got that steady check coming in, well, shoot."

"Tell me about it," Don Condon said. "I heard that."

"It's not that they stop loving the Lord or feeling like they ought to or that they don't feel guilty enough anymore to know they ought to be paying a little hush-money to make up for the shit they been doing."

Jimbo looked back up at the cornice on the Peabody lobby bar ceiling, the one that had taken his eye earlier, and felt the right way into an explanation gathering in his brain. He opened his lips a space for it to come, and the words which carried it did their appointed task. It's still working, Jimbo said to himself with gratitude, you give it a chance to focus, and the good Lord knows I have learned to do that. Wait on the Lord, and He will answer.

"It's a different set of values at large now in the country, Don, and in what makes our demographic tick. It came to me one night when I was channel surfing a TV screen in Marked Tree, Arkansas, where I was still trying to work the divine laugh. And let me tell you, it had done gone flat by then and was not functioning worth a nun's nipple, and I knew it. It was like an old man remembering what it had been like to be able to look down and it was up and ready to go and it had happened without him having to think or worry about it. He understands that success used to be a by-product, coming uninvited, but now it's all he can think about.

"Hell, you're a young man yet, but I bet it's been times already you've waited on yourself to be able to do what you want to do with a woman ready and willing and just lying there as open as a book, and you'd had to try to think yourself into getting ready to do what needs to be done. Am I lying, son? Tell the truth now."

"No, you're not," Don Condon said, "much as I hate to admit it. I've had to reason with my dick on more than one occasion. Come on, I've had to say. Now do what you're supposed to do, damn it to Hell."

"Anyway, to leave that metaphor behind," Jimbo said, pleased to see the candidate for the PR position register a response at Jimbo's use of the word metaphor—surprise, surprise, son, I ain't no dummy, Jimbo whispered in his mind, I did my time in school, same as you did—"I happened upon a John Wayne movie, see, there on that tube in Marked Tree, one of the old John Ford productions, right in the middle of a scene of a bunch of cowboys with their heads bowed praying about something.

"That caught my attention, but mainly what impressed me, see, the thing of it was, that bunch of cowboys was in a saloon. Bottles all kind of lined up across the back of the bar, shot glasses sitting on the counter, and all that paraphernalia of needing to get hammered by alcohol, but these old boys in that saloon were seeking divine connection rather than a drink of whiskey.

"It came to me just then, like a revelation. I'm not talking God speaking to me, don't get me wrong. But the idea that hit me between the eyes like a well-swung billy club was about our demographic, folks that admire John Wayne and what he stood for."

It was coming up in his throat, the catch that arose each time he thought on a thing transcendent, and Jimbo Reynolds paused to swallow it back. Praise Jesus, it still works, he told himself, all these years back down the line, and it's as strong as it ever was, from right here in the lobby bar of the Peabody all the way back to standing in the side yard of one of those damn shacks in East Texas as a kid, looking up at that empty sky and wanting something. A bicycle, something sweet to eat, a shirt in the pattern everybody else was wearing, something, for Christ's sake. Praise be to the Lord.

Don Condon had seen what was happening and was looking away to give his prospective boss a little privacy in his moment of emotion, and Jimbo was glad to see the man had antenna. That's what I'd be hiring him for, when you get right down to it, for whether he could read a situation. That's all PR amounts to, and that's a bunch.

"It's like Reagan was," Jimbo said, his voice strong again, "back when he was himself like before that brain rot eat him up. Or Little Bush's daddy, climbing up on that submarine after the Japs shot him down, and even Little Bush himself, too, of course, chopping away at those trash cedar trees every time he gets back to his ranch. Cowboy virtues, you understand, that's what I'm talking about."

"Damn," said Don Condon. "What an insight."

"Hard work," Jimbo Reynolds said, "sweat, simplicity, not thinking and worrying about stuff, no putting up with the mindsets of pansies like Montgomery Clift in those old movies, or Bill Clinton feeling everybody's goddamn pain, or women like Hillary Clinton herself, that whore of

Babylon."

"Her legs," Don Condon said, setting his drink down deliberately on the table before him and beginning to move his hands slowly straight up and parallel to each other about six inches apart, "start at her ankles and go right up from there the same exact thickness all the way to her knees. There's not curve one in her calves, either damn one of them."

"Thank God for pantsuits," Jimbo Reynolds said. "Cowboys, I said to myself, there in that Holiday Inn Express motel in Arkansas, cowboys. A church full of cowboys. A cowboy church. That's what I'll set up, and that's what'll fetch them, and that's what I'll preach, the cowboy virtues. And let me tell you, hoss, it has gone like gangbusters from inception right up to this very moment, ten minutes after six in the Peabody Hotel lobby bar with two stiff drinks in me and another one about to be on its way."

"I want to be a part of that enterprise," Don Condon said. "I want to contribute to its success, and I want to facilitate your efforts to make it grow."

"I'm not lying to you, son," Jimbo Reynolds said. "That was my moment in the garden, the time I was on that knife edge of asking the Lord to let this cup pass from me. And John Wayne with the help of John Ford's staging and cinematography put my feet on the path to righteousness and to continuing financial stability and growth.

"It is not my style to exaggerate or shuck and jive. I face the truth, whatever it costs me. If I tell you a chicken dips snuff, you can start looking for the Copenhagen box stuck up underneath its wing."

"I got to get me some new clothes," Don Condon said. "I'm thinking about the proper apparel for a new job."

"Memphis, Tennessee will clothe a man in whatever raiment it is he needs to wear," Jimbo Reynolds said. "Why, look what this city did wardrobe-wise for Elvis."

3

They would be coming, Beulahdene Jackson knew, and she knew that fact in her bones, the same way she could predict the onset of heavy weather even on a day the sun was shining bright and the air tasted clear and sweet in Memphis on the river. Something inside whispered to her not in words but a feeling, and Beulahdene had come to trust the truth in that feeling over the years, that thing like a small sickness or pressure around her heart. And it had a color, and that color was a shade of light yellow. Words could and would lie, but that feeling did not. Falsehood was not in it.

Whether they would come more than one at the time, Beulahdene Jackson did not know. It could be two, three, four, not likely more than that. It could be just the one. And if only one, that would carry the most weight and the greatest menace. Knowing that was a feeling, too.

They would not have come a few years before, not there to the corner of Montgomery and Peach, where Beulahdene had been able to buy the little house where she had lived these years since. The government check had started coming back then, and with what she had saved from the money she had made working for all the white ladies in their houses in Midtown over the years, she had been able to put enough down to move into the brown house on the corner, the one with siding and the front porch and the backyard where she had grown tomatoes and okra for a long time. Not any more now, though.

When Beulahdene Jackson moved in, many of the Jewish people who walked to their church each Saturday, what they called a synagogue, had lived in the neighborhood still. Some of them, anyway, and everything was kept up, and the yards were mowed, and any window that was broken in any house was always replaced the next day. Walls were painted, new roofs were put on, the sidewalks were not all broken up by sycamore and oak tree roots, no pieces of glass scattered in the street got left there long.

But a new synagogue was built by the Jewish people, somewhere out in East Memphis, and they all moved away so they could walk to that new one on the weekends, since they couldn't drive their cars to it. Why they couldn't drive to church in all the big cars they owned and drove everywhere else Beulahdene never did get straight. But they couldn't for some reason, and that was their business and none of hers. So she didn't let that worry her mind.

But they had left, almost all at once, and everything changed in the neighborhood. The old synagogue was now where the white Baptist young folks went to learn how to be preachers, though it looked the same as it ever did, except for the signs in the front of the building. The foreign writing the Jewish people had carved on the building itself was still there, saying whatever it said that nobody could read but them. But they weren't there to read it anymore, the Jewish people, and Montgomery and Peach was not the same place it had been when Beulahdene Jackson moved into the little brown house. No more tomatoes in the backyard, no more families walking to the synagogue at the end of the week, no more okra in the hot Memphis summer, sticky to the touch when you cut it off the stalk.

A little boy knocked on the front door first thing that morning, right before seven o'clock. Beulahdene Jackson didn't open her door to see what he wanted, of course, but she got a chance to study him close by looking through a crack between the lace window curtain and the edge of the window frame off to the side.

He was a light-skinned boy, and he looked nice, even sweet in his face as he stood turning his head from side to side trying to look through the pane of glass cut into the door. That was not a good thing to have in your door when the house was located where it was, on the corner of Montgomery and Peach. The policeman who had had the meeting with the neighbors that still lived there had told Beulahdene that directly when he had done the inspection for security measures on everybody's house, the ones still being lived in. That's what he called it, security measures. And he called it community outreach, too.

"That there piece of glass is an entry way, Ma'am," he said to her, pointing at Beulahdene's door and writing it down on the piece of paper which he had left with her later on. Everybody got their own piece of paper, everybody living there who went to the meeting with the police officer. Beulahdene put the form, the inspection report, in that top drawer of the chest in the bedroom where she slept, the place she kept all of her important papers. The letters from the Social Security, the insurance form for her house, the agreement she paid on every month for the burial arrangements for when the time would come when the Lord decided to finally do what He had to do. There were letters there, too, from kinfolks and from David, but she didn't read them anymore much. They were in her head already and had been for a long time. She didn't have to look at letters now.

"I'd say you need to get you a new door, Mrs. Jackson," the police-man said. "A steel one, like the one you got in back. That'd be my recommendation."

"Yessir," Beulahdene told him, smiling at herself for calling some-body "sir" who looked no older than a child, and knowing she wouldn't do what the policeman recommended about the front door to her house. That pane of glass was small, but it let in the light, and you could look through it and see whoever was passing on the street outside, going up and down Montgomery, summer and winter. If you wanted to, that is, though there wasn't many people going by a person would want to see anymore these days, not on Montgomery Street.

The little boy was wearing those pants like they do now, too big by several sizes for what would fit him, almost falling off of him as he stood on the front porch, his hand up the pane of glass to shade his eyes so he could see inside Beulahdene's house into the front room. He didn't look long, though, and as he left the porch, hopping down on the sidewalk without using the steps, Beulahdene could see through the crack beside the curtain that his big pants were so long in the leg the cuffs were frayed and worn out from dragging on the concrete wherever he walked.

"Lord Jesus," Beulahdene Jackson said out loud, "hold my hand."

He is little, she told herself, he's just a child trying to find a little yard work to do to make him some spare change to jingle in his pocket. Or to buy him a treat, an ice cream or a bottle of pop in this hot weather, that's what he wants, what he's looking for, that's all it is to it.

But as she washed the dishes she had used for breakfast and ironed herself a blouse and a house dress and the towels she had been meaning to get around to for a week, she sang over and over a hymn, He Comes to the Garden Alone, to keep her mind occupied.

I'll look at all my papers in that drawer this morning, she told herself, check on everything being where it ought to be. I will dust every surface in my house this morning where it ain't been touched for two weeks. I've been letting down too much here lately. A bad habit will come on you before you know it if you don't keep things up to where they ought to be.

He's real young, she said to herself, he's a little boy, he don't mean nothing, he's just working his way down old Montgomery Street this morning, door to door to door, looking for an odd job.

4

Two calls had come in at almost the same time, and J.W. Ragsdale and Tyrone Walker were both available, sitting at the two desks in the Midtown station pushed together across from each other. Tyrone had his head down, making notes on a legal pad, and J.W. was staring balefully at the cursor blinking away on the computer terminal before him.

"I hate this shit," he said, loud enough for people across the aisle between the two rows of desks to hear, if they had wanted to acknowledge it. Nobody did, not even Tyrone Walker, not over an arm's length away.

"I hate it," J.W. said again, shifting his gaze to Tyrone.

"I know you do, J.W, and I heard you, and I feel for you. But there it is to deal with."

"There it is, all right," J.W. said, "look at it, saying do something, do something, do something. Blinking like a blind man."

"You just reading that into your computer," Tyrone said. "It doesn't care one way or the other what you do or don't do. It does not give a shit."

"I do despise cost-cutting measures," J.W. said. "Whatever happened to secretaries, ranks two and three? That's what I want to know."

"Abolished and superceded," Tyrone said, "as you know, J.W. All those low-level clerk positions are gone, and the ladies that would've been filling them are all in law schools and MBA programs, learning how to kick ass and just dying to do it once they get that piece of paper letting them loose to do it."

That's when both calls had come, the phones on both J.W.'s and Tyrone's desks ringing at almost the same time. J.W. let Tyrone pick up first, and then he lifted his instrument to his ear. At least it would the voice of a human, if you could call Myra Summers one of the species.

"Yeah," J.W. said.

"You supposed to say your name, then homicide," the voice in J.W.'s ear said. "Or it's all right to say Memphis Homicide first and then your name and rank. Whichever way you want to go with it. Whatever."

J.W. said nothing. The cursor was still blinking and would do that until Memphis fell off its bluff into the river, provided electricity kept getting to the computer. As Tyrone said, it didn't give a shit.

"You still there?" Myra said.

"Yeah."

"Two come in, and y'all figure out how you're going to divide up the goodies, I reckon. You always do. That's what Major Dalbey says about y'all, anyway."

"It's called multi-tasking, Myra," J.W. said, "that part of the decision tree is."

"It is not. That's a different thing. Anyway, one is at 2935 Peabody, a woman smothered by a ceiling fan."

"Smothered by a fan?"

"Yeah, that's what I said. I don't know what it means, but the uniformed policeman says it's a homicide, not no accident, the way it looks to him."

"What's the other one? Somebody mashed by a refrigerator?"

"It's at 408 Montgomery, corner of Peach. It ain't no doubt about it, neither, according to what that officer says."

"I'll take that one," J.W. said. "Put down Ragsdale on your slip there. And then you put down Walker's name on the slip for the fan deal on Peabody."

"I know that. You don't have to tell me how to do every little bit. I know how to do, and there ain't no slips anymore, either. It's all computerized now, everything is."

Myra hung up, and J.W. looked across the desk at Tyrone, who was turning his telephone back and forth as though exercising his wrist.

"That all right with you, partner?" J.W. said, "me catching the Montgomery Street one?"

"I don't care," Tyrone said. "But why'd you pass up that fan deal? Sounds different. Woman smothered by a fan."

"I hate a mystery," J.W. said. "Just keep it simple for me and my computer. I'll just take some honest blood on the damn walls every time."

"No intellectual curiosity, Sergeant Ragsdale," Tyrone said, getting up from his desk. "That's what holds you back in your career in law enforcement here in Memphis."

"That ain't what you singled out last week to explain my shortcomings. You mentioned my Mississippi upbringing then."

"Just add this new one to the list," Tyrone said. "Consider it an update. I'll see you back here later, J.W."

"Nice blazer," J.W. called after Tyrone as his partner walked away between the row of desks in that part of the Midtown station. "What they call that material? Burlap?"

"Linen," Tyrone Walker said. "Linen."

When J.W. pulled up in front of the address on Montgomery Street after taking a right off Poplar just past the old Memphis Tech High School, he could see a couple of uniforms standing on the front porch in the shade out of the direct sunlight. He recognized the female as someone he had noticed before, mainly because of the way she filled out the seat of her regulation blue pants, but the officer she was talking to was a street cop he hadn't seen before.

The officer had taken his headgear off and set it on the banister of the porch, and he was running his hand through his headful of dark curls on which he obviously set high store.

"Howdy, Shaquita," J.W. said to the woman who had turned to watch him come up the sidewalk to the house. "Hot enough for you?"

"Yessir, Sergeant Ragsdale," she said. "It most certainly is."

"Put on that headgear, officer," J.W. said to the other one, looking at his name tag, "and square it up. You're in the eye of the public, McComick."

"Yessir, " McComick said. "Like you said, it's hot today. Trying to catch some breeze out here."

J.W. looked at McComick until the officer dropped his eyes as he juggled his hat into position.

"Who's here?" J.W. said. "Whose city vehicle is that yonder?"

"The M.E.," Shaquita Lawson said, "and the assistant M.E. with him."

"Is it Hoot?"

"Yessir, him and somebody I ain't met before, a lady assistant. She's a new one, I believe.," Shaquita Lawson said.

22

"I bet old Hoot's wearing a tie today then," J.W. said, "along with his pretty white coat."

"I never noticed," the male street cop said. "I did see his white coat, though."

McComick's Memphis Police hat was now firmly in place at the regulation angle, but J.W. ignored what he'd just said. Damn if I'll buddy-buddy right off with a police officer that needs to be told to keep all his clothes on when he's in uniform.

"What we got here, Officer Lawson?" J.W. said. "Run it on down for me."

"Sergeant Ragsdale," she said, flipping pages in a small composition notebook in her left hand, "we got a deceased female, African-American, blunt trauma and stab wounds, as I ascertain, the cause of her death."

"Let Hoot Sarratt tell us, Shaquita," J.W. said. "He's got to do something to earn his keep."

"Yessir, it's in there in the front room, half on and half off of a sofa. Neighbor looked in the window and saw her an hour or so ago."

"Why'd he say he looked?"

"Says he saw glass on the porch when he was walking by headed for Pop Eye's up on Poplar. Says he knew that wasn't right. She would've swept up anything that was broke or was a mess, you know, on her porch."

"How old a woman was she?"

"Old," McComick said. "Not real old, but old."

"How old was she?" J.W. said again, still looking at Shaquita Lawson.

"She was eighty-three. Name of Beulahdene Jackson. Lived alone."

"Busted out the window in the door to get in," J.W. said. "I guess early morning. Have y'all done your door-to-door yet?"

"Not across the street yet," Shaquita Lawson said. "Just the one neighbor we talked to so far."

"Well," J.W. said. "Officer McComick, you see that line of houses over yonder. Go to it."

McComick stepped off the porch and marched down the sidewalk at a good clip, hat firmly in place, and polished shoes winking in the sunlight.

"Who is that, Shaquita?" J.W. said, watching McComick head for a yellow stuccoed house directly across the street.

23

"He's new to us," Shaquita Lawson said, "new to Memphis, but he's been on the job in Nashville for several years already."

"Why ain't I surprised?" J.W. said. "You the first one in the house, Shaquita?"

"Yep, we was out here on Poplar just passing the intersection of Cleveland when the call come. So we responded."

"How'd it look when you went in? Same old, same old?"

"It looked usual, but it looked a little funny, too." J.W. didn't speak, and Shaquita Lawson went on. "You know, all kinds of stuff was throwed in the floor, drawers upside down and scattered, knick-knacks and things here and yonder, ransacked and all, TV throwed down on the floor."

"Just one of the brothers looking for a way to buy him some medicine, I reckon," J.W. said.

"Yeah, but the way he got out of the house was what was different. See, what he did was to go out through a side window up pretty high off the floor."

"Didn't use the door he come in through?

"Don't look like it, no. He kindly jumped up and busted through that window, knocked out the casing and the curtains on it, left bloodtrail on the glass he busted, and by the time he hit the ground outside, he had to've fell eight feet."

"High jump artist, showing out, huh?"

"I guess. Didn't make sense to me. Glad we got the blood, though."

"Let's go on in, Shaquita," J.W. said. "See what our crack M.E. can tell us."

A smallish man was leaning over the body sprawled in the middle of the room. Viewed from behind he looked normal in configuration, but J.W. knew that if you turned David "Hoot" Sarratt sideways for examination, he would appear to be carrying a fullterm pregnancy, maybe twins, beneath the white coat he was wearing.

"Hoot," J.W. said. "You got on your tie today."

"Yeah, Sergeant Ragsdale, I do," the Memphis M.E. said. "I woke up feeling kind of formal this morning."

"I can see that," J.W. said, and he could see why, too, as he looked at the woman standing to Hoot Sarratt's side, some sort of shiny instrument in her hand. She didn't look up immediately at the entrance of

J.W. and Shaquita into the room of the crime scene, and J.W. was glad she hadn't, since he got a chance to see her in profile, face and torso both.

Her forehead, nose, and chin looked as though they had been cut out by some artisan a few centuries back as a model for a silver coin, one probably high in value. We're talking the equivalent of a silver dollar here, J.W. noted, not a commemorative state of Arkansas quarter with a flying duck on it. Somebody took some pains on getting that profile done right, he paid some attention to his engraving, and he got it exact.

Although he couldn't tell from the advantage of his current viewpoint, J.W. Ragsdale knew that if and when she turned to look in his direction, the woman would have the cheekbones you are liable to see in good number on women in Mississippi and Alabama and Tennessee, but hardly one in a thousand north of a line you might draw on a map marking the division between the Delta and the state of Missouri and all points Midwest.

"How you doing?" J.W. said in the direction of the woman, not meaning to say anything yet to her but discovering himself doing it without meaning to act like he'd seen her at all. Hell, keep on talking, you've showed your hand now, damn it. Two of a kind with Hoot Sarratt, not a dime's worth of difference in his response to a good-looking woman from that of the man wearing a tie spattered with egg yolk.

"What you seeing there?"

"Well, a dead woman," the female assistant said, "probably been that way for five to six hours."

"This here is Nova, Sergeant Ragsdale," Hoot Sarratt said, grinning at J.W. as though he'd just seen him trying to sneak something out of a location where he had no business putting his hand. "Let me introduce y'all to each other."

"Hello," J.W. said. Shaquita Lawson, standing beside him, cleared her throat and looked down at her fingernail, holding her fingers straight out the way a woman will do in contrast to a man who will turn his palm up and curl them back toward himself to take a look-see. Why is that, J.W. wondered.

"This is Nova Hebert, my assistant. That homicide detective there is Sergeant J.W. Ragsdale, up from Panola County, Mississippi."

"Nova?" J.W. said, trying not to babble, but feeling it about to get away from him. "Like the name of the Chevrolet? That one G.M. made with Nissan back in the seventies?"

"Yes, you got it," the female assistant said, looking back down at what she'd been doing when J.W. and Shaquita Lawson came through the front door. "That's what they named me for, though I didn't know Nissan had anything to do with the Nova."

"Oh, yeah," J.W. said, "sure, that's why it was a good economy-sized car, see. It had a lot more than Detroit going for it."

Thinking as he spoke, goddamn, why can't I keep from rattling on about a car that there ain't been any made of for over twenty years? Thirty, maybe. Shut your fool mouth, dummy.

"Why would your folks name you for a brand of automobile?" Hoot Sarratt said, still grinning like a jackass eating briars. "Didn't they know what that name nova means in Spanish?"

"No sir," Nova Hebert said. "I expect they didn't know about that. There was a lot they didn't know about a lot of things."

"What it means in Spanish is it won't go, see," Hoot said. "You got to break it down first, though, see, to its constituent parts. No, that means no in Spanish, just like it does in English. Then va, that means go. So no go, that's what that name means."

"It's a nice name," Shaquita Lawson said. "It sounds pretty to say."

"Thank you, officer," Nova Hebert said. "So does Shaquita."

"Not nearly as pretty as Hoot, though," J.W. said, thinking he had to get this thing refocused on the only one in the house that seemed to be showing any sense of dignity at the moment, the dead woman in the middle of the room.

"What did the job?" he said. "Whatever it was that hit the victim on the side of the head, I guess it was."

"Naw," Hoot said, sounding a little miffed at J.W.'s comment about his nickname which had always seemed fine to him. It was jolly and short and nobody ever had a problem remembering it. "It wasn't that that did it. You tell him, Nova."

"She bled out," the female assistant with the profile said, pointing with the instrument in her hand at several spots on the body before her, moving her hand up and down with short, precise jerks as though she was sprinkling drops of water on some object.

"See all these amounts of blood in profusion at the throat, the upper torso, both right and left lateral? Her heart was pumping for some space of time, probably even after the killer exited the scene."

"Something scared him," J.W. said. "Made him leave before he was finished picking stuff up."

"We don't know about that," Hoot Sarratt said. "That ain't part of our job, right, Nova? We just process the scene, tell you what we see, and leave the rest of the job up to you homicide detectives."

"You got that right, Mr. Medical Examiner," J.W. Ragsdale said. "I've never seen you meddle yet in what I've got to do."

"You got to stay focused, J.W.," Hoot said, over his pout about the aspersion cast on his name. "Focus sharpens the mind, understand, lets a man do his job right."

"You can see footprints in the blood trace all around the room," Nova Hebert said. "So the perp was here for a while as the victim was bleeding out."

Nobody said anything for a space, but for Hoot Sarratt's humming tunelessly as he looked from his assistant to J.W. and back again, beaming like a basketball coach who had witnessed his only child sink two game-winning free throws in an overtime period.

"Then," Nova Hebert said, pointing toward the small window set high in the north wall of the room, the one with the pane of glass missing and the curtain hanging partway outside the house, "he did his high jump through that hole he made for himself."

"Suppose it was a western roll or a Fosbury flop he did, J.W.?" Hoot Sarratt said.

"Yeah, Hoot," J.W. said. "You pick up on the funny part, all right. Shaquita, let's you and me walk around in the rest of the house. See what we can see."

"He went headfirst through that window," Shaquita Lawson said, "like it was something after him."

"Like it was biting him on the ass," J.W. said. "He was motivated, all right."

I wish I hadn't said ass in front of that woman named Nova, J.W. thought as he left the living room of Beulahdene Jackson's house, headed for the kitchen, that kind of talk is for sure a no go.

27

5

By the time J.W. Ragsdale arrived back at the Midtown station a couple of hours later, Tyrone Walker was already at his desk punching on his keyboard.

"You done got it figured out, I see," J.W. said. "Made your arrest and listened to a full confession, just like on TV. When's the execution date?"

"Just as soon as he figures out what he wants for the last supper, J.W.," Tyrone said, giving his keyboard a last flurry of punches and looking up from across the desk. "I wish it was that quick, all right. It'd save us a whole bunch of trouble."

"What'd you find out about that fan smothering the lady?"

"This is your kind of deal, J.W., for sure," Tyrone said. "The way you love to hear lies and people making up crazy stuff. See, here's the way it happened, according to the husband, the man who called 911 all in a uproar."

"Run it down for me," J.W. said. "I need some uplift after what I been looking at on Montgomery Street."

"All right, Mrs. Sirhan Barsamian was napping on the king-size bed in the master bedroom, it being that time of day for the lady, and she was lying under a big ceiling fan, one of the top-of-the-line units from Hunter.

"Turns out it hadn't been mounted right, there in that nice house on Peabody and when Mr. Sirhan Barsamian came home after a hard day at the International Food Mart, he found that the fan had shook its way loose and descended upon his lovely bride enjoying her nap in all that cool air underneath it."

"Did it cut her throat or something?" J.W. said. "I wouldn't have thought wood blades would slice through anything. They'd knock hell out of you, of course, but that ought not to kill you. Was that the first story he told you?"

"Naw, J.W.," Tyrone said, leaning back in his chair and shaking his head from side to side for dramatic effect, "the fan smothered her, that's what Mr. Sirhan Barsamian told 911, and the officer responding, and me when I got there. And he would've told Jesus the same thing if He'd showed up."

"What? The fan laid on her face? That don't make sense. How did he expect to get that by you?"

"See, it was a language problem, J.W. It's like most misunderstandings in this old world we live in. It just comes down to problems in communication. A failure to communicate, like old Strother Martin says in that Paul Newman flick."

"That's before my time. What then?" J.W. slapped at the breast pocket of his shirt as though something had just stung him, felt nothing, realized what he was doing, and began searching through the drawers of his desk to see if there might be a piece of hard candy left to sacrifice to his nicotine hunger.

"You done ate all that candy up," Tyrone said. "And I never have had any over here, and I don't now. So don't be asking me."

"All right," J.W. said. "I guess you hadn't got any Juicy Fruit, either, do you? Not stick one."

"No," Tyrone said. "What had happened, you understand, was that high-dollar Hunter ceiling fan, model number A one four seven, worked itself loose, fell on Mrs. Sirhan Barsamian as she peacefully napped, and choked her to death."

"How? Couldn't she fight it off? Not a stick of gum left, huh?"

"No, you know I stopped using it. Chewing gum metabolizes as a carbohydrate, even the diet brand, and the body converts and stores that crap as fat."

"What a shame," J.W. said. "How did the fan do it, then? This model whatever it is."

"A one four seven. I just entered it into my report."

"You're an efficient bastard, ain't you?"

"I give good report, J.W., unlike some detectives of homicide. Anyway, that fan had wrapped its chain that hangs down so you can adjust speed and all that business, clear around that woman's neck and choked her to death. And then tied a knot in the chain so it wouldn't work loose and let her catch another breath."

"Bullshit."

29

"That was precisely my experienced and expert opinion and response. The very remark that came to my mind, and I said it."

"He thought we'd buy that, this Food Mart guy?"

"This is a different culture than what the man's used to, J.W., here in Memphis. I expect where he's from people fly around on carpets and turn into bullfrogs just on a whim. Why wouldn't we buy it, he figured."

"You got to give him credit, I reckon," J.W. said, "for being a good storyteller. What finally broke him down?"

"He gave it on up, Sergeant Ragsdale, after I pointed out to him how all the finger and thumb marks had started rising up on his wife's neck just as pretty as a picture. Even an old-school police officer would've seen it."

"Did he start squalling and stuff?" J.W. said, refusing to rise to Tyrone's bait. Old school. I'm so damn old school I don't know what old school means. "This grieving Food Mart man?"

"That he did, yes, and praying in a foreign language and trying to explain to his dead wife why he'd done what he did and how he hadn't seen a single alternative."

"Do you suppose the AK forty seven fan did fall down on her and Mr. Barsamian saw his chance and like a good Memphian took it?"

"Not AK forty seven, J.W. It's A forty seven. We're not in Vietnam now, so don't start having an AK forty seven flashback on me. But no to your question. The fan came down after the wife was already done. The fool left his tools stacked up on a dresser drawer thing right there in the room."

"He dismantled the fan, then, to cover up the strangling he'd done put on her?

"Mr. Sirhan Barsamian did just that. And you know what else? That fan was well-secured, too, before it came down. He had to use a screw driver, a wrench, and a wire cutter to get it to tumble."

"Phillips head?" J.W. said, turning to his computer to get it cranked up to receive his notes so far on the Montgomery and Peach killing. The way the machine began to whir and groan put J.W. in mind of an old man rising from bed after tossing around all night and not sleeping a wink.

"Do you sleep good at night, Tyrone?" he said. "Can you still do that?"

"Of course," Tyrone said. "I got them half-grown twins to wear me out when I get home at night. I sleep like a baby every time I get a chance to lie down. Why do you ask?"

"Brag on," J.W. said. "Your time's coming."

"I guess the thing over at Montgomery and Peach is not going to be so easy for you as the fan smothering was for me, huh?"

"No," J.W. said. "All we got's some blood from the perp and some pissant bloody footprints."

"No real prints, I reckon."

"No, you know they all wear them little old rubber gloves now, Tyrone. The dumbest crackhead in Memphis is learned to do that these days."

"Damn television," Tyrone said.

"Easy for you to say, buddy. You got a woman living in the house with you. A single man like me would be a lonely bastard without his TV set."

"You are a romantic, J.W., to believe that myth," Tyrone said. "I think your computer sounds ready to do it."

"Yeah," J.W. said, turning toward his keyboard with the reluctance of a teenage cotton chopper in Panola County, Mississippi picking up his hoe for the first time on an early morning in July. "I wish I had me Mr. Sirhan Barsamian's wire cutter about now. I'd show this sucker something."

6

The rent house was set high on the bluff in South Memphis and had been there for close to a century, once neighbor to others like it up and down and across the street and on the streets behind and before it. Now of its kind it was alone, though between it and the river were rows of condominiums and single-family dwellings, well-fenced, with double and triple garages filled with SUV's, high-end sedans, and speciality sports machines for land, water, and air.

To the south of the rent house itself was a development of single-family, stand-alone homes surrounded by a masonry and wrought-iron barrier topped with spikes, well over nine feet in height. Anyone entering through the gate had to stop for permission from personnel in a fortified booth, 24-7, and pass under a sign announcing the name of the development, Nathan Bedford Forrest Estates.

Coy Bridges could see from his vantage point high up in a small room of the rent house, which had once been servants' quarters, though Coy didn't know that, that the man in the entrance booth to N.B. Forrest Estates this morning shift was some kind of a Mexican, maybe not really from Mexico, Coy told himself, but from somewhere like that. Guatemala, maybe, or Honduras, who knows, Puerto Rico, or Costa Rica, one of those places.

No, not Puerto Rico, that belonged to the United States, didn't it, so if the entrance guard was Puerto Rican he wouldn't be in Memphis, for sure. He'd be up in New York City with the rest of that bunch, sitting on some steps in front of a tenement, eating a purple snow cone.

The guard this shift was definitely dark-skinned, all right, wore his uniform tailored to fit tight at the waist and close to his shoulders. Coy couldn't see from here the man's footwear, but he figured it would be highly polished half-boots with one cuff showing and the other one stuck down in the mouth of the shoe. The dude was a young one with no real belly on him yet, and that was the way Mexican type males liked to show out when they got any opportunity to wear a uniform, military or industrial. Muy macho.

"Bob," Coy Bridges said without taking his eyes off the guard in his little fort at the entrance of Nathan Bedford Forrest Estates, "come see who's in the booth this shift."

The guard was reaching his arm out the window, leaning pretty far over, to take something from the driver at the wheel of a Mercedes convertible drawn up at the entrance. The top was down, and the mane of blonde hair on the woman at the wheel was flashing in the morning sun as she shook her head and said something to the guard.

"It's Enrique, I imagine," Bob Ferry said, coming up to stand by Coy and look out the window of the former servants' quarters of the big old rundown house he'd rented from the real estate lady two days ago.

"Enrique Valdez, yep, there he is."

"You know that Mexican?"

"Not personally, no. I know who he is, though, of course, and I know when he's on duty. Weekdays from four a.m. to eleven."

"How'd you know that?" Coy Bridges said. "Damn, look at that little blonde bitch in that ragtop Mercedes. I'd love to crack that."

"Only way you'd get close to something like that, Coy, is to break into her house in the middle of the night. Wait, no, I take that back. If it was daylight and you were to get past the gate there somehow, she might let you do a little yard work, if you'd do it minimum wage off the books. And you would."

"That's another reason I'd like to bust her open," Coy said. "Just that very thing you said then."

"Dream on," Bob Ferry said. "You sure ain't never going to meet her socially. Never see her, you know, on an equal footing."

"I'd make her think footing," Coy Bridges said, leaning further toward the window to watch the Mercedes move off up the street and out of sight. He bumped his forehead hard enough against the glass to make him jerk his head back.

"And how I know Enrique Valdez is on the job this time of day is how I know everything I know," Bob Ferry went on. "I studied it out, wrote it down, and committed it to memory."

"Got it by heart, huh?"

"Heart hasn't got a damn thing to do with it, Coy," Bob Ferry said. "When the subject is business, you got to leave everything out of the equation but your brain."

"What good does that do us?" Coy said, stepping away from the window and reaching in his pocket for a cigarette, "knowing that greaser's name and what hours of the day he's working. We ain't going in there in the morning. That ain't what we supposed to do."

"You know I've asked you not to smoke around me," Bob Ferry said. "I'd appreciate it if you put that out. And yes we are going in there in the morning, and we're going to do it more than once, too."

"Why?" Coy Bridges said, stubbing out the Marlboro carefully on the window sill to save it for later, maybe. "We done know his address."

"Knowing a number is not knowing an address or the house at that address, Coy," Bob said. "That's nothing but the first little bit of what you need when you're setting out to plan a project."

"You're one to plan, all right. I'll give you that."

"I am that, and I'm proud of it. Another thing I'm proud of is that I have never spent a single night incarcerated, which is more than I can say for lots of folks."

"You don't know what you been missing, Bob," Coy Bridges said. "You have no idea."

"I guess that's something you've learned by heart, Coy," Bob said.

"I've learned it by everything, starting from the ground up."

Both men fell silent, looking out of the third floor window of the servants' quarters of the mansion built in 1892 by Ruben Weiss, a cotton factor in Memphis in the time before the first automobile turned a wheel on a street in the city. Hot on the south bluff already this early on a summer Sunday morning, and they watched Enrique Valdez below in the entrance booth slide the window closed to conserve air from the cooling system.

"When're we going in there the first time, then?" Coy Bridges said. "In the preacher's house, I mean."

"We'll talk about that when Tonto wakes up," Bob Ferry said, "and when Earl gets back from whatever whorehouse motel on Lamar he spent the night in. We got somewhere else to go before that, though, you and me."

34

"Yeah, where?"

"To church this morning We got some worship time to do before anybody moves a peg to do anything else on this deal."

"Not no, but nuh uh for me on that shit," Coy said.

"Oh, yeah, Coy. You and me are going at eleven this morning to the Sun-Rise Ministry of the Big Corral. But don't worry. You don't have testify or sing a solo or kiss a cross or nothing like that. This is business."

"It's always business in a damn church."

"What an attitude to have on a Sunday morning in Memphis," Bob Ferry said. "Enrique does look good in his outfit, doesn't he? You can see the creases in his shirt from way up here. Just like the edge on a knife."

7

Jimbo Reynolds had been leery about the space at first. No matter how you chose to view it, no matter how you tilted your head to the side, narrowed your eyes and tried to sneak up on it as though you weren't looking to see anything and then all of a sudden there it was, jumped up and staring back at you, the building was still just a big warehouse that some component of the Memphis manufacturing base had moved out of, first a little at the time, a little more at the time, and then all at once.

The final departure had been in the usual pattern of such tuck-tails-and-run. Equipment was abandoned, window fittings had been ripped out for sale because of the value of the aluminum in their make-up, a couple of delivery trucks that wouldn't run stood where they were last parked, their wheels naturally gone early and gone entirely, but surprisingly some cargo in the trailer vans was still there.

The financial holders, the banks and mortgage concerns, stuck with what was left, had grown more efficient over the year, Jimbo figured, knowing they had to secure what they could of commercial failures as quick as they could if they wanted to keep anything that might sell for a penny or two on the dollar.

What was good about the warehouse marking the corpse of MidSouth Floor Coverings, Inc. was readily apparent to the trained eye, however. The building was big, it had a roof that looked sound, and there was a shitload of parking in front and on both sides of the metal-sided structure. Enough pick-ups, minivans, outdated Detroit four doors, privately owned school buses, and the rest of the variety of transportation used by the religious demographic in question could be accommodated to provide a good-sized congregation. If you could turn them out, of course. But that was Jimbo's strategic problem and opportunity, not the responsibility of the facility itself.

A good salesman does not blame his product or his tools. He hustles and moves what he has to work with. That Jimbo knew, and that he lived by. All Jesus was given to work with on the banks of the Sea of Galilee was two fish and four loaves of bread. But He didn't whine about it, or try to blame staffing problems or kick it upstairs. No, He went to work and convinced that bunch of Jews that there was enough for all of them to eat. And they believed it and acted like they were in the buffet line at a Morrison's Cafeteria franchise. What they ate filled them up, and that's what counted to them. Jesus sold that idea, and they all bought it, and people were still buying that bullshit.

The first facility that Jimbo Reynolds had his eye on was a great big old Episcopalian church right downtown in Memphis not two blocks off of North Main Street. That had been the problem, of course, location. The value of location, location, location in questions of real estate was time and circumstance dependent, Jimbo knew, and the Grace-St. Marks structure had become a victim of time and tide and an outdated vision of what would work.

The money folks that once inhabited downtown Memphis had started a steady move-out in the 1950's, following the dollar eastward and fleeing persons of color, and the erosion of property value and suitability of Grace-St Marks for a location of worship had accelerated like a 1965 387 Olds dropped into low and floorboarded the very minute after Dr. Martin Luther King, Jr. was killed not far down the street.

So the Episcopalians deconsecrated the old Grace-St. Marks, couldn't sell it, and did not let the doors of the church hit them in the ass on their way out of the building, out of downtown Memphis, and out of the proximity of persons of African persuasion.

The truth was in 2003 Jimbo Reynolds could have bought or, better yet, leased the whole thing for a few hundred dollars, nave and arches and transepts and choir lofts and pews and memorial plaques, and stained glass windows, those busted out and those still whole, all of it from the tip of the stonework up top to the bottom of the crypt below.

But, wait, he told himself, would a cowboy church thrive here? Would people of his target demographic show up for services? And if they did, where would they park? And if they found places to park their vehicles, how would they respond when they left the place of worship and found their wheels missing and their side mirrors broken out, and their windshield wipers twisted into strange and wonderful shapes, and their batteries gone? And that would be if they were lucky enough not to find just an empty space where they'd parked on the broken and oil and brake fluid stained streets of that part of Memphis.

So, no, Jimbo had said to the realtor trying to peddle Grace-St. Marks to him. Get thee behind me. A good thing available at a bad time is not a good thing any more. A great edifice for a wrong purpose is nothing but a pile of stones.

Jesus knew that. That's why he rode a donkey into Jerusalem instead of a blooded Arabian horse and why he had arranged for folks waving palm leaves at him rather than silk scarves and embroidered rugs.

A sense of occasion and what's right for it, that what makes success, Jimbo Reynolds thought as he sat on the edge of one of the bales of hay on the platform against the west wall of his leased galvanized steel warehouse, former home of the ex-MidSouth Flooring Company.

The wide double doors before him across the way were propped open with their own bales of hay, and they were coming in, his target demographic, a steady stream of them, those who came to seek, to worship, to fellowship with one another, to partake of the rodeo meal after services, and to quell for a space those feelings of fear and dislocation which drove them through the streets of Memphis on their way to the Big Corral.

Family groups were most in evidence, and Jimbo lifted the Stetson from his head in a steady motion to tip in homage and welcome toward the mamas and daddies and young'uns moving inside together like clots in an artery. Most of the men returned the gesture, those wearing western headgear—not many of the ones with ball caps who seemed to consider those coverings to have been welded to their skulls at birth—many of the wives and mothers did a little curtsy, those who'd learned that was what cowboy women did in greeting, the kids for the most part slouched in like robots, testimony to what was wrong in America these days, and the singles and the couples scattered in the crowd displayed the usual ignorance of how and when to act. Their behavior came from what Jimbo knew were deep-set psychological feelings of inadequacy and nowhere to belong, but God bless them, they were always the biggest givers. The unhappy try to buy good feelings by giving beyond their means, and a secure man is as stingy as a goat.

38

Blessed be the miserable. Praise them.

The western band behind and around Jimbo on the platform was providing a steady musical accompaniment to the procession of worshippers this morning into the great galvanized cathedral of the Sun-up Ministry of the Big Corral. The Cowboy Combo of Grace included two guitars, a fiddle, a snare drum and cymbal set-up, a bass, and a piano, and they sounded upbeat and particularly tight this morning. They had been practicing, Jimbo noted with approval, to get used to the new fiddler, a good one and one abut two-hundred percent better than the old one, Rabbit Handwerker, who Jimbo had finally run off for good this time. He could fiddle, you had to give Rabbit that, when he was there and when he was sober. But he never could understand limits and the need to observe them now and then.

This tune the Combo was working this morning during the entry of the congregation was a softly intoned "Red River Valley," instrumental only, but Jimbo let the words run through his head as he greeted the gathering crowd of worshippers from his perch on the hay bale. "From this valley they say you are leaving," Jimbo thought as the fiddler squeezed he haunting notes of accompaniment from his instrument. "I will miss your bright face and your smile."

"Folks," Jimbo said aloud, rising from his lounging position, the small wireless mike on the collar of his shirt picking up his words and broadcasting them from the banks of speakers throughout the building, not a distortion to be heard in any part of any sound. "Welcome to the Big Corral this morning. I hope y'all had a good breakfast right around daylight, and that you slept as sound last night as a wrangler does that's rode fence all day and rounded up half a hundred strays in the meantime. I mean to tell you that cowboy's tired. He's earned his rest, and I know you have, too."

Most of them were seated now, all the pews Jimbo had salvaged from a closed U.C.C. church in Raleigh filled, the crowd overflow pushing toward the limits of the folding chairs arranged in banks to the right and left and behind the rows of wooden pews. The last few found places to sit, the Cowboy Combo of Grace segued from the "Red River Valley" to the first bars of a more traditional church service offering in song, "Peace in the Valley," and Jimbo told himself to remember to congratulate Joe B.

Wyatt, the lead guitar and vocalist, for the arrangements. Nice transition and nice thinking. The boy has a vision.

These folks are here for a total experience, just like they are anytime they enter a themed establishment, and whether they realize what's happening to them or not, they are gratified by good attention to the details making up the moment.

"I'd like to ask all you cowhands and your ladies and your young'uns to bow your heads in the presence of the man who runs this spread for all of us. Let's have a little palaver with Him this morning."

The knocks and scrapes of boots on the concrete floor, the rustle of hats and sombreros being removed, the hushed swish of petticoats beneath the western skirts and dresses of many of the women, a cough or two and some throat clearings, a child's bright thin voice lifted in a question immediately stilled by his mama, these sounds rose and mingled into a single murmur as soothing to Jimbo Reynolds as that first bite of Maker's Mark bourbon at the end of a filled and harried day. Slow down, it said. Ease up. Rest.

"Boss," Jimbo said into the wireless Sanyo mike at his throat. "It's me again, wanting you to straighten out some things for us. We're here together, this bunch of wranglers and mothers and tikes, old and young, big and little, men and women, and me along with them waiting and needing to talk with you, Boss."

Jimbo looked out from beneath the edge of his left hand, the one lifted to his forehead as though to ward off the slanted rays of the sun as he stood alone at the end of the day on a solitary butte, cattle grazing and milling peacefully about him. The Stetson in his right hand Jimbo Reynolds held waist-high and to the side a bit, propped against his hip as he stood in a calculated lean, just a hair off the vertical the way John Wayne habitually assumed a stance when not mounted on a horse or backed up against a saloon bar. The angles of his body and their intersections presented interesting contrasts, Jimbo knew from long practice, suggesting a cowpoke at rest, yet one capable of sudden and powerful motion if need arose. Jimbo worked out, he went to the iron three times a week, he watched what and how much he ate, he appeared on the edge of being dangerous, middle-aged as he was, and he was conscious of the image he presented. Jimbo Reynolds looked right, he looked fit, he looked good.

Peering up from beneath the edge of his left hand, his chin tucked prayerfully as it had to be, Jimbo could observe the closer rows of worshippers in the steel-sided Cathedral of the Sun-Up Ministry of the Big Corral, and he could tell they were doing what they should. Every head was bowed, every eye was closed, every ear was open to the words he was delivering.

"Boss," Jimbo said, "we come to You as Your people, as Your range outfit, and we offer You on this pretty morning in Memphis with the sun shining and the birds singing and our hearts beating together all that's due and all that's owed You. We promise You a fair day's work for a fair day's pay, and we look back behind us at the week since last we gathered in the Big Corral at what we've tried to do, and at what we've got done.

"Boss, You gave us our riding orders a week ago, and we paid attention to the work You set before us and the way You laid out for us how we ought to go about carrying out Your orders. Boss, some of us have rode fence, and we've made sure any downed wire was put back where it's supposed to be. We nailed it back to them heart cedar posts, and we stretched the wire tight. The dogies are still on the right side of the barb wire You wanted us to keep up. We took care of that. We rode Your fence."

At this, several "amens" arose from the congregation seated in prayer before Jimbo Reynolds. Jimbo hit his Stetson on his hip as though to knock loose some trail dust or grass burrs clinging to it. He did that again, and then once more, and went on.

"Some of us, Boss, You set to keep an eye on coyotes, range wolves, hawks and eagles, all manner of varmints that might try to take some of Your stock.

"Boss, we done that. There ain't been a one of your calves lost this week to nothing looking for an easy meal to take. Set Your mind at ease, Boss. We been on the job."

"You tell him, Range Foreman," someone called from back near the rear of the auditorium, the voice lifted in a tone of resigned satisfaction, "we doing what we can to carry out the Boss's will."

"Amen, amen," the words came like the start of a rain shower, more this time and from all quarters of the congregation, the higher and lighter voices of women laid over the throaty barks of the men.

"But we're tired, Boss," Jimbo said, lifting his left hand to quiet some of the outpouring. "We're tired. It's the end of the day, and the sun is setting, and Cookie's got the beef and beans on the plank table, and we're longing to eat and seek our bunks and take our rest as the whippoorwills call and the cattle low, bedding down on the prairie.

"But, Boss, we're here to tell You at the end of a long day of doing Your will and carrying out Your orders, that after we get our rest, we going to be here tomorrow, looking up at You in the dawn of a new day with the dew on the grass and roosters crowing and cattle grazing on a thousand hills, we'll be here, Boss, I'm pledging for all Your hands and all Your outfit, asking You what You want us to do this week. We're ready, Boss, we'll do our job, we'll satisfy Your will, we'll do it the cowboy way."

"Cowboy up," the first cry came from somewhere deep in the crowd, from back beyond the rows of wooden pews, all the way from the folding plastic chairs for overflow, and other worshippers chimed in as quick as a top hand slapping a tie-down rope around a yearling's back-legs on a branding takedown.

"Cowboy up," the chant lifted and strengthened, and Jimbo Reynolds let it go on until it seemed that every cowpoke and lady and child in the building had to be giving voice to achieve the level of vocal thunder being generated in the steel-enclosed space. "Cowboy up, cowboy up, cowboy up."

Now, Jimbo said to himself, the internal clock of exquisite timing he possessed giving him the sign, now. Cut if off when it's at its peak, don't ever let it start to dwindle and fade on its own. Do that, and they'll be in danger of realizing that the commotion is self-ignited and there ain't a damn thing but them doing it by themselves. Thank you, Lord, Jimbo Reynolds said to himself, as he raised his Stetson high as though to get the attention of a herd of white-faced steers barreling toward him. Thank You for giving me that clock. I never knew to ask You for it, but You knew what I'd be needing to further my career path. You had the foresight. I give You the glory.

"Amen," Jimbo boomed into the Sanyo throat-mike, the sound from the banks of speakers as true as a dinner bell's ring at day's end. "Amen and amen."

In the rear of the building, the great steel-sided cathedral of the

Sun-Up Ministry of the Big Corral, Coy Bridges and Bob Ferry looked at each other from where they sat side by side on two pale green molded plastic chairs in among the stragglers who'd arrived too late to make it into the rows of salvaged wooden church pews.

Jimbo Reynolds's announcement of "amen" had cut off the chants from the crowd of "cowboy up" as though a spigot with a new washer had suddenly been closed down iron-tight by a strong man, but people were still making noise, talking among themselves, beaming at each other as they jostled in their seats, rubbed shoulders, slapped each other on the back, nodded heads vigorously as though to seek agreement as to what they had witnessed and were now full-fledged part of, wiping their foreheads with the backs of their hands like a hard task had just been successfully completed, and showing all the signs of being members of a worshipful congregation at a Sunday morning service in the Mid-South. The Lord was moving, and they felt it.

"Who was he talking to?" Coy Bridges said to Bob Ferry, "that tall jaybird up there on the loading platform?"

"God," Bob said. "He was talking to God, fool."

"He never said God's name," Coy said, leaning closer so Bob could hear him over the buzz of voices and the scrape of boots on concrete and the sobs of two kids right in front of him. "I never heard him anyway say it."

"Yes, you did," Bob Ferry said. "That just shows how far you've drifted away from the Lord, Coy. By now you wouldn't know God if He walked up to you on the street and asked for a cigarette."

"Don't say shit like that while church's going on, Bob."

"This is not a church, Coy," Bob Ferry said. "It's a flooring company warehouse recently vacated."

"You said Reynolds was talking to God. And look at these folks all around us in here. Tell me these crazy fuckers don't think they're in church."

"They don't think period," Bob Ferry said. "And besides, all they are is a reverse truth-barometer."

"Truth-barometer?" Coy Bridges said, his voice lower now as the jubilation of the worshippers of the Big Corral began to subside. "What you talking about?"

43

Coy was beginning to feel like he'd like to backhand Bob Ferry on the side of the head, see how he'd like to have his teeth rattled around a little, but he couldn't do that where they were, of course, and the thought was not a new one anyhow. Ever since he'd met Bob Ferry in Huntsville, Alabama, where Tonto Batiste had arranged for all four of them to get together on this deal, Coy had often had the urge to come up strong beside Ferry's head after some smart-ass statement he'd made.

But the sawed-off little dip had a way of saying things you knew were against you somehow, they were meant to put you down and make you look dumb as a fence post, yet the way he put them you couldn't really tell what he was saying exactly. Coy knew at those times that if he acted the way he knew he was being tempted to and ought to that the other ones would never listen to what he was saying and they sure wouldn't back him up.

There'd come a time, though, and it would be the right time, and when it got here, Coy promised himself, he wouldn't just be swinging flatfooted. He'd get up on his toes and put everything he had into it. He'd rock Bob Ferry's world.

"You said," Coy said, this time almost in a whisper since Jimbo Reynolds, up on the loading platform in his cowboy clothes and boots and waving that big white hat in his hand, was now talking again and the crowd had knocked off the talking to listen, "you said he was talking to God, but I never heard God's name mentioned a time. What's that mean, huh? That's what I'm wanting to know."

"God hasn't got a name, Coy," Bob Ferry whispered back. "He'll answer to anything."

"Bullshit," Coy said. "God's name is God. Every asshole in Memphis knows that.'

"Jesus Christ," Bob said and put his hand up to his mouth as though he was about to laugh out loud and had to choke it off there in the church so as not to be rude.

"That's God's son, that ain't God who you just said," Coy Bridges said, feeling the prickling sensation build in his shoulders and hands and the buzz start up in his ears No, he told himself, no, not now. Later, later on I'll bust Bob Ferry so hard he's be squealing God's name out loud over and over again, just begging Him to notice.

44

Up on the stage, the Cowboy Combo of Grace began playing a tune which most of the congregation seemed to recognize well enough to sing along with, and after that one was finished, Jimbo Reynolds sang one by himself, to the tune of "The Streets of Laredo" but with different words. He talked some more, again in a manner which to Coy Bridges made no sense, so he stopped trying to listen. Instead, he watched the worshippers around him, who liked what they were hearing, judging by the way they all sat up in their seats and leaned forward with their lips parted and their eyes glistening as though they might miss something they just had to take in or lose out forever on having a chance at it.

Beside him, Bob Ferry was listening, too, Coy could see, but Bob was showing no signs of hearing anything he judged worthy of taking seriously. He had the same little twisted turn to his mouth he always had when he wasn't the one mouthing off and was having to listen to somebody else say something. Not believing what he was hearing, but listening so he could file it away in his head to bring out and laugh at later, like a man who would eat a dish of food he didn't like just so he could point out how bad it tasted when he was finished and how the cook didn't know shit about how to do it right.

At the end of his sermon or talk or whatever it was, Jimbo Reynolds, the one everybody kept hollering "range foreman" at, sat back down on his bale of hay and sang along with the cowboy band a tune Coy Bridges had never heard. It had lots of words and verses, and it mentioned the wind and rain and cattle and sunshine and sage brush and lost calves and tumbleweeds and cowboys by themselves riding horses in cold and stormy weather. It had the name of God in it, too, Coy noted, in lots of places.

Down both sides and in the middle and across the back of the steel building and the far side of the rows in front, a team of men in full western regalia proceeded from one member of the crowd to the next, not skipping a one, including each child in its own seat or on somebody's lap. The colors of the team's shirts and hats and bandannas and boots and the cut of the chaps most of them wore varied greatly, but one item each cowpoke carried was identical to all others. It was a silver galvanized bucket attached to a metal handle fully four feet long, and as the cowboy working the row of seats where Coy Bridges and Bob Ferry sat came steadily closer the words written on the sides of the container he moved from one

45

worshipper to the next could be easily read. "God's Bucket" was printed in deliberately scrawled letters designed to look homemade around the top edge and below that was another statement. "He Paid YOUR Entry Fee."

Bob Ferry had a bill waiting when the bucket reached him in its journey, a fifty, Coy noted, and that made him want to bust Bob up alongside his head again. Coy had only a couple of quarters and some dimes picked out of his pocket to drop in, and they made a loud and terrible rattling sound against the side of the bucket, disappointing Coy's hope that the wad of bills already in the container would soften the sound of his change. Coy couldn't stop himself from showing something in his face, because the cowboy holding the bucket spoke to him, and he did so way yonder too loud for Coy's taste.

"Just give what you can, hoss, this time, and make it up the next. The Boss ain't worried about counting up the amount of each cowboy's contribution. He ain't in it for the money. He's looking for a giving heart."

"Amen," Bob Ferry said, booming out the word loud enough that others in the vicinity joined in "That's right, Pecos, amen and amen," some woman next to Coy said.

The cowpoke with the bucket moved on, and Coy twisted his head from one side to the other, trying to get his neck to pop, but it wouldn't. "Who's Pecos?" he said.

"The man with the bucket," Bob Ferry said. "Didn't you see his name tag? That one over there's Shorty, and Wichita just passed by. There he goes."

"Not a one of them's got a real name," Coy Bridges said. "They made every one of them up."

"What's in their buckets is real, though," Bob Ferry said, "and they get filled up and poured out every time the Big Corral opens the barn doors."

"And he keeps it in his house?" Coy said. "For a fact?"

"The Range Foreman don't like banks," Bob said. "That's what his assistant's been telling us. Banks ain't the cowboy way."

"Praise Jesus," Coy said. "Praise Him."

"Amen and amen," Bob said, and that made Coy feel for the first time this Sunday morning they were riding the same trail.

8

Randall Eugene McNeill felt the braided wire pulling him slowly but steadily toward the mouth of the cave, struggle against it however much he did or could do. The wire was fastened somehow to his feet, around both ankles, with enough slack to allow him to move his feet apart eight or ten inches, but no more than that.

Although he couldn't see the wire in the dark, Randall Eugene McNeill knew its colors, three strands to the braid, one red, one black, one green and he knew that if he were pulled feet first through the opening of the cave into the passage into the earth, dark and musty and cold behind it, that he'd never see light or feel fresh air moving across his face again.

A whine was forced through his lips without Randall Eugene willing it, and that frightened him more than anything else about what was happening, more than the wire braided red, black, and green, more than the hole of the cave mouth, framed by boards like those set around a window, more than the dank, dark passage leading somewhere beneath the ground, more than the fact that he couldn't move and his arms lay dead beside him no matter how much he told them to push his hands down toward his feet. Take it off, unwind it, Randall Eugene begged his arms and hands, get it away from my feet. Don't let it pull me, don't let it drag me underneath the ground.

Calling on all he could of his waning strength, forcing his lips apart as far as he could manage, Randall Eugene tried to cry out, but the sound he was able to make was weaker than the whine that had been pried from him, and he felt a sickening lurch as the braid of wire pulled him further toward the window into the cave, the dark mouth into the earth, the teeth of boards framing it.

"Why can't you get up, sleepy-head?" his mother was saying. "I'm about to pull your little toe off, Randall Eugene, and you still won't stop trying to sleep."

"Mama," Randall Eugene McNeill said, "it's you, it's just only you."

"Who'd you think it was, baby? One of your girlfriends?"

"No, I ain't got no girlfriends," Randall Eugene said, pushing his hand toward the foot of the bed where his mother stood. She was dressed for work and ready to leave the house, a raincoat covering all of her uniform and her purse hanging from a strap on her shoulder. Her hair was combed out straight, and her make-up was on.

"Don't talk like that, son," she said. "You know better than that."

"Well, I ain't got no girlfriend. I'm just telling the truth."

"Don't say ain't no. Who're you trying to fool? You weren't raised to speak that way, and you do know better. Anybody hearing you who didn't know any different would never believe you're in that gifted and talented program."

"All right, I'll do it," Randall Eugene said. "I'll get up."

"You've got a lot to do today, remember, Sugar. You have the counselor to see this afternoon, and don't you forget to tell her what I said about your meds."

Randall Eugene began to speak, but didn't, stopped by the way the wall of his room across from his bed looked different somehow. Had his mother changed it in some way, put different paper on it, painted a design where there was only a pale blank space before? There was a pattern evident now, regular small squares in alternating colors, black and red, changing as he watched them to separate shades of gray.

"Why did you do that?" Randall Eugene said, pointing toward the wall by lifting his head as though to indicate with his chin what he wanted her to see.

"Do what? What're you talking about? That picture over there? The one of LaFrance? Is that what you mean?"

"No, nothing," Randall Eugene said, watching the pattern on the wall shift from squares of gray back toward white, fading quickly into blankness again as though to vanish before his mother would be able to see what was happening before her in her own house. Another thing that he knew only he could detect, a state of change which always eluded everybody but him. She couldn't see it. She wouldn't see it, and if she did, she'd be afraid to admit it. "I guess it's just the way the light's doing."

"As little light as you let get in this room, I don't know how you see to find your way around. When you were little, you couldn't let enough light get through your windows to satisfy you. Now you act like an old bear trying to hibernate."

Randall Eugene picked up the shirt his mother had put across the foot of his bed while he was asleep and looked at her.

"You're allowed to talk, young man," she said. "The polite thing would be to say mama I need to get dressed now. And if you did that, I'd leave the room. But I know if I do, you'll just crawl back under the covers and go to sleep."

"No, I wouldn't," Randall Eugene said. "I used to would've done that, but not no more."

"You couldn't sleep again last night, honey?"

"I could sleep all right, but I didn't want to. What I'd like to be able to do is never go back to sleep again. That's what'd satisfy me."

"If you keep going to that counselor lady and taking your meds, you'll grow out of this, Randall Eugene. I know you would. It's just a stage of development."

"Don't call it meds. I hate it when you call them that. And don't say development."

"You hate it when I say anything these days. Meds is what it is. I know what I'm talking about. Now get up and get dressed and do it quick now. Eat your breakfast and be ready in fifteen minutes. I've got to be in the surgical unit in less than an hour. Move it, Randall."

I know why the window, Randall Eugene told himself as he watched his mother leave the room, I know that part all right, up and down and sideways and backwards. But why the rest of it? A cave, a cave? A frame around the hole? Wires on my feet? The wall moving?

I have got to cool down, he lectured himself as he dressed and walked by the plate on the table in the kitchen where she'd left something for his breakfast. He picked it up, not looking at whatever was there, and succeeding in scraping it into the garbage pail under the sink without having to see what it was. He couldn't avoid hearing the sound it made, though, as it hit something flat in the garbage container, a piece of cardboard maybe. It splatted, it sounded heavy and wet, and Randall Eugene's stomach dipped and rose as though it was headed all the way to his throat.

I have got to cool down. I've got to get something else into my head, something big enough that nothing can get around it, nothing can make me think, not a sound, not a sight, not a smell.

They said he wouldn't do it. Antwan mainly, standing there laughing, his teeth so white when he threw back his head to show how funny he thought it was.

"Dog," he said, "you ain't going to do shit. You too much of a white man to do nothing but talk."

"Naw, naw, wait a minute," Damon said. "Do Run Run be going to show us something. Show us some shit, ain't you, Do Run Run?"

"You got that right," Randall Eugene said, all of them standing there on the steps going up to the big doors in front, the ones under the stone carved with the Gothic letters spelling out Central High of Memphis. "You just watch my natural ass."

"Oh yeah, oh yeah," Damon said, "Do Run Run going to show us something, all right. He going to show us his vocabulary."

Then they all laughed and fell about the steps, spinning and staggering like they were about to fall, hands thrown up in the air, pushing, pushing, pushing. Three white girls coming up the steps toward them changed the way they were walking to take a path further away, and Randall Eugene saw that Amy Amonette was one of them. She looked right at him, and he looked off as though he didn't see her, but he knew she could tell he did. He turned his back to her, but he could feel her eyes sliding off of him, and he heard her say something to one of the other ones, Elizabeth Hubbard, maybe.

"Fuck that monkey shit," Randall Eugene McNeill said to Damon. "Dog, you don't know what's up with me." The street in front of the steps was doing it again, slow this time, but Randall Eugene knew if he let it know he saw it, the street would do it more and more quickly, too fast for him to keep up and hold it contained in his eyes and then the sound would start up. He couldn't afford the sound this morning, not today. Don't look at it, move your eyes away and face the building, but don't hurry so it'll be able to know you see. Look at the words cut into the stone above the door. Let the stone keep your eyes. It's not moving.

"Unh uh," Antwan said. "That ain't the word, that ain't what we waiting to hear you say. Don't say fuck. Say something like molecule. Say economic trend, Do Run Run, say economic trend. Say honors program."

That's when they really laughed, and he walked off down the steps, taking them three at a time, and by the time he was down to the street, all of them had turned to head into the building, Damon saying over and over, monkey shit, monkey shit, fool, fool, fool.

When Randall Eugene stepped up on the porch, he could see her peeping at him from where she was looking out from a crack in her curtains, thinking she was hidden from anybody standing in front of the door. The sun hit her glasses, and he couldn't see her eyes, and he was glad of that.

Randall Eugene kept looking straight ahead, but he was still able to see the curtain to his left move just a hair, so he leaned forward and put his hand up to shade the glass part of the heavy wooden door. It was too dark to see anything inside, standing as he was in the bright sunlight, but the old lady couldn't tell that.

Seeing him do that would scare her, Randall Eugene thought, and it would keep her indoors with all her locks fastened. When he went back to school, getting there late and coming into the classroom where the officers of the Bones Family, Antwan and Damon and Ja'Nce, would be sitting against the back wall in a row, one-two-three, he'd be able to tell them the house he'd picked out had somebody in it, watching too close for him to go inside.

"Motherfuck," he'd say, "if I'm going to have some old bitch call the blue knockers on me for busting out a window. I want it to count for something when I be breaking in. I want to be able to take my time, do a little shopping for a thing to show you dogs, something worth something, to prove out where I been. Word up."

Yeah, Randall Eugene told himself trotting across Montgomery to the other side of the street, that'll work, get them notified I mean business. I ain't just moving my mouth up and down to keep the flies off my face. I be meaning to show I'm Bones material, and I mean to do it big.

He'd just hit the curb with the sole of his shoe, when it happened and it caught him before he could get up all the way onto the sidewalk and out of the hold of the pattern in the cement of the street. How had it happened so fast that he couldn't see it taking place? That was the fastest it had ever been, and that told Randall Eugene that the pattern had been deceiving him ever since it started up. It had always been able to move too fast for him to stop it, to hold and contain it, and put himself at a distance from it. When the pattern wanted to set up like cement in the sun, it could have done that, and the reason it hadn't was that it wasn't ready yet. It was waiting until he stopped being so afraid of the pattern and had come to believe he could live with it, and it would move then when it was ready.

Here on Montgomery Street the pattern this morning had decided it was time, and it let him get almost all the way out of the street and up onto the sidewalk before it took him. But now it had, and he was in a pawn's position, and the hand when it wanted to move him would do that. It would give him up for an advantage or not for one, maybe throwing him away just to fool the white king and make him think he was winning. The question is not where it will move me, Randall Eugene said to himself. I know that. The jar the curb gave me traveled up my leg and told me that. What I don't know is when, and the pattern knows that, and it wants to think about that, along with the message it told the muscles and blood and bone of my leg.

I know a thing and I know it is true, from the sole of my foot to the pit of my stomach to the top of my head, Randall Eugene whispered to himself, straining to listen to the one talking to him. The message lodged in a spot just behind a part of his skull directly above his eyes, and it brought with it the look they would have on their faces as he tried to explain why he still hadn't done it, still hadn't done the deed he had to do before they'd let him in, before he would be able to feel both parts of his brain come together and touch and be as one with each other as the white and yolk of an egg in the same shell.

"Do Run Run," Antwan would say, "go sit over yonder with the rest of the bitches and read some shit out of a book. Read it real loud and nice, say it like a white girl doing a book report."

Randall Eugene could see himself listening to them laugh at what Antwan said and waiting for the next one to say what he'd thought up, something even better than that, all of them ready to call him what he was.

He stepped off the sidewalk on Montgomery Street, taking himself away from the broken shards of clear glass and the cracked pieces of concrete, now part of the pattern which had been following him and waiting for him to know and allow he was part of it. Randall Eugene lifted both hands to his forehead to press the scene he'd imagined to come at Central High School back into his head along with the other ones already there, all the ones telling him he was a freak and a misfit and a white boy and a bitch and a final piece of the pattern waiting to step into the pawn position and be one with it. He looked up into the hot blast of sun hanging over Midtown Memphis, and he spoke out loud to it.

"Fuck it," Randall Eugene McNeill said. "I'm going back over to that lady's house, and I'm going in, and I'm bringing something back out with me to show their punk asses what kind of a man they messing with."

And that he said out loud, and the other words he whispered to the evidence of the pattern on the wall in his room and in the concrete of the street and in all the tools and formulas and equations and translations in the world, and those words he said but could not hear and heard but could speak and understood but could not know.

But when Randall Eugene got inside after the pattern had moved him there, the inner side of the door behind him, the air in the house smelling of where an old lady lived—paper flowers, some kind of chemical, maybe a floor cleaner, old toast, stale and burnt, a still dead odor of things shut up and sealed away in plastic wrap—nobody was home. Nothing told him to be quiet getting in, so he hadn't tried to be, breaking the window set in the door with a brick from the ones lining a flower bed, hammering it hard and hearing the glass fall inside to the floor, snaking the wire of the coat hanger down, down to where it caught the deadbolt and flipped it up, a hard sharp sound in the middle of the morning.

He went directly to the small dark colored table against the wall, watching his hands pick through the accumulation of things set there, placed by somebody in a shape to show them off. Pictures of men and women and children in funny clothes, everybody dressed up pretending to be young but showing they couldn't be by the way their eyes looked staring into the camera lens, dead for years but trying not to be and fooling nobody. A framed letter, medals with ribbons fastened to them, a coin, a necklace, a pin carved with a white woman's head. Paper weights made of colored glass with flower petals frozen in the center of them, blooming forever, but dead, dead, dead.

From all this collection, Randall Eugene's hand picked up one thing, a book bound in leather with two words made of curlicued letters on its cover, and his hand lifted the book to show it to his eyes to read, and the words said Precious Memories, and his eyes read that but his brain would not tell him what that meant, and he knew he had to understand it, and he believed if he looked a little harder and longer, the meaning would come to him and say its name.

It hung there on the surface of his sight, almost connecting, but it never did, because she was in the room now, and Randall Eugene knew he would never be able to take its meaning now because she spoke, and her words got in the way of letting him know what Precious Memories meant.

"Son," she was saying, "son, don't touch that, don't take my book, you hadn't got any use for that."

She held a butcher knife in her hand, and it should have been trembling because the woman was old and afraid, but it wasn't. A shaft of sunlight from the window broken in the door touched the edge of the blade, and it hung there steady as a stone set in a ring, winking with light, and Randall Eugene watched himself step toward her and take the knife out of her hand.

What will it do now, he wondered, my hand with the knife in it, the wink of the sun gone now from the blade edge, and then it showed him, all the light in the room did, gathered into one beam, like it does when someone is on a stage ready to begin an act or sing or dance or play an instrument, and it showed him what he would do and it let him see him doing it.

And then the old woman was lying on her sofa, but it wasn't like she was asleep. No, she was falling halfway off the piece of furniture, but her fall was frozen in a way it couldn't be, a way gravity wouldn't allow. How could she do that, Randall Eugene said to himself, amazed by the act the old woman could perform, stop in mid-air halfway to the floor, holding, holding, holding everything in the room fixed and set and captured like one of the pictures on the table of the old people pretending to be young and alive and smiling, though they were dead.

"Go on, now," a man said in a deep voice. "You've done what you came to do, son. You've got what you wanted. It's in your hand now. You have it to carry all by yourself."

Randall Eugene knew the voice, and he knew the man, and he had for as long as he could remember, and the man was standing in the entry way to another room.

Randall Eugene had not seen that room before, how had it gotten there, he had looked that direction before, hadn't he, when he came into the place where he found himself now?

He was dressed like he always was, the man in the entry way, a dark suit, a shirt so white you wanted to look away from it to save your eyesight, a tie with broad muted stripes and he was solid and bulky across the face and forehead, and his cheeks and chin shone from being freshly shaved, the thin mustache two precise lines above his lips, large and prominent and parted to speak.

"Dr. King," Randall Eugene McNeill said. "I have always wanted to meet you, but I thought I never would be able to."

The man nodded once, but his eyes did not move from where they were fixed on Randall Eugene's eyes, and then he lifted one hand and held it out as though to take the leather book from Randall Eugene.

"My name is Randall Eugene McNeill," he said, speaking as if he was introducing someone whose name he had heard only once and had to concentrate to remember. "Dr. King, I'm Randall Eugene, that's me."

"No," the man in the entry way to the other room said, "you're not him, young man. Your name is Do Run Run."

And then the blood, just a thin line, began to come from the knot of the man's striped tie, the place where the bullet had struck Dr. King on that balcony in Memphis, the one at the Lorraine Motel, and Randall Eugene watched it grow like a flower blossom, a red carnation like the ones in the corsages the girls wore to the Central High prom, and it was stronger and wider and deeper, and the blood was a stream now, not a flower at all, and it moved in steady spurts.

All the light in the room began to gather into one point, which twisted and glowed so brightly that Randall Eugene had to close his eyes or be blind, but he could still see it through his lids, moving past his face now, and he followed it as it floated up and out a window set high in the wall, and Randall Eugene knew he must follow, and he did, and he watched himself take two strong steps and leap from the floor, the leather book held before him as he went through the glass and frame of the window, following the ball of light outside, and now it was gone, and the sky was as black as midnight, as dark as Dr. King's suit and the blood against it.

The light was gone forever, and Randall Eugene knew that, he knew that was true, as true as the leather book he now had to carry in his hands into the pattern worked into the street that ran through all the world.

9

J.W. Ragsdale sat in the Owl Bar on Central at a table well away from the crowd of police officers, detectives, and the odd dispatcher and clerk clamoring at Cliff Perry for more drink. He was nursing his first beer, a Buckhorn or Stag or some other brew occupying the low end of the price spectrum. J.W. hadn't looked at it close enough to tell when Cliff put it before him, but he knew that Cliff knew his preference well enough to make the correct selection and he knew that Judy had not showed up to work that shift, leaving Cliff to fight alone the battle of Thursday night in the Owl after one a.m. against the powerful thirsts of Midtown Memphis peacekeepers, law enforcers, and support staff.

Judy was supposed to be there, Cliff had told J.W., but goddamn it she wasn't and hadn't even called in to let him know she wasn't.

"Maybe she couldn't, Cliff," J.W. said. "You know, sick, or disabled to work for some good reason."

"Sick, my ass," Cliff had said, pointing toward the solitary beer on the table in front of J.W, "She's lying up drunk with that Mexican, Herrara or Hernandez or whatever his name is. You better let me get you a couple more of them bottles while I'm at it, J.W., cause once that damn pack of head-knockers gets here, I sure ain't going to be running around in front of the bar serving tables."

"Just the one, Cliff," J.W. said, "will do me. I'm technically on duty. But I got to say I'm disappointed to hear you talk the way you been doing, Cliff."

"Better get that extra one now," Cliff said again. "What're you talking about, the way I been talking? What the shit does that mean?"

"Calling Judy's gentleman friend a Mexican, for one thing," J.W. said, curling one hand around his beer bottle and lifting the other one in a stop sign gesture to discourage Cliff Perry from fetching another one. "The gentleman is Hispanic ethnically, and you can't presume to know what flavor of Hispanic he may happen to be."

"If that's all that's bothering you, I ain't worried then."

"You should be. Show a little sensitivity, Cliff. Shit, you're talking like a racist redneck asshole, and it appalls me."

"Appalls?"

"Appalls," J.W. said. "Yessir, and calling my comrades in arms by that demeaning term, head-knockers, Lord, Cliff, what I am suppose to think? That kind of coded speech marginalizes a whole category of service providers."

"Oh, hell, I get it. You been at a departmental workshop, ain't you? Had some kind of a consultant talk at y'all. That's where you hearing this stuff."

"I have," J.W. said. "Run by a lady PhD from St. Louis, and a little session of soul-searching would do you some good, too, Cliff."

"Here they come," Cliff said, turning toward the door just slammed back against the wall by a cadre of mustachioed uniformed cops baying for whiskey. "You and that beer are on your own now."

"Fuck you, Cliff," J.W. had called after the departing bartender, "and your low and mean use of hate speech."

But that was fifteen minutes ago, and the beer level in his bottle was at a hair short of two fingers, Cliff was too busy to look up, and J.W. Ragsdale would be damned in hell with his back broke before he'd walk over to the bar and fight his way through the mob of cops to ask for a refill.

And where was Tyrone Walker, late again but with a foolproof excuse like every married man always has at his immediate disposal. Something with the wife, something with the kids, something with the goddamned house.

A man on his own, J.W. considered, looking at the last swallow of beer in the bottle, has not got a single thing between him and the obligation to get to work on time. Be late once, and they're convinced you're either laid up drunk or getting over that condition. Be single, and be suspect. Be divorced, and be a dickhead. Be double-divorced, and be damned to an early hell.

"Hey, Sergeant Ragsdale," somebody said. "Looky what I got for you. Cliff sent you over a beer."

"God bless the boy. I can use that," J.W. said, knocking back the last warm swallow in the bottle before him and taking the cold one from Jim

58

Drake, who was leaning over the table at a perilous angle.

"Mind if I sit down?" Drake said. "Or are you thinking some deep thoughts about how to fight crime in the big city? Figuring up ways to effect a turn-around, like Pencil Neck Cogrun's always saying."

"Yeah, sit down, Jim," J.W. said. "And don't get me started to thinking about Cogrun. I'm trying to enjoy a quiet drink here before Tyrone shows up, rearing to go."

"You better think about him, J.W.," Jim Drake said. "Once Pencil Neck gets finished up at the night law school, he's going to be a force to be reckoned with. That's what he's always telling everybody. He figures to move up in the organization. Push the envelope. Go to Republican fundraisers. Get that nose polished up."

As he talked, Jim Drake was leaning in toward J.W. across the table, his voice raised to be heard over the din at the bar of shouts, curses, laughs, and grab-assing from the crowd of police personnel hammering down shots, hits, and drafts. Up close and personal as Jim Drake was having to be with J.W. in order to be understood, J.W. was able to see clearly flecks of yellow paint in Drake's thinning pompadour.

"What you been painting today, Jim?" J.W. said, patting at his own hair to give Drake hint and direction as he spoke.

"Nothing, that's from yesterday. An old boy's garage out in Southhaven. I ain't bothered to wash my hair with paint thinner yet this week. Just only hand soap."

"I wouldn't if I was you," J.W. said. "That yellow hairdo gives you kind of a punk look. You could go undercover with some of these youthful offender bunches, and you'd blend right in. Get you a cover story in the Commercial Appeal. I can just see the headlines. Hell, you might even get you some pussy out of it."

"Aw, there was a time when I used to worry about getting paint on me, back when I was running women all over Shelby County, but I don't give a shit no more, J.W."

"Well, whatever gives a man an edge I don't begrudge him."

Jim Drake turned to look at the bar where a particularly loud outcry from one of the female officers had just risen above the general baying of Thursday night late in the Owl.

"Who's that? LaPearl?"

"Naw," J.W. said. "LaPearl wouldn't have bothered to holler before she knocked the piss out of whoever just grabbed her by the ass. She don't give no warning. That's got to be one of them new enough to still be surprised when a colleague disrespects her person."

"Yeah," Jim Drake said. "You're right, but listen, J.W. I got to tell you this story about Major Dalbey, if you ain't already heard it. That's why I come over here in the first place and disturbed your meditations."

"What? You mean about the Atkins Diet when he was on it that time?"

"No, better than that. The major's off that now anyway, and he's found something better, he believes. I never thought that story about him and the Atkins stuff was funny, anyway. Who gives a fuck about diet humor?"

"All right, fire away," J.W. said. "I'm about to get sleepy enough to call Tyrone on his cell phone, anyway."

"It was Dan Mayfield that did it," Jim Drake said, beginning to laugh at what he was about to tell, "right before he pulled the pin and retired."

"Where's he living now, Mayfield?" J.W. said. "Where'd him and Carroll move to?"

"Bells, Tennessee, where else? He hates it so much he was bound to go back yonder. Anyway, Mayfield calls up Major Dalbey at home see, one night, and he says, Are you Marlon Ray Dalbey, sir?'

"The major goes yes.' From near Holly Springs, Mississippi? Mayfield says. Yeah,' says the major. So what?'

"Did you go to high school there in Holly Springs?"

Yeah, who are you?' says the major.

"I'm getting to that, sir. Did you date a girl when you were at the police academy in Memphis, name of Jenny Lucille Brady?"

I don't remember no Jenny Lucille Brady, no, I don't. Who's she?'

"I remember her, sir, and I remember her well. She's my mama, and she's in a care facility now, young as she is, all disabled to work and her mind about two-thirds gone. All Mama remembers is a few things."

"Why you telling me this stuff? I'm sorry for your mama if she's in the shape you're talking about and all, but I don't know her."

"Sir, Major Dalbey," Dan Mayfield says, all solemn and his voice just low and quiet like he means everything he's saying. You know how

60

Mayfield can be."

"Yeah," J.W. said. "He could lie better than any cop I ever knew on the force. And did, too. But what happened then?"

"Well, Mayfield says to the major, Sir, I'm telling you this for one reason, and here it is it's because you're my daddy.'

"Jesus H. Christ," J.W. said, almost knocking his new beer over, "I bet Major Dalbey had a instant stroke. I bet the side of his face went all numb on him."

"Wait, J.W., wait," Jim Drake said. "It went on and on. Mayfield kept calling from cell phones he borrowed from people on the street, and pay phones and convenience stores that let him use the phone, and it got to the point where Major Dalbey would recognize his voice and just slam the damn phone down, and Dan Mayfield would call right back and try to keep on talking, like the connection had been broke or some shit."

"God Almighty, I never heard any of this before," J.W. said.

"Course not. Mayfield never told nobody about it until he retired and went back to Bells."

"He was afraid the major would get him fired."

"He was afraid the major would get him killed," Jim Drake said.

"Anyway, the next to last time he called him to talk about being his son and all that horseshit, Mayfield told the major he had gone to the care facility and picked up his crazy old mama and had her in the car and would bring her to Major Dalbey's house. Said all she would say over and over was Marlon Ray, Marlon Ray, Marlon Ray, and then kind of cry a little bit and look happy, smiling and all."

J.W. was laughing so hard that a few of the drunk cops at the bar of the Owl looked around to see who was causing the disturbance.

"And J.W.," Jim Drake said, "Mayfield had taped this shit, a lot of it, and he let me listen to this part. I guess he lost the rest of it or something. And when the Major heard this unknown son of his was going to bring his crazy mama by the house for a reunion and to meet Gladys, Major Dalbey said, you do, and I'll kill your ass with ordnance you never heard of. You'll be a dead motherfucker, and so will your nutty old lady."

"How drunk are you crazy bastards, anyway?" Tyrone Walker said, sliding into the other chair at the table where J.W. and Jim Drake were reared back laughing. "I heard y'all out in the parking lot before I even hit the door. I could hear you outside hollering over that bunch in the vice task force up yonder at the bar."

"That makes me proud of myself, Tyrone," J.W. Ragsdale said. "Being louder than vice. But you got to wait a minute here. I got to get the end of what Jim's been telling me." Then, shifting back to Jim Drake. "You said that was the next to last time Mayfield called him. Something else must've happened. What?"

"Well, of course, there didn't nobody show up at the major's that night, and Mayfield left it alone for three or four days. And then he pulled the last stunt during that big summit meeting of all the brass with Mayor Herrenton and that bunch of suits he runs with."

"You mean the congressman with his fact-finding committee and the big report on progress against crime they working on making and all that shit?"

"Yeah, Harold Ford, Jr and a bunch of aides and you name it, every damn big dog and hanger-on in Memphis and West Tennessee, they was all in that big meeting. And Dan Mayfield said it came to him like a gift, what to do, when he heard they were taking questions and e-mails and calls at the press conference at the end of the thing."

"Aw, naw," J.W. said. "Nuh uh."

"Oh, yeah," Jim Drake said, leaning across the table to speak directly into J.W.'s face, the flecks of yellow paint in his hair glittering like Mardi Gras makeup. "Mayfield know Myrtice Watson was screening the calls and like everybody that's been around her he knew her soft spot."

"Old folks in nursing homes in Raleigh," J.W. said.

"Mayfield said he was a concerned senior in the Golden Sunset Gardens facility in Raleigh, and hell you know that's where Myrtice's old lady stays. Mayfield said he wanted to say one thing to Major Marlon Ray Dalbey of the Midtown station, and Myrtice patched him through on the loudspeaker, announced who the senior wanted to talk to, and the Major says yes sir, how can I help you, and Mayfield says one thing."

"Say it," J.W. said. "Tell it on out."

"Mayfield says real pitiful and like he was asking something, you know. He said, Daddy?'"

After J.W. and Jim Drake tailed off a little from their fit of laughter and table-slapping, Drake rose to leave.

"I got to go, y'all," he said. "Be careful out there, like it says on the TV."

"Don't tell me what led up to this, J.W.," Tyrone Walker said as they watched Jim Drake head for the remnants of the vice task force still drinking at the bar, "I don't want to know, and I won't listen to it."

"All right, Tyrone," J.W. said. "I won't bother you with frivolity. I know you're a serious man. What's the deal tonight you got me into?"

J.W. knew what it was, of course, having read Tyrone's e-mail six hours earlier, just before he left the Midtown station for his little house on Tutwiler, supper, and a two-hour nap in front of the TV. Time was when he could have grabbed something to eat, drunk beer at the Owl for two hours, joined Tyrone for a stake-out for the rest of the night, and then showed up for work in the morning, not that happy but functioning. These days he had to shoehorn in a couple of hours of lie-down time somewhere along the way. That fact he kept to himself.

"So you believe Ronnie Katz is back in Memphis?" J.W. said.

"I do, J.W., and I got it on good authority."

"Who'd that be?"

"His ex mother-in-law, that's who," Tyrone said. "Marianne Felder and I have been keeping in close touch for over three years now. I talk to her, or she talks to me, I ought to say, a couple of times a month, sometimes more."

"Three years, huh? Ever since Ronnie Katz fled the wrath to come."

"Yeah, as soon as he got on that first leg of his flight, and Marianne realized it, she started letting every cop and every politician know about it, from the bottom to the top."

"But Mrs. Felder settled on you, finally, for sure, didn't she? Why'd she do that, you reckon?"

"I expect it's because I got a capacious soul, J.W., and I know how to listen."

"Capacious, huh?" J.W. said. "I wish I'd had the opportunity for schooling you had, Tyrone. I could sling them words around, too."

"You got to take opportunities, J.W. You can't just stand way off at a distance and admire them. You got to get mad at them."

"I expect that middle-aged lady with all that blonde hair took to you because she thought you was cute. Maybe wanted to change her luck."

The last few cops at the bar of the Owl had paired off, male and female, the ones of them that were going to or felt like they were still able, and the noise level had dropped enough to make the building seem more like what it really was, a big empty space surrounded by concrete block walls with no windows and poor ventilation. J.W. felt a need to move beginning to rise in his viscera, and he looked Tyrone in the eye and gestured toward the door.

"Yeah," Tyrone said, and the two homicide detectives left the Owl Bar and got into the unmarked city car Tyrone was driving and pulled out onto Central Avenue headed east.

"Best thing about my personal vehicle is I can leave it almost anywhere in Memphis and nobody will mess with it," J.W. said. "It'll be right there when I get back."

"That old Buick would be right there if you were to leave it parked for a month with the keys in it," Tyrone said. "And it wouldn't be out of respect for property rights, neither, J.W."

Neither man spoke for the next several minutes as Tyrone drove the deserted streets of Midtown, a little wet after a rain shower, working his way deeper into the upscale residential area near Cherokee Gardens, J.W. thinking about Ronnie Katz who'd located himself safe and unknown and now returning to a place where people were bound and determined to put him under the jail if they ever got the chance.

Tyrone switched off the car lights, drove for a couple of blocks on a side street called Pebble Brook, parked under the dark overhang of two big oak trees, and switched off the ignition.

"This spot must be a place where rich kids stop after a date and work on each other," J.W. said. "Nice and private."

"Don't get your hopes up," Tyrone said. "I ain't interested in making out, and besides, rich kids in this part of Memphis don't have to do their thing outside in a car, and they sure as hell don't go on what you call dates anymore, either."

"Is that right? They don't know what they're missing, then. They never had the chance to grow up in Batesville, Mississippi, learning all their night moves like I did."

"You are so out of it, J.W.," Tyrone said. "It's pitiful listening to you trying to live in the past."

"This is where Ronnie Katz's kids stay, I guess," J.W. said. "I remember the street name."

"Yeah, after Ronnie had their mama killed and then hauled ass for Belize, this here is all the poor little things had left to get by on."

"Looks like the governor's mansion," J.W. said. "Over yonder in Nashville."

"It's better than that," Tyrone said. "It's new and up to date in every respect and in every way. We're parked by the tennis court, for one thing, in there behind all these trees and shrubs and stuff."

"You really think Ronnie Katz would put himself in range to come back here and see his young'uns?"

"Not the first time he's done it," Tyrone Walker said. "Mrs. Felder says he's been back at least twice in the last fourteen months."

"Why?"

"Pure dee love, J.W. It is a strange and powerful force, love is. It'll make a man take all kind of chances. Besides, Ronnie Katz doesn't want to miss out on the key times of his kids growing up. The magic moments, you understand."

"Which one is this?" J.W. said. "A sweet sixteen party?"

"No, little Ronnie has just graduated from M.U.S. He'll be off at college here in a couple of months."

"He will? Where'll he going? University of Memphis?"

"No, hell, J.W. Ronnie Katz's boy's not going to some redneck place like that. He'll be in Lexington, Virginia, come September. W and L, J.W. That's where the young scholar's headed."

"W and L," J.W. said. "What's that mean? Whips and leather?"

Tyrone started to answer, but fell silent as up ahead the low beams of an automobile appeared around a picturesque bend built into Pebble Brook Way by a high-dollar environmental contextualist J.W. couldn't summon up the name of. He knew he'd read about the man in a feature story in the MidSouth Life section of the Commercial Appeal several years back one Sunday morning in his rent house on Tutwiler. He had given the Commercial Appeal piece his attention in a weak moment, he remembered. He promised himself now he'd ask Tyrone if he knew about the man and his wonderful way with natural space, as the lady Commercial Appeal writer had called it, after this business with Ronnie Katz was over.

Probably Tyrone hadn't seen the story, and that would give J.W. a little leverage for hoorawing his partner. Something to do.

And another thing, J.W. told himself as he watched the lights on the car ahead go out as it pulled to a stop the other side of the drive leading onto the grounds of the big house which Ronnie Katz, once the pre-eminent real estate attorney in a large part of Memphis, used to call home, it would've been interesting to see how Tyrone handled that thing he'd said about whips and leather. That was spur of the moment, and it was pretty damn good for a Batesville High graduate.

"Whose limo is that?" J.W. said. "You reckon that driver knows who he's carrying?"

"He'd say no, and so would the man who owns the car," Tyrone said. "I guarantee you that."

The passenger in the limo was getting out, the two homicide detectives could tell, though no light came on in the limo when one of the rear doors opened.

"He sees this car," J.W. said. "He's not taking a step toward the house yet."

"There's cars parked all along here, J.W.," Tyrone said. "I can see three other ones from where we're sitting."

"Yeah, but not a one of them's as shitty as this one, and he can tell that."

The figure at the rear door of the dark limousine ahead pushed the door closed, the sound barely audible in the dead quiet of Cherokee Gardens, and took a step onto the expanse of manicured space between the street and the house.

"That's a quality machine," Tyrone said. "You hear that door close?"

"Like a rat pissing on cotton," J.W. said. "Like a Lincoln."

"Unh uh. It's a step up from that."

"How do you want to do it?" J.W. said. "You going to wait until he gets in the house?"

"No, I don't want to have to get through the door and look for him inside. I want to take him while he's messing with the keys and stuff."

"You suppose Ronnie's packing?"

"He always was before, J.W.," Tyrone said, easing the door open, "all the time he was strutting around Memphis. I expect Mr. Katz is strapped all right, but he's never had the balls to pull trigger on anybody, not even his own wife."

"O.K.," J.W. said, propping his door open, "you go on ahead, do what you're going to do, and I'll see to the driver. Ronnie might've hired him somebody that ain't too shy to bust a cap or two."

With that, Tyrone Walker was gone, his first two steps taking him to full speed, and J.W. marveled as he had the first time he'd met Tyrone, all those long years ago in E.H. Crump Stadium where the All-Tennessee, All-Mississippi high school exhibition football game used to be held. The first time Tyrone Walker, the All-Tennessee tailback from Central High of Memphis, took the handoff from the quarterback, he was through the hole inside the right tackle before J.W. could get up on the balls of his feet from his position at inside linebacker for the Mississippi team.

"J.W. Ragsdale," Bobby Herbert, the coach for the All-Mississippi squad said at halftime, "the first time that colored boy touched the ball he went by you like an Illinois Central freight train."

"Yessir," J.W. said. "But I got him down the next time."

"Yeah, twelve yards up the field," Coach Herbert had said, looking around the locker room for signs of appreciation for his wit, but as J.W. remembered the scene, no one would meet his gaze.

As J.W. sprinted toward the driver's side of the limousine, he could see the man behind the wheel lifting both hands up before his face as though to ward off something unexpectedly thrown toward him, palms out and empty, and that was a relief. No reason in sight to make J.W. have to think about how to dodge fire while figuring out a way to get the limo driver out from behind the door, out of the car, and under control without having to go terminal on him.

At about the time he put one hand on the door handle and began to gesture with the other for the man behind the wheel to open up, J.W. heard the sound of a collision coming from the expanse of yard toward the house, putting him in mind of the way the breath might sound exiting from a man who'd just fallen off a truckbed and landed flat on his back on hard-packed ground. Deep, sudden, and tailing off into a higher note at the end. Mr. Tyrone Walker had got to where he was going.

The limo driver was out of the car, turning around with his hands held up to the back of his head, and spread-eagling without having to be told a thing about what steps to take next. Yet people will claim over and over that watching TV doesn't teach a soul a thing, J.W. thought as he cuffed the driver and helped the man into the back seat of his own limo, not forgetting to put a hand on the man's head to save it from banging into the roof. He knew the arrestee would expect that. People do pay attention to TV, they can learn, and they like doing things right.

"Stay right there, buddy," J.W. said. "See can you think about where you went wrong in your life the very first time you can call up. I'll get right back to you, and you can tell me when it was."

As J.W. walked away, he could hear the limo driver beginning to tell his story of woe about being nothing but a working man doing a job. The breath was whistling back into the man Tyrone had facedown on the lush Bermuda of the yard as J.W. walked up. As soon as he drew in a good lungful, the man would start talking, J.W. knew, if he truly was Ronnie Katz, and he'd be protesting his treatment and threatening dire consequences for anybody near him.

It is born and bred in any man that ends up being a lawyer, J.W. mused as he stirred the figure before him on the ground in the side with the tip of his shoe, just like a suck-egg dog will rob every hen's nest it can find, no matter how much you whip him off of it and try to break him of the habit. He is natural to it, and it to him.

"I had a dog one time, a red-bone hound," J.W. announced, "down in Panola County, Mississippi, when I was a kid. And he would suck every free-range egg he could find on the place, and let me tell you, he could find them all."

"Is that right?" Tyrone Walker said, getting a good purchase on the cuffs he had fastened on the man on the ground and beginning to pull him to his knees, assisting him in the effort to rise by tugging strongly at the man's coat collar from behind, as well.

"I'm not going to ask how that observation is relevant to the situation, Sergeant Ragsdale," Tyrone said, "since I expect you're not going to need any encouragement to tell me."

"Thing of it was," J.W. said, reaching out to help get the cuffed man stood up and pointed in the right direction, "I had the idea one day to break him of the habit, that dog name of Bobo, by busting open a egg before he got to it and pouring about half a bottle of Tabasco sauce in it.

Setting up a surprise for him, see."

"Did you get that done?" Tyrone said, and then speaking to the man in front of him, "Come over here in the light so I can see your pretty face."

"I did, and Bobo found it, and he ate it, and you know what?" J.W. said. "He wasn't even fazed. Didn't turn a hair. He liked it, see, but that kind of backfired on him on down the road."

"How's that?" Tyrone said. "Damn, Ronnie," he went on. "You look terrible. You lost too much weight, son. What you been eating?"

"Yeah," J.W. said. "Bobo was never satisfied with a plain old raw egg ever again. If it didn't have that zing, he didn't want it, from then on. Got so damn discouraged with the quality of them Panola County eggs, Bobo just stopped eating them. He decided they wasn't worth the trouble no more. It was kind of pitiful to watch him run up on one and then just kind of turn away from it."

The man Tyrone Walker had stood up in the reflection from a streetlight still hadn't spoken, his head thrown back as though he was exhausted from a burst of physical activity that had left him drained and in need of some deep breathing. He coughed twice and broke into a sob.

"Evening, Counselor," J.W. said. "I know you done met Sergeant Walker, but let me introduce you formally, give y'all a chance to talk about life in the islands, you know, shoot the breeze a little, get acquainted."

"Belize is not an island, Sergeant Ragsdale," Tyrone said. "You don't actually think Ronald Q. Katz would be so conventional as to run off to a Caribbean hideaway, do you? He wouldn't do that. It's much too usual, and Lord, the price of real estate on a tropic isle. Just prohibitive."

"I do believe Mr. Katz, Esquire, has learned the same lesson old Bobo Hound did," J.W. said, "back down yonder in Panola County. He seems to have stopped doing what he always loved to do before. It's lost its suption."

"How's that?" Tyrone said.

"He ain't made a peep. He ain't said a word, and we been standing here in the yard probably two or three minutes. Back in the old days, Ronnie would've said four or five paragraphs by now. He would've done got out a writ on your ass, Sergeant Walker, for knocking him down on that old wet grass and getting his pants all muddy and stained up."

"Sergeant Ragsdale," Tyrone said in an earnest voice, "I do believe

69

Ronnie Katz has seen the error of his ways and has come back to Memphis to atone. He is prepared to submit himself to the due processes of the justice system of the great state of Tennessee. Do not misjudge this man."

"I do expect you're right, Tyrone," J.W. said. "He's learned his lesson, and as soon as he stops blubbering, I think he's going to request to talk to counsel. Let's give him a ride downtown and get every thing all cranked up and good to go."

"They've turned lights on in the big house, I see," Tyrone Walker said. "You want to transport him and the limo driver together?"

"You go on with Ronnie," J.W. said. "I'll wait for a squad car to get here and pick me and the driver up."

Then addressing Ronnie Katz, by now in an advanced state of tears and moaning, "Good seeing you this evening, Counselor. Isn't this a wonderful time of the year to be coming home to Memphis again? Lord, just smell that Mississippi River funk."

Tyrone began to direct his seized felon toward the car, and J.W. called after him. "One thing I want to know, Tyrone," he said. "How come you get all the easy ones like old running Ronnie here and I get the poor old dead ladies like Miss Beulahdene?"

"The ones I get ain't easy, J.W.," Tyrone said. "I just make them look that way."

"Oh, that's it, huh?" J.W. said. "I knew it was something scientific."

10

Six a.m., Ronnie Katz in custody, and he should be in bed, J.W. knew, trying to get a little sleep before showing up at the Midtown station again sometime before noon, but he still felt wound a turn too tight to face heading for the rent house on Tutwiler. He'd likely toss around for an hour before passing out in bed, and he'd dream crazy shit that would leave him grumpy all day.

Turning the car left on East Parkway instead, he headed toward the Jewel Box out toward the airport, a drinking establishment known for being either the latest place you could get a drink at the end of a long night or the earliest place you could find one at the beginning of a new day.

Three or four cars were parked in front of the building, leftovers of the evening just completed, and two pickup trucks loaded with ladders, cans of paint, and tarps were pulled in at the side, early birds of the day just dawning.

A house painter had to maintain a certain level of alcohol in his blood to be able to function, J.W. considered as he alighted from his Buick, and every painter he'd ever known paid due attention to that professional fact of life. Maybe it was some kind of chemical need the body was required to satisfy, J.W. thought as he marched up to the bar and took a seat. Probably all the reagents and dyes in paints get into a painter's brain and spleen and liver and all those other innards, and set up an imbalance only alcohol can counteract.

Maybe scientists were working away right here in Memphis, maybe out at the Schering Plough Laboratories or Buckman Chemicals, trying to figure out why every house painter in the MidSouth and beyond was either a damned old drunk or doing his best to achieve that calling. Were women ever house painters, J.W. wondered and decided not, since he had never seen one up on the side of a building swabbing away.

"You can't blame a painter for doing what his body system makes him have to do," J.W. said to the bartender before him, who was taking a deep drag on an unfiltered cigarette. "You can't judge him, and you can't hold him responsible."

"I don't hold nobody responsible for nothing," the bartender said. "What can I get you, friend?"

"Heaven Hill and water back," J.W. said. "I like that attitude you just expressed, too. I flat out tell you I do."

"Why, thank you," the bartender said, stubbing out his cigarette and going to his pocket for another one. "I do make one exception to that rule, though, I got to say."

"What's that?"

"I do judge the tobacco companies, Philip Morris in particular. Them fuckers have give me cancer."

"Well, an exception proves the rule," J.W. said. "Nothing wrong with that. Make that Heaven Hill a double."

Two seats down the bar, one of the painters from one of the pickups outside was taking his medicine and trying to get the attention of a woman seated at the corner to his left. J.W. could see from her reflection in the mirror above the bar of the Jewel Box that the woman was past being drunk, and had entered the stage where she had consumed enough alcohol to make herself sober, a stage which would last up to a half hour provided she kept drinking. If she stopped suddenly now, took her foot off a steady pressure on the accelerator and touched the brake, she'd fly right through the windshield, seat belt fastened or not.

"We could go get some coffee at my place," the painter was saying, "but it's way out in Whitehaven, and my kids is all there asleep. I got the custody of every last one of them, and I just love them to death."

I have got to get that Heaven Hill stuck in front of me quick, J.W. said to himself, suck it up fast, and get the hell out of the Jewel Box and go home. Where is that cancer-stricken bartender?

"I know I'm the one that smoked the cigarettes," the bartender said, placing two glasses before J.W. "I ain't quarreling with that fact. I lit them, and I sucked in the smoke from ever one of them, I grant anybody that. But I didn't make the damn things taste so good and put them in a pretty package for people to buy. No sir. That part of it wasn't me."

"Or," the painter down the bar was saying to the woman currently stuck in the intermediate zone of fully-achieved drunkenness, "or we could go get some of that coffee out of that thermos in my truck. Sit out there for a while. That's a workable option."

Doing her part, the woman took another strong sip from her drink, the bartender leaned in closer to J.W., waiting for a response to his judgment on Philip Morris, the painter turned to look in the direction of the two men to his right, his tongue jammed in his cheek as he pondered the next thing he might say to get the woman to join him in the promised land of morning coffee in the cab of a pickup, and J.W. shifted on his bar stool.

"Tell you what, buddy," J.W. said to the bartender, "here's your money for the Heaven Hill, but I want you to give it to that lady down yonder."

"You don't want your double H.H.?"

"You don't want your cigarette?" J.W. said, and then looking down the bar at the woman at its corner, called to her, "Sugar, just keep drinking your whiskey. Leave that old coffee alone."

"What you looking at?" the painter said. "Who you talking to?"

"I ain't looking at nothing," J.W. said, heading for the door out of the Jewel Box. "And I ain't talking to nobody. All I'm saying is hello and good morning, Memphis, Tennessee."

11

Like most opportunities in life, Jimbo Reynolds considered as he watched them piling into the rows of seats in the auditorium before him, playing to a crowd of school kids is double-edged. There is an upside, and there is a downside. There is good to be gleaned and advantage to be taken, and there is a poison-hard chunk of inertia to be overcome to get the sorry little suckers to listen.

It is like, he thought carefully, as he passed through a mental file of comparisons that might or might not prove apt as illustration of the general truth he was seeking to understand and present to his audience, his audience in this case himself alone, and that to a true thinker devoted to honest comprehension the toughest audience of all it is like choosing to pursue a truly good-looking and genuinely sexually attractive woman rather than just settling for a skag.

A skag, now, has her purpose, and she has her use. She is easy, she presents little resistance, and she is above all grateful and ready to accommodate. She will do what you want her to do, and she will do it quick, and she will do it with zest and enthusiasm. What, Jimbo Reynolds put to his internal self privately as he sat, watching the crowd of high school kids clamber across, over, in, around, and through their own mass as they filled the rows of seats in the Memphis Central High School auditorium, what is wrong with this picture, this portrait of dalliance with a skag?

Nothing, nothing at all. Each thing in its own place is appropriate, and God makes no mistakes in His provision of the wonders of His world for a man's use of them.

But there's a doubleness in this bit of reality, as there is in all things.

A man truly attuned to the truth of that doubleness, a man in touch with the downside as well as the up, must know the other face of a situation or a thing and must embrace it, if he is to enjoy the full savor of existence in and partaking of God's world.

Defending the rose are its thorns, the sweetest fruit hides its flesh within the toughest rind, and the best pussy is always the hardest to come by. Jimbo stepped back mentally from what he had just thought and looked at it. Damn, that's good, he judged. Let's take it to the next level.

The beauty of the rose and its scent, the savor of the mango and its juice, the incredible delight of the reluctantly spread thighs of a beautiful woman finally conquered, these are the richest treasures God grants a man willing to commit fully to the work at hand.

So, in this case, the invitation to him as Ranch Foreman of the Sun-Up Ministry of the Big Corral to make a presentation at the weekly assembly of all students in Central High School of Memphis came as a double-edged opportunity. Don Condon had arranged it, of course, as part of his PR campaign of service outreach for the Sunrise Ministry. The publicity is free, Don had pointed out, coming out of such pro bono gestures, but the space in the newspaper is just as big as if you had paid top dollar for it.

"It can't be a chapel service," Dennis Ryan, the vice principal of the high school had told Jimbo. "I hope you understand and appreciate that fact, Mr. Reynolds. We are a public institution, and we revere the separation of church and state. And we honor that constitutional imperative at Memphis Central High School."

"Call me Jimbo," Jimbo said. "And let me tell you, Dr. Ryan, you ain't going to find a cowboy anywhere who's more of a believer in the constitution of the United States than the old boy talking to you right now. If you were to ask me to preach the gospel to these young'uns in a public school setting, I'd just walk off with my fists balled up. I wouldn't say a word back to you, except so long."

"That's reassuring," the vice principal said. "There is some reluctance in segments of our faculty and staff about the matter, as you might well imagine. It's been hotly debated in some quarters."

"I know that, Doctor," Jimbo said. "I praise the vigilance of the standard bearers in your faculty. But what I'll do at your assembly of these young students will cause no problems for you. I just want to talk about the West, what it means as a symbol and a reality in our great nation. What I like to do is call up pictures to inspire the imagination and spirit of our youth. They're hungry for positive values, they need them big time, and they want them, whether they know it or not."

"Pictures?" Dr. Ryan said. "A series of tableaux?"

"Yes sir," Jimbo said. "Let me give you a couple. I'll talk about a cowpoke, alone on the trail, working cattle, doing his duty, tending to his job despite storms and stampedes and rustlers, and all this for small reward. A true American hero, and I'll explain how that's part of our character as a people. And the way I'll end up, after evoking all them truths from the way of the cowboy is this. Just picture it. Our president, the leader of the free world, given a few hours to relax after the burdens of all he's got to handle, and what does he do? Why, he puts on his old work clothes, sturdy jeans and rough old cowpuncher boots, and he picks up an axe, and he attacks that scrub cedar which will spring up and ruin a man's pasture land. And he does it with energy and force and determination, getting all sweaty and dirty, and he goes about it in the cowboy ways just as he does back in the oval office when he's figuring out how to combat the efforts of terrorists to pop up and ruin our country and our way of life.

"That sounds good," Vice Principal Ryan said. "I believe that'll work. It promises to be most acceptable."

The tumble of one kid over another one, the scrape of footwear against the floor, the hammer of auditorium seats being banged down, the squeals and shouts and groans of teenagers being forced to move from one place to another, the overall sound of the grunt and grab-ass and hoot of the young—all the menagerie of moan—began to subside, and Jimbo Reynolds made his first studied and choreographed move, thinking I hope Don Condon is taking good notes on that yellow pad he carries everywhere with him.

Standing up from the hay bale on which he'd been leaning, Jimbo had had to bring that prop with him and promise to take it away when he left the premises Jimbo Reynolds stretched his arms out at length, yawned big, took off his Stetson and fanned it back and forth a couple of beats as though to get a little breeze moving, and then he turned his back to the assembly of Central High School and looked up at the ceiling area of the rear of the auditorium as if aware of something of great interest and moment residing there.

He held that pose for fully half a minute, acutely aware that the focus of the crowd's attention was closing to a fine bead on the back of his head.

Let it build, he told himself, let it build. But don't let it boil over, don't let it move beyond that magic moment of maximum concentration. You'll know it when it's there, and you'll know when it's fixing to get away from you, and you know that your knowing is the measure of your being a salesman who can forevermore close the hell out of the deal.

Almost, almost, hold it, hold it. Let it sizzle. Now, bust it wide open.

"Partners," Jimbo said, swinging around almost lazily as he pivoted on the heel of his left boot to face the audience, and seeing all those heads and all those faces and all those eyes turned in calibrated perfection settled precisely on him.

"Partners, sometimes out on the trail, out on the range at the end of a day of doing my job, I look up at the sky, and I see things."

I'm on the upside, Jimbo said softly to that part of his brain which judged his actions and his affect and which did it truly and did not lie, I'm here. Use it. Use it hard.

"I see things other folks don't seem to. They tell me I'm wrong, some of them do, the weaklings, the ones whose life is nothing more than that of the cattle I have in my care. Cattle eat, they water, they doze. They eat, they water, they doze. And finally, they die.

"They die, all right. They die if you can call eating and watering and dozing being alive.

"I don't. No, I call that the way of cattle, I call that being a piece of meat waiting to be cut up, fried over a fire, and consumed as fuel."

Some kid near the front of the audience tried to laugh at that, hoping for a reaction, but none came, and his cackle cut off as though somebody had just jerked hard on a rope around his neck.

"What I call life is not that. What a wrangler knows to be real is not what a steer or a bull or a heifer or a calf can ever know. How could they? They're meat, moving around.

"I call life being able to see what's not there and knowing that's the real thing, that's the truth, that's the miracle. What comes out of what's nothing to cattle is what's real to a cowboy. If you don't know that, all you're doing is eating and watering and dozing as you creep toward a lonely death. And, partners, that don't mean nothing."

Out in the audience of Central High School students, a third of the way from the rear of the auditorium near the middle of the row of seats in which they sat, Antwan leaned over to speak into Randall Eugene McNeill's ear.

"What that fool talking about, Do Run Run?" he said. "What's he saying?"

Randall Eugene shook his head once quickly, as though to discourage something trying to light on his face, and leaned forward in his seat. A prickle of heat had started up in his head, at a point just below the hairline, and he could tell if he positioned himself at just the right angle, the heat might grow, might spread out and up from its location, and that if it did, it might be able to come near the place where that chunk of ice had settled in as though to fasten itself securely in his head and stay forever.

If the man on the stage dressed in cowboy clothes kept talking and said a thing which Randall Eugene knew he had to hear, though he couldn't say what that thing had to be until he would hear it put into words, then the heat could prosper and become stronger, it would be able to announce itself to the chunk of ice, and the ice would have to notice and acknowledge it, and Randall Eugene would be allowed to come along, too, with the heat and be a part of what it was doing as it worked against the ice. Ice is water in a pattern. If it melts, it flows, and it escapes the pattern.

"Shut up, Antwan," Randall Eugene said under his breath so as not to miss the next thing the man in the cowboy suit might say. "Hush."

"What?" Antwan said. "What you telling me, dog?"

"Shut the fuck up," Randall Eugene said. "Shut the fuck up, and don't call me dog."

12

J.W. Ragsdale spent most of the morning at his desk in the Midtown station with his head down in the files, going over what little there was on the homicide on Montgomery Street. Some blood evidence, unanalyzed, that probably wouldn't amount to anything once it was, the report from the neighbor who'd first noticed the broken-out door panel, a claim from a lady up the street, a Mrs. Deedee Sawyer, that she'd seen a man dressed all in red from head to foot including hat and shoes, "casing the place," as she put it, for the last week leading up to the time Beulahdene Jackson was murdered, a statement from an ice cream van driver to the effect that a middle-eastern looking man, or as he put it, a raghead, must have done it because Mrs. Beulahdene was known to be such a strong Christian.

It must be the same song playing over and over again at a high volume that drives ice cream van drivers nuts, J.W. considered as he flipped through the thin sheaf of papers in the file. You listen to the same minute's worth of Pop Goes the Weasel, repeatedly coming at your head at a high velocity for six or eight hours, and you'd be bound to start seeing all kinds of strange characters roaming the streets of Memphis, especially in those parts of town populated by folks willing to buy something to eat out of a truck with a hole cut in the side of it.

I wonder if the ice cream van guy actually saw an Arab-looking dude in the neighborhood, J.W. thought, and I wonder why the uniform cop who wrote up this report would've even taken a statement from him, much less have stuck it in this file for me to have to read. It is a lost ball in the high grass, education is these days. Nobody has to learn anything anymore. Criminal justice studies they call it. Lord have mercy.

"Hey," J.W. called across the space between his desk and a row of others. "Hal, do you know this street cop name of Brian Allen?"

"No," Hal Meechum said, not looking up from the computer before him. "J.W., I don't. I don't know none of them damn kids anymore, and I'm glad I don't."

"He's got curly black hair," J.W. said, "and he messes with it all the time like a woman does. You bound to've seen him in here. He's always following Pencil Neck around real eager and asking for advice all the time."

"I bet Pencil Neck gives it to him, too," Hal Meechum said. "Now you mention that part, I know him when I see him. Not to talk to, though, don't get me wrong. Why you interested in Brian Allen, J.W.?"

"Because he's a fucking idiot, that's why."

"Well, hell, J.W., if you're looking for idiots among our uniformed officers, you don't have to settle on the one in particular. They're like starlings around here, idiots are."

"Yeah, but this bird is the one who's deposited all this shit in my file," J.W. said. "And I want to counsel with the young professional."

"I'll tell him you're looking for him if I see him," Hal Meechum said and lifted a finger to poke at his keyboard. "What does it mean when the computer says it's a fatal error, J.W., and why's it all the time saying that?"

"If it ain't an International Harvester cotton-picker manufactured before 1975, don't ask me nothing about a machine," J.W. said. "Besides, I got to get out of here and let some air get to me. Don't be scared to touch and mash them keys, Hal. Stand right up to the sons of bitches. Show them who's boss."

Outside as J.W. pulled out of the Midtown station on his way toward the nearest Corky's Barbecue, he almost had his Buick sideswiped by an SUV gleaming like a chariot in the July sun. Standing on his brakes, J.W. briefly contemplated the satisfaction to be gained by chasing the visiting Ohioan down, flashing his badge, and kindling the latent and deepest fear of every Yankee tourist in the South. Being pulled over by a hulking officer of the law looking to be just on the edge of exploding into redneck wrath and vengeance. What would I say to him, J.W. considered as he eased his underpowered sedan into the traffic of Union Avenue just before noon on a blistering first of July, something calculated to cause an instant bowel twinge in the Ohioan, something like "Hey, friend, you in a hurry to get somewhere? You got a destination you just dying to get to? You need some help getting there?"

But no, J.W. told himself, moving into the flow of traffic headed toward the river, I'd probably get the accent wrong, forget to shift my weight from one side to the other like all these sheriffs do in the movies when they're fixing to terrorize some innocent victim from north of the Mason-Dixon Line, and then I'd likely get myself sued for bad acting. Besides, I couldn't catch that SUV in this buggy if I chased it all the way to Little Rock.

And it wouldn't be neighborly, middle of the week leading into the fiftieth anniversary of the birth of rock and roll right here in Memphis, Tennessee. That's what they'd all been calling it anyway, the Chamber of Commerce and the talking heads on local TV and the visiting reporters and news teams, and all the rest of the menagerie, particularly the collection of Elvis freaks from parts north, south, east and west and from every damn place else on the globe where the music of the King has reached and touched and swelled up like a summer gourd in season.

On July fifth, fifty years ago, in 1954, Elvis had parked his truck in front of Sun Recording right here on Union Avenue, a little further on toward the Mississippi River from where J.W.'s Buick was currently cruising, and he had walked into the front door, talked to the lady at the desk and to Sam Phillips and the two other guitar bangers in attendance, and then put it onto acetate for eternity to have to deal with. "That's All Right," the first one, the big one, the bird that brung him, and now it's fifty years later, and there is still money to be made in Memphis from what that redneck boy from Mississippi had caused to happen on that hot day.

Hotels and motels and restaurants and bars and hookers and folks eating their lunch in the University Club and executives sitting high up in ice cold offices in East Memphis and players selling crack and meth in small plastic bags all owed a debt to what happened in 1954 on the fifth of July on Union Avenue in Memphis. They could forevermore live with it.

"Thank you, Elvis," J.W. said out loud as he maneuvered the Buick into the parking lot of the barbecue restaurant he sought. "The rest of the sorry bastards won't say it, but I will. Thank you. You going to keep me busier, too, in the next few days, I do realize and acknowledge. They's bound to be some extra killings coming up here during all this celebrating in the birthplace of rock and roll, and they'll all owe "That's All Right" a debt of gratitude."

Rock and roll do stir things up. It does, and it always has. In Thy name, we gather in Memphis.

81

13

"Damn, it is hot in this old ription of a house," Coy Bridges said. "It feels like it ain't never had the first cupful of air conditioning blow through it."

All four of them were sitting in what used to be the drawing room of the rent house across the street from the Nathan Bedford Forrest Estates. It was late afternoon, just past five o'clock, and the sun stood fixed in the sky west toward Arkansas as though it had been nailed there by a master carpenter intent on having his work last forever. Heat had burned any shade of blue from the atmosphere, leaving the sky as blankly white as the sheet covering an unidentified body in a morgue.

Bob Ferry had bought four plastic-webbed folding chairs at a Dollar Store in South Memphis, arranged them in a circle, and all four men were now looking into the empty space they surrounded. Bob had also purchased a large ceramic ashtray mounted on a wrought-iron stand, and he was pulling matches one by one from a matchbook and flipping them toward the bowl of the tray. Only one so far had landed where he aimed.

"There wouldn't have been any air conditioning back when this place was built, Coy," Bob Ferry said. "So naturally there couldn't have been any cool air blowing out vents anytime in the history of the house."

"History," Coy said. "History. What you talking about? They could've stuck window air units in every hole punched into this building, every damn window."

"They did," Tonto Batiste said, "at points along the way. You can see the brackets where they've rusted on the bricks."

"They not there now, though," Coy Bridges said. "I can flat guarantee you that."

"I don't mind the heat that much," Earl Winston said. "That's not what gets me."

"Let me guess what it is, then," Tonto said. "The humidity, right?"

"Yeah," Earl Winston said, "the way the air kind of sticks to you, you know, like a wet dishrag."

"That's what I figured," Tonto Batiste said. "I judged you to be a man sensitive to humidity, Earl. I thought you'd come up with that."

"Leave Earl alone, Tonto," Bob Ferry said. "You don't want to get him cranked up now, do you?"

"I don't give a good goddamn one way or the other, Bob," Tonto said. "I'm just damn sick of sitting here waiting and listening to new slants on humidity."

"It's not long now," Bob Ferry said. "It's coming like a loaded freight train, gentlemen."

"Why not tonight then?" Tonto said. "Go in there, do it, get out, and get gone."

"Because today's not Sunday, that's why. Sunday's not until day after tomorrow on the fourth of July. We don't want to grab the eggs until the chicken's laid all of them, every last one."

"Will anybody go to church on the fourth of July?" Coy Bridges said. "I keep thinking about that. I know I wouldn't."

"You wouldn't go to church on Judgment Day, Coy," Tonto said. "You'd be too busy getting your head full of dope and humping some ugly whore in a crackhouse."

"Tonto," Coy said. "You better be glad I just tell myself you're trying to joke when you say something like that about me. And you don't know how to tell it right so it's funny."

"I know how to do everything I do," Tonto Batiste said. "Just hold that thought in your head."

"Now, now, gentlemen," Bob Ferry said. "It's just hot and every-body's nerves are on edge. Just a couple of days longer to wait now, and we'll be dividing up all that money and going our separate ways before you know it.

"And yes, these folks will be in church on Sunday, and that's particularly because of what Reverend Jimbo Reynolds has been advertising for the last three months. And they'll be ponying up the donations big time, and we don't want to miss letting them do that."

"What's he calling that again?" Coy Bridges said. "That July the Fourth deal?"

"The Reverend Jimbo Reynolds is calling it what it is, Coy," Bob

Ferry said. "If you haven't heard about it on the radio, you haven't tuned in to a single station in Memphis in a long time. Sunday, July the Fourth, in Reverend Jimbo's church is going to be the Sun-Rise Ministry of the Big Corral's salute to America."

"Howdy, partner, come palaver with Jesus, the Biggest Cowboy of All," Tonto Bastiste said, moving his hand in short jerks from left to right as though reading words on a banner hung in the air before him.

"You see," Bob Ferry said. "Tonto's been doing his research. He's been paying due and accurate attention to what's going on spiritually in Memphis. He's modeling good behavior for all of us."

"He's the top hand, Jesus is," Tonto Batiste said, "according to what the Reverend's been advertising. Never was a man that couldn't be throwed. Never was a horse that couldn't be rode."

"So Don Condon is behind all this noise, huh?" Coy Bridges said. "He's into everything, ain't he?"

"Donny Boy has always had an eye for the next chance," Tonto said. "First time I saw him in Huntsville, he was figuring a new way to put a saddle on Jesus and ride the boy home."

"I'm getting sick of hearing about Jesus all the time," Earl Winston said. "Especially when it sounds to me like you throwing off on him, Tonto."

"What do you care about Jesus, Earl?" Tonto said. "That's the first time I heard you say a thing religious. What, you turned Jesus freak?"

"I ain't religious, no," Earl said. "But I like to hedge my bets whenever I can on things. What if some of the shit they say about Him is true? You ever think about that, Tonto?"

"No," Tonto said. "Not being a lunatic, I haven't."

"You calling me a lunatic?" Earl said, banging the front leg of his folding chair down against the floor and pushing it back with a scraping sound on the scarred hardwood of the drawing room.

"You two cool off now," Bob Ferry said. "Never discuss religion or politics while you're on a job. You know that. Now shut up about Jesus and talk about something else."

"Yeah," Coy Bridges said. "Let's talk about pussy."

"No, you're right, Bob," Earl Winston said. "There ain't no reason to bring up touchy subjects when you're getting ready to do a home invasion.

There's a lot of planning goes into home invasion, and you liable to lose your focus. Forget something you need to remember, or leave something out. You know, shit like that."

Earl looked around him for confirmation, pushing back into his chair so that the front legs rose again into a more comfortable position and lifting both hands before him in a calming gesture. OK, OK, they said.

"Let's talk about pussy," Coy Bridges said, looking directly at Earl and then shifting his gaze to Bob Ferry who was flipping another paper match toward the ash tray.

"We heard you the first time you said that," Tonto Batiste said. "You don't need to tell us the same thing again, over and over. Jesus Christ."

"Well," Coy said. "What you got to say about pussy, anybody? Let's get started."

"What about this for something to talk about while we sit here sweating our asses off," Earl Winston said. "Did I tell y'all my daddy, that sorry old son of a bitch, gave away my dog without telling me about it?"

"No," Bob Ferry said. "Really? When you were a kid over in Arkansas?"

"Naw," Earl Winston said. "Back in April, that's when."

"Jesus Christ," Tonto Batiste said and got up from his folding chair. "That does it for me. I'm going to the Green Frog and drink whiskey until I fall off the fucking stool."

"I wish you wouldn't do that," Bob Ferry said. "Tonto, think about it. It's too close to countdown to be getting messed up."

"I don't give a shit," Tonto said. "I need some relief. I don't want to hear another goddamn word about Earl's sorry old daddy giving his dog away. Jesus Christ."

Tonto banged the door behind him as he left the room and headed outside, and the three still in the room watched Bob Ferry's last paper match sail through the air and miss its target.

"Tonto said Jesus Christ again the last thing he said as he was going out the door," Earl Winston said. "Did y'all notice that?"

"Yeah, Earl," Bob Ferry said. "Jesus Christ."

14

It was a midweek service, prayer meeting night, and Jimbo Reynolds didn't know why he even bothered to do it, outdated as the concept was. The parking lot was not one-third full, if that, and the walk-ups for any church function would be negligible, as always. So why did he feel like he ought to keep rolling out for display something so old fashioned and decrepit as midweek prayer meeting? Don Condon had smiled like a possum when Jimbo first told him he still ran Wednesday night prayer meetings out of the Big Corral.

It didn't make economic or demographic sense, Condon said, and Jimbo agreed silently with his PR director as he leaned on his hay bale and watched the slow trickle of old women, the odd old codger or two, and the assorted other prayer meeting attendees move into the steel-sided cathedral of the Big Corral. Not a bit of sense, he knew for certain, not a lick.

But, of course, he admitted within in that part of himself he kept to himself and never let anybody else see other than the stray woman or two he now and then accorded what they considered a privileged and personal and unique glimpse into the inner workings of his heart and mind as he angled to bed them, Jimbo actually did know why he still included the off-weekend night prayer meeting in his repertoire. He was catering to a weakness in himself, something left over from childhood, like looking at a black and white snapshot of himself as a kid on the front porch of one of the rent houses he'd grown up in back in those dead days in East Texas, the skinny little self-doubting loser he'd been.

Put it another way, Jimbo told himself as he observed the last few supplicants totter in through the open doors of the Big Corral, put it like this.

You have a bad tooth, and it's sore and you're conscious of it all the time, but it's not really actively paining you. So do you leave it alone and hope for the best? No, not hardly. You poke it with your tongue to make it fire up and send a message to your brain to make the hurt come. You go even further sometimes, depending on your mood. Not only do you poke with the tip of your tongue at what's betrayed you. You take a good hard suck at it until it roars in your head like a siren.

So, there's not a dime to be made by holding night prayer meetings, there's not a man or woman showing up who's worth getting to know for the purposes of love, money, or networking, and there's not even a dab of ego satisfaction to be gained from putting on a show good enough to wow the audience.

But you do it. You do it, and you do it because Wednesday night prayer meeting at one point in a life long dead to you used to work. You felt something, you were moved, you thought there was something outside you magical called God, and you could get in touch with it. You didn't have to be stuck in East Texas in a three room house with a busted down floor and a well outside for water all by yourself forever.

But you learned there was no magic. You couldn't get in touch with it, and you didn't, and it was a rotting tooth not to be healed, but at least you could make the sucker crank up and roar. You couldn't get away from the pain, but you could make that pain come along with you at your command. You exercised your option.

That was something that Don Condon probably didn't appreciate personally, probably couldn't. Hell, he had most likely even visited a dentist while he was still a kid and therefore couldn't comprehend the rotten tooth analogy. That disadvantage aside, Don was proving to have a nose for promotion and money. He knew what folks would notice and how to sniff out where the money was in a given location, though he was a tad hairpie fixated, Jimbo pondered as he looked out over the cathedral space before him. The boy did have a weakness for the private parts of the female, and he would root around as patient and dedicated as a hog at a swill bucket looking for access to them. Look at him now, back by the entrance doors, his head thrown back so as if to allow maximal nasal access to any whiff of something that might be coming into season.

But give the PR man credit, Jimbo Reynolds remarked to himself, and due recognition. A man's strength is directly connected to his weakness, and what builds him up is exactly what can tear him down. If Don Condon wasn't so hard-wired to hunt pussy down to wherever it was hiding, high or low, here or yonder, he wouldn't be such a hound on persuading folks to belly up to the bar of this ministry and lay their money down, every last dime of it. Don Condon will have the bottom coin and the widow's mite, and he will not cull any woman walking around with that hairy surprise tucked up underneath her step-ins. He wants it all, and he is not to be satisfied with one penny or one hump less.

Thank you, Lord, thank you, Master, for the rich variety of motivations among the creatures you have put on this earth. I swear I do believe You knew what You were doing. Go after that dollar, Don, and go after that snatch.

They were all about in the building now, the old ladies by themselves, the ones with a grandkid or two along they were raising because of the bonedeep sorriness of their own offspring, a few younger women in the chairs toward the back, victims in one way of the other of no-account abusive weak men, a few others harder to characterize but all losers and misfits and abandoned in their own particular and pitiful way. It was the midweek prayer meeting crowd, the army of the lost. Wednesday, the bleakest day of all seven. So much behind you, so much still to come, and no relief in sight. So it was time to crank up the music, lead them in prayer, call for some witnessing, collect what little there'd be dropped in the buckets tonight, and put this week's prayer meeting out of its misery.

Jimbo Reynolds rose from his lean on the hay bale, took off his Stetson as a signal to the combo to launch into the "Red River Valley" as modified and improved for Big Corral use, and looked out over the crowd before him, standing in the need of prayer.

As he did, the introductory notes from the piano and the guitar beginning to swell through the sound system, Jimbo noticed one last figure step through the door at the rear of the building. It wasn't an old woman, or a young one, and it wasn't a member of the largest demographic of the Big Corral not white, not to put too fine a point on the matter and the late worshipper was not choosing a seat in the last row, as is traditional with the tardy at any church service, but came directly up the aisle between the rows of mostly empty chairs, and sat down in the front row in the seat closest to where Jimbo Reynolds stood in a hipshot John Wayne pose on the platform on which all worshipful eyes focused. Don

Condon, Jimbo noted, trailed a bit behind the stranger and took a chair a row away, looking up at Jimbo on the platform and nodding once.

Should I think what I ought to do if this punk tries something, Jimbo considered briefly, and then pushed the thought aside. No, no negativity, he told himself, expect the best to happen, and lots of times it will. Look for the nugget that might nestle at the core of all the dirt and debris around it. Pluck the flower between the thorns, focus on the gleam of light, not the darkness surrounding it. Be of good cheer.

Besides, if the little punk tries something disruptive, I've got five old boys behind me working away at the "Red River Valley" who'd like nothing better than to swarm off this stage and kick the living hell out of a single little colored kid looking like this one does. He's probably zoned out on a headful of crack, and he's wandered in here thinking he's found a jungle honky-tonk.

The band reached the last few notes of the improved version of "Red River Valley," closed it out with a final tinkle on the piano keys and a lingering whine from the steel guitar, and a premonitory hush fell in the building as the real business of the prayer meeting cranked up.

"Folks," Jimbo said in the tone of voice he had worked so hard to develop over time for the initial moment of a worship service—resonant, yet a little gently playful "it's been a few days, hadn't it, since the last time we got together for a palaver with the Boss. Things have happened since then, ain't they, good things and bad things. Some of the stock has strayed off, broke through a part of the fence we didn't make strong enough to hold them in, now we got to find a way to round them up again and bring them back home.

"I look out there at you, and I see some cowboys and some of their women folks and young'uns having to deal with what happens when a varmint gets into the herd. Maybe a prairie wolf, maybe it's a thunderstorm that's come up, could be a real gulley-washer of rain has set in, maybe drowned a calf or two. Maybe a bolt of lightning has struck where we hadn't expected and hadn't wanted, and we're wondering how in the name of tarnation the Boss let that happen. We're questioning His judgment, we're saying, Boss, now if You'd have give us some warning of what was going to happen, we could've maybe got ready for it. We could a looked ahead, and fixed that fence. We could a made sure the herd was bedded down, well-fed and watered, and none of this trouble would a plagued us. Them calves would still be grazing on the hill, kicking up their heels, lowing away and praising Your creation.

"Let me ask you range hands, and you ladies, and you young'uns, ain't that right? Ain't you sorry now that you didn't get all your chores done when you ought to've done?"

A moan arose from the worshippers, the supplicants, those Memphians in need of prayer and intervention, and it was not loud nor boisterous, but Jimbo could feel that it was real, and that it was working the crowd like a good dose of salts wending its way through the digestive tract of a sick heifer, bloated on an overfeed of green timothy.

"Yessir," came a cry from a couple of rows back, a woman's voice lifted over the general groan of acknowledgment and complaint. "I done fell short."

"Yes, ma'am," Jimbo Reynolds answered, "You did. You did fall short, you left undone that which should have been done. You shirked your duty, you took your eye off the particular thing, and you let matters slide, slide, slide. You did that, you did all that. You did.

"But, ma'am, you know what? And here's an assurance from the Boss, and I offer it to you as His Holy Range Foreman. And it's this. We have all fallen short."

The young colored kid in the front row, Jimbo could observe from his advantaged position on the platform, sat with his eyes closed and his head leaning back, and he swayed from side to side in his chair, clasping his hands together, wringing one palm against the other.

Not going to be any problem with this young doper, Jimbo breathed to himself, not at this prayer meeting. Better than that, not only will he not disrupt the proceedings, he's going to help me out later on here, he's going to let me get the spirit of generous giving moving in a while, if I handle it right. If that doper boy ain't under conviction, I'll ride a hog out of here sidesaddle.

"Folks," Jimbo said, dropping his voice an octave lower as he spoke more closely into the cordless button microphone attached to the tab of his shirt collar, almost in a croon now, a hint of sweetness blending with the authority of his request, "folks. I'd like to lead you in the Cowboy's Prayer. Those that know it, I invite you to join me as I offer up what the cowboy might say to the Boss when he's standing in the need of prayer. Those that don't know the Cowboy's Prayer, or haven't learned it yet, I direct you to look at the back of your program. But, cowpokes and ladies and children, just listen to the ones that do know it. Don't just read it out loud from what you'll find there on the paper. You got to have the Cowboy's Prayer by heart for it to mean like it ought to and can."

"Amen," came the cry first from an older woman near the front of the rows of seats, and then scattered from all over the group, the word was repeated. "Amen, Range Foreman, amen and amen."

"Boss," Jimbo Reynolds said, lifting his voice as though to be heard by a superior some distance off, tending to some other business but present in the moment in every true regard, on call to listen when need arose, "Boss, I sit my mount at the end of day."

The music of voices from the audience came to Jimbo's ears, chiming in as the prayer he recited gathered and grew, and a brief huskiness touched his words as he spoke. Something is happening here, Jimbo felt the thought welling up as he spoke, it ain't all about the money and what it buys a man. I swear it's not. I feel it right now, just like being with a sexed-up woman. It's of the body, but something else is happening, too, not just the drive of the gonads and the deep, true thrust of the hips and the belly and the thighs. Praise be, praise be, Glory.

"The sun is sinking in the West, my day is almost done. I let loose the reins, Boss, I slip my feet from the stirrups. You will lead me to that pasture where the grass is lush, green, and belly-high to a tall horse. I know You wait in the corral, Boss, to welcome me home. Your great bunkhouse at the end of day is my reward for all chores completed and all work done. I ache to lie down, Boss, on the great soft pallet on the floor of Your love, and drift off into the final sweet sleep of the cowboy come home."

As the last word of Jimbo Reynolds's recitation of the Cowboy's Prayer reverberated in the steel-sided cathedral of the Big Corral, the true tenor of Chip Overstreet's voice lifted like a bugle from the Cowboy Combo on the platform, delivering the first line of the "Boss's Answer to the Weary Cowboy," a tune written by Chip himself as he was coming down from a week-long drunk he had thrown two years ago in Hazel Green, Alabama.

Damn, that's good, Jimbo Reynolds thought as he sneaked a look at how the young doper punk in the front row, Don Condon sitting relaxed now behind him, might be responding. I ought to give personal credit to Chip for that rendition, and I would, if it wouldn't ruin him for a month to hear a compliment like it always does.

"Well done, thou good and faithful cowpoke," Chip sang, the guitar, drum and piano providing a strong foundation for his voice to rest on and rise from. "You've mended all the fence, you're saved the lost heifer, my love for you's intense, I'll never let you suffer."

At the end of the prayer meeting, a short one, given the small crowd but one which made the collection buckets rustle and ring well beyond what Jimbo had expected, the young black punk kept his seat as the rest of the worshippers shuffled toward the doors and struggled out of the building, some stepping lively, some wandering with deep reluctance back onto the streets of Memphis, all moved to return to the Big Corral to give generously, Jimbo did hope and pray with a heart full to overflowing. Let it come, Lord. Prop me up.

"Son," he said, looking down from his platform toward the only person other than Don Condon still in a seat, "have you got something working on you? I sense a burden. Do you need to talk to the Range Foreman and get it off your heart?"

"I saw you before," the black kid said, looking up at Jimbo now, his eyes so dark there seemed to be no distinction between pupil and iris. Their whites were deeply bloodshot, Jimbo noted, telling the old sweet story of the killer weed filtered through a bong bowl. Don't kids even bother to pour some Visine into their peepers anymore, particularly when talking to their elders in a worship setting?

No, they don't, he told himself, but it's not because they don't know any better. They do it on a purpose. They're just showing a badge, like a marshal walking into a saloon in Dodge City in the old days. Here I am, it says. Look at me for the dude I am. Ain't I a consequence? Lord, the arrogance of a young punk, Jimbo Reynolds said within, shaking his head in sorrow as he contemplated the kid before him. If you only knew what an ass-kicking is waiting on down the road for you, you little shit.

"Where'd you see me, son?" Jimbo said. "That picture of me on one of the billboards? Which one was it? On Elvis Presley Boulevard? On Lamar? Or whereabouts did you see it? I'd like to know, me and my partner, Cowpoke Don Condon would, to see how the message of the Big Corral is getting out. Wouldn't we, partner?"

"Yessir, Range Foreman," Don Condon said. "We sure would. Do you think I ought to stay here and counsel with you and this young man, or should I go pass along howdy and so longs to our people?"

"Do the so longs, partner," Jimbo said. "Me and this young wrangler is going to want to palaver for a spell." Then to the young doper as Don Condon walked quickly down the aisle toward the exit, Jimbo thinking he's smelled some he's fixing to check out, "I bet it was on Lamar, right, son?"

"No sir, it wasn't a picture. I saw you in person and heard you talk."

In person, Jimbo noted the phrase, that's a good thing to hear. In person. Reckon who he believes I am? A rap star?

"It was at Memphis Central High when you talked to us this week. In the auditorium at assembly. To the summer school program kids."

"I saw you, too, son," Jimbo said. "I picked you out of the crowd where you were sitting. And I talked directly to you, son, there in that room full of all those fine young people."

"How did you know to do that? How did you see me? How could you tell I needed to hear what you said?"

I be damned, Jimbo thought. This little doper here believes what I'm telling him. Ain't that a sight and a kick in the ass?"

"I didn't pick you out all by myself," Jimbo said. "The Boss told me to look for you, said I'd know you by your eyes, told me I'd know you when I saw you. And He was right. That's why He's the Boss. He don't shoot no blanks."

"Do you know my name?"

"No, I don't know what handle your mama and daddy slapped on you at birth, son. Names don't matter. Labels ain't a consideration to the Boss. The Boss is got everybody's name in his logbook already. I know you because you got all the signs of a man working under a strong conviction, and let me tell you something, son, in all humility but with all assurance. There ain't no way for a cowboy to hide when he's under conviction. He forevermore stands out from the herd."

"Sir," the young doper said, standing now in front of his chair and moving toward the platform where Jimbo Reynolds stood, both hands outstretched in Jimbo's direction as though he was feeling his way in the dark in an unfamiliar room, "my name is Randall Eugene McNeill, and I got to ask you something, please."

"Don't call me sir, son. The handle is Range Foreman, and Randy McNeill, that's a good name for a cowboy. I like it."

"That's what I want to ask you about. Was there ever a cowboy like me?"

"Like you how?"

"African-Americans. Was there ever a black cowboy, a colored one?"

"Lord, son," Jimbo said. "Was there ever any colored cowboys? You mean to tell me you never heard of Black Ned Callahan? Or Rufus Smiles? Or Texas Jack Youngfield, trailboss for Charles Goodnight out of Pecos? What have you been studying in school there at Central? What they been telling you?"

"Nothing," Randall Eugene McNeill said. "Nothing I can remember that'll do me any good now. It's just been one thing and then one thing and then one thing."

"Here's what'll do you good, Randy," Jimbo said. "Let's get down on our knees together on this dirty old floor in this old steel-sided building, and let's see if the Boss is home. I expect He's going to be. He don't never wander off."

"Thank you, Range Foreman," Randall Eugene said, collapsing to the floor as though a razor-sharp knife had just severed both hamstrings. "Thank you, thank you."

Can I spot it when a man's under conviction, Jimbo asked himself as he hopped off the platform, no matter what color the sinner happens to be? I ask you now, have I still got it? Huh? Tell me the truth.

Here's some of that variety I honor in this world. My PR director out hot on the trail of some quiff and me here getting my pant knees all dirty praying with a doped up brother. I don't care which one of us is doing righteous work. I know who's having the most fun with it, though, and it ain't no lasting satisfaction where Don's got his nose.

15

The micro-waveable lunch packets Major Dalbey included in his regimen of weight reduction left a lingering odor in his office which lasted at times for up to two hours. This fact was especially true of the Italian supreme selection from the medley of quick meals Major Dalbey enjoyed, and that was also his favorite.

Each time J.W. Ragsdale was summoned to the boss's office, he'd learned to look at the clock automatically and figure out how close to noon he was cutting it. Today was very close, only a little after 11:30, and J.W. began pawing around in his desk drawers for whatever he could find to pop in his mouth and get working strongly enough on his olfactory apparatus to ward off at least a little of the byproduct of Major Dalbey's lunch entr,e.

"Which one did he cook up today?" J.W. said to Tyrone Walker, who was on the phone and waved him off, turning his chair to the side to look away from where J.W. was leaning across the desk toward him.

"It's Supremo," Princess Wilbur said from the desk behind J.W.'s. "The big gun, that's what."

"Princess, are you sure?" J.W. said. "Cause I ain't feeling all that strong today in my belly. I don't know if I can take that stench right now. Don't play with me, please."

"I'm speaking from experience, Sergeant," Princess Wilbur said, delicately typing at her keyboard as she finger-tipped around and with a full set of two-inch chartreuse nails. "I know when I smell the Italian Supremo, and I wouldn't joke about that. I don't have to guess what's stinking."

"Why does he have to want to see me now?" J.W. said. "Why didn't I stay where I was a little longer before coming back to the station? Why don't I ever think ahead further than a minute and a half?"

"Don't ask me to analyze your shortcomings, J.W.," Princess Wilbur said. "I ain't no shrink. Where were y'all this morning, you and Sergeant Walker?"

"Aw, up yonder off Jackson in one of them old big places turned crackhouse. Got a call in on a working girl punched full of holes."

"Fresh kill?"

"Naw, shit. Been dead a week anyway," J.W. said, then deciding to go on the offensive against Princess Wilbur a little. "How you keep them pretty green fingernails all perfect, kind of work you do, Princess, on that keyboard?"

"I buy them by the boxful from the Korean, that's how," she said, extending a hand toward J.W for his closer inspection. "Why you worried about the major's lunch grossing you out when you spent all morning poking around a ripe one, J.W.? That don't make sense to me."

"It's a question of right things in right place, Princess," J.W.said. "Like you and them plastic fingernails."

"Ain't plastic. Acrylic."

"All right, say acrylic, whatever they are," J.W. said. "Think about it this way. A kill a week ripe has got a right to smell bad, but damn it, what a man eats for lunch ought not to leave a stink high enough to gag a turkey buzzard, Princess. That's what I mean."

"Well, it's your turn to see the major, not mine," Princess Wilbur said. "Here's you a stick of Big Red gum to cram in your mouth."

Major Dalbey was holding both hands about six inches from the top of his desk, moving them back and forth in slow sweeping motion, when J.W. walked through the door. The Supremo smell hung in the air strong enough to be seen.

"What you looking for, Major?" J.W. said. "You look like you're after buried treasure."

"It's buried all right, J.W.," Major Dalbey said, "but it sure as hell ain't treasure. It's a letter from Ovetta Bichette."

"Oh, Lord," J.W. said. "What does Ovetta Bitchhead want?"

"Don't call her that name, now," Major Dalbey said, after he'd finished a half-hearted attempt at a laugh. "You liable to get me in the habit of thinking that, and it'll pop out of my mouth sometime just when I don't need for it to do. And here's what the honorable councilwoman is concerned about. I found the letter right in front of me."

"If it'd been a snake," J.W. said.

"Yeah, right, you'll think snake when you hear it. Here's the part you need to know about. Listen to this."

J.W. chewed down on his wad of Big Red and leaned back in his chair, lifting a hand to his face as though he was moving into a state of deep concentration. Held that way, maybe his fingers up to his nose would block out some of the heaviest load of the Supremo smell.

"Here it is, after all the first bullshit blah blah blah that Ovetta starts up with. To my knowledge, partial though it may be at this point, not one lead has been established in pursuing the matter of the murder of Mrs. Beulahdene Jackson, late resident of North Montgomery Street. Investigations have been perfunctory at best, and it's become clear that the priorities of certain officials of the Memphis Police Department are directed not toward protection of those most vulnerable, African-American citizens of fixed income, but toward pandering to the white power structure of this city.'"

Major Dalbey stopped and looked over his glasses at the sergeant of homicide sitting before him, reared back in his chair with his eyes focused on the ceiling as though he saw an event of great interest depicted in the panel boards there.

"What do you think about that, J.W.?"

"I think that Ovetta Bitchhead is running for mayor again, Major," J.W. said. "I would put money on it. And I think she didn't write that letter herself, neither."

"Don't call the bitch bitchhead, J.W. I already told you that. Know something else? This letter I been reading to you from ain't directed to me. Nuh uh. This is a copy the Chief has sent to me of the original she sent to him."

"That don't surprise me none," J.W. said. "I figured it'd be addressed to the Chairman of the Joint Chiefs of Staff, calling in a airstrike on the Midtown station. I figure we've got off easy this time."

"Yeah, ha, ha," Major Dalbey said. "Meanwhile what is going on with that case? Give me something to work with."

"Nothing much," J.W. said. "Ain't nothing going on you don't already know about. I figure the way we going to find out who did it and put Ovetta back in her box is to wait until one of the little shitheads who did it's buddies drops the word on him. It'll happen, like it generally does."

"Or it won't," Major Dalbey said. "At least not quick enough. What's the M.E. say, what's the lab rats' take on this thing, what about the damn neighbors? They ain't said nothing?"

"Some blood evidence, but that don't mean nothing until you actually got hold of the perp. This ain't TV, Major."

"I know it ain't TV, goddamn it, it's my career," Major Dalbey said. "I wish to God that Ovetta Bichette was in hell with her back broke."

"She'd still be whining," J.W. said, "writing letters and position statements and shit. She'd drive the devil crazy."

"I know it, J.W. I know it," the Major said. "Listen, go talk to the M.E. again, find something you can dummy up to make it look like progress and get it back to me asap."

"Asap," J.W. said. "All right, I will jump on that, Major, and get back to you. I've always wanted to write a fiction story or two. This could be my first one."

"First, my ass," Major Dalbey said. "I read the reports you and Tyrone turn out. Real entertaining, they are sometimes, too."

"Thank you, Major," J.W. said. "We just fling on in and do the best we can to get that writing done."

On the way out of Major Dalbey's office door, drawing in the first real breath he'd allowed himself in the last several minutes, J.W. considered the task before him. The easy part would be the writing up portion, since Tyrone Walker had a knack of making a description of total inertia seem to be an accurate account of a lively and ongoing investigation well on its way to conclusion.

Studying English in college was a damn good thing for a homicide detective's partner to have done, and J.W. was grateful to whatever professor in Tyrone's past at Memphis State had taught him how to make shit sound like Shinola. That was a skill worth the having of it.

The hard part was finding something for Tyrone to work with, J.W. knew, since he would not sit down and write a barefaced lie from scratch, and J.W. wouldn't ask him to. Shading the truth now, or as Tyrone Walker put it, interpreting the facts of a matter, that was a different thing. It allowed some breathing space. It stepped back from the bare bones of a matter and let the facts about them cool off enough to be able to worry down and live with.

Closing the door to Major Dalbey's office behind him, J.W. permitted his mind to touch on the subject of the medical examiner it was now his assigned duty to see, and doing that caused him to let a smile grow on his face as he walked back to his desk to record where he was headed. Nova Hebert, that was her name.

"What's wrong with you, J.W.?" Princess Wilbur said, turning to get Tyrone Walker to notice what she was seeing. "Why you grinning like that? Something bad must've happened in the Major's office. Look at him, Tyrone, how cheered up J.W. looks. That ain't right."

"The reason J.W. looks so strained in the face, Princess, is because he's doing something not natural to him, smiling like that," Tyrone Walker said. "The muscles that generate that kind of facial activity hadn't had any practice functioning for years in J.W.'s case, see. They're quivering and about to tear loose from their sockets."

"Y'all go to hell," J.W. said. "Both of you. I got to go to the morgue."

"That's why you're grinning?" Princess Wilbur said. "You a gruesome bastard, if that's why you smirking so hard."

"I'm going to have to leave before y'all run out of ammunition," J.W. said. "I can tell the pressure of trying to think of some other way to low-rate me is getting to you. Y'all ain't got that much gray matter to keep it up much longer. It's pitiful to stand here and watch y'all strain so hard."

J.W. figured that by the time he got over to the city morgue on Gayoso Street, located Nova Hebert, the blonde M.E. who'd handled the crime scene description on Montgomery, and found whether or not she could give him something for Tyrone to whip into shape for Major Dalbey to use on Ovetta Bichette that it'd be time to slip out for the day. So he took his Buick from the lot rather than a city car, as complicated a pain in the ass it was to get reimbursement for use of a private vehicle.

Pencil Neck Fognan liked nothing better than making some detective squirm and beg, trying to justify a rebate for fifteen or twenty dollars, but the prospect of that seemed worth the trouble today to J.W.

First of all, he hadn't even felt like talking notice of a woman for a long while, much less talking to one, ever since Diane Edge had moved off to Washington, DC, almost a year ago. J.W. had known that getting involved with a woman of Diane's education and class and particularly her profession was a bad idea to start with, one sure to cost him on down the road. But he's done it because he felt like it at the time. Just said fuck it, and flung on in. The upside in hand now would be worth the downside to come, he'd figured. Thing was, he had underestimated the weight the downside would develop by the time had come for him to pay the freight costs.

Diane Edge was a lawyer, an educated one, and divorced once, so she had no misconceptions about what it meant to be with just one man for a while. She liked to tell jokes and laugh and drink gin at the end of the day, and take car rides down into the Delta to see what crop was growing and how it looked and to listen to blues in honky tonks and eat the best barbecued pork shoulder in Mississippi and thus in the world.

But Diane was smart, too, so when the DOJ offered her a job in DC, she took the first plane flying out of Memphis so she could start work the next Monday morning.

They had spent the last weekend before she left together, and got drunk and made love and cried and said they'd see each other all the time and spend vacations together. And when J.W. carried her to the airport and promised to call Diane's cell phone that very night, she stopped after she'd gotten through the security checkpoint and waved back at him and blew a kiss and said "I love you" for him to lipread. J.W. could still see the sandals she was wearing and the off-white dress with the design of red seashells on the bodice whenever he closed his eyes and wanted to call the scene up.

He hadn't seen her since then, and she'd finally stopped calling and leaving messages on his machine, and J.W. hadn't been in bed with a woman now for nine months, and no, he'd told Tyrone Walker several times, I ain't lonely and I stopped missing her right after she left Memphis.

Tyrone hadn't said a word the last time J.W. swore everything was just jake with him, thanks for your concern. He'd just looked at J.W. for way too long, shook his head a couple of times, and looked off and begun to whistle the tune to an old Jimmy Clanton song from a long time ago. "Just a Dream," J.W. recognized it to be immediately, but he didn't make a sign that he knew what mood music Tyrone was providing.

So driving toward the location on Gayoso where the medical

examiners hung out with cadavers and body parts, J.W. switched on the Buick radio and pushed the button set to an oldies station, one of several in the Memphis listening area, and considered the fact that it was damn different to see a woman and feel that little tingle of interest kick up in the lower section of his belly again.

About time, too, though it was not likely to come to anything existing in the real world where a man and a woman might get together and feel like there was something out there besides themselves that wasn't themselves and could be worth getting close to. Or might be possible to get close to. Or at least you might think, despite all experience to the contrary, that it might be possible for at least part of a day or two.

Then, J.W. told himself, beginning to hum along to some tune on WRVR he didn't recognize but felt like he might have known once a long time ago, that ought to qualify and damp down what I'm expecting enough to let me live with it for a while. Don't look at it close, fool, or it'll show you what it really is.

"I need to talk to a M.E.," J.W. said to the clerk II in the outer office of the morgue on Gayoso Street, a young man dressed in a yellow jumpsuit that looked to have been double-starched before it had received a careful ironing. The cuffs were turned back at precisely the same width and angle, and they were perfect. So was the manicure and the light purple polish job on the clerk II's nails.

"You do?" the clerk said. "Any M.E. in particular you're looking for, sergeant, or will just anyone do for you?"

"Naw," J.W. said, making a big production of looking through his notepad for the name, flipping pages and then backing up as though he'd missed one. "Not just anyone of them will ever do for any job, I don't believe."

"You got that right, Sergeant Ragsdale," the clerk II said, delicately pointing with one of the perfect nails on his left hand at J.W.'s police ID. "It's been my experience that a substitute for anything will never do. Do you know his name?"

"It's a woman," J.W. said, settling on a page in his notepad to read from. "I believe it's Hebert, her name is. Nova Hebert."

"Oh, Nova, oh my yes," the clerk II said. "I'll call her and let her know you're coming back in there to see her."

"It's about a case," J.W. said. "Tell her that's why I'm here."

"Why, of course," the clerk II said and pushed a button on his telephone keypad, "what else could it be?"

J.W. looked around the room, cool and casual, as though not listening to the clerk II talk to Nova Hebert, and then began flipping through his notepad again.

"The medical examiner says come on back," the clerk II said and hit a switch to buzz open the lock to the steel door behind him. "Don't you just love her hair? It's completely natural, Nova's hair is, that curl and that color. I'd give a lung for it."

"I'm here to talk to the M.E. about a dead woman," J.W. said, headed for the door. "That's the reason I'm here."

"I believe you," the clerk II said, tossing his head and lifting a hand as though to ward off something unseen in the air. "Trust me, Sergeant."

The temperature on the other side of the door was much lower than that in the anteroom, and J.W. always enjoyed that contrast when he stepped into the working part of the police morgue. Besides the cool, it was generally quiet here, too, except when some of the M.E.'s and lab nerds might be horsing around with each other and telling stiff stories. Then they could get loud, laughing in the way that J.W. had noticed only science types do, high-pitched and in too much volume for what they were laughing at would justify.

It was not that way this time of day, though, the morgue rush hour generally coming later in the night hours, and the only sound was that of somebody laying down a metal instrument on metal and the whine of a bone saw cutting off abruptly and then cranking up again.

About halfway down the aisle between rows of polished steel tables, coming toward him at a brisk pace, J.W. saw Nova Hebert, and he wondered how it was you could instantly recognize somebody you either wanted to see or didn't want to see as soon as you saw them. He hadn't seen Nova Hebert more than two or three times in his life, and he'd only talked to her for a minute or two and that in the little white house on Montgomery with blood all over the floor and walls, but he could have picked her out of the crowd at a Memphis Grizzlies game with one glance.

Was it one thing in particular about somebody your eyes settled on, maybe, he asked himself as he watched her come toward him, and then that made you remember a connection? The hair, say? Or the way she walked? Or the way she tilted her chin back as she looked at the person she was about to speak to? It was an interesting question, and he'd have to ask Tyrone Walker about it someday when they were on a stakeout trying to come up with something to shoot the shit about and make the time pass. He wouldn't use any names, of course. Keep it theoretical.

"Good afternoon, Sergeant," Nova Hebert said. "Keeping cool in all this weather?"

"I don't mind the heat," J.W. said. "I don't care if I sweat some or not." Jesus, why did I say that, first thing out of my mouth? Panola County upbringing, I reckon, like every damn thing else I do. "I mean sweating in the summer."

"That is the time to do it in Memphis all right," she said. "Which one do you want to ask me about?"

Nova Hebert had on a city-issue lab coat and white shoes like nurses used to wear, but that didn't seem to be holding her back any, J.W. noted. Her hair was contained in a net-looking arrangement which didn't allow its interesting thrash much room to operate, but that too was no real obstacle to its being a focus of interest.

"It's the one on Montgomery the other day where you were working that scene with Hoot Sarratt," J.W. said. "The knife thing on that lady in her house."

"Oh, yeah," Nova Hebert said. "Blunt force, too, but that wasn't what did it. It was the bleed-out."

"Yeah, that's what you said then. Anything to stick on to that?"

"Nope," Nova said. "A little blood from the perp, like we saw then, but nothing else we found since. I don't see help for you from anything we ran into."

"Thing is," J.W. said. "I need to find me something to talk about, you understand, for the boss's benefit."

"You want some progress to report, I suppose is what you're saying."

"You got that right. I need some progress bad. At least the boss does, because his boss does, and the councilwoman riding his ass, she needs to hear something to shut her up a little bit. I need to get creative."

"I wish I could help you, Sergeant," Nova Hebert said, snapping the rolled-up part of first one rubber glove, then the other one against her wrist as she stood facing J.W. in the big room full of steel tables. J.W. could hear water running somewhere, but he couldn't tell where from. "Nothing new, though, to tell you."

"Nomar Garciaparra," J.W. heard himself say, as he watched the lady M.E. with all those curls pushed into a hairnet, looking up at him.

"What?"

"The way you're messing with your gloves," J.W. said. "Doing first the one, then the other with your hands. It's like Nomar up at bat, the way how he does when he's getting set for the pitch to come."

"Yeah," Nova Hebert said. "But Nomar's working with Velcro, hearing that nice ripping sound every time he pulls it loose. That's a lot more satisfying than these rubber gloves."

"The Red Birds are in town tonight," J.W. said. "I can get tickets."

"All right," Nova Hebert said. "You want to meet me at the main gate about 6:30?"

"Catch batting practice?"

"Yeah," she said. "That's always the best part. Getting ready for the game to start up. Watching it crank."

"Yeah," J.W. said, watching Nova Hebert turn and walk back down the aisle between the steel tables in all that cold air of the morgue. "Oh, yeah."

16

The van was wrong. Bob Ferry kept saying that to anybody close enough to hear him, pointing out the wrongness of the color, a bright, almost luminous shade of green, the fact that the lettering on the sides, front, and back declared the plumbing business the van represented was located in Forrest City, Arkansas, but that the tag was Shelby County, Tennessee.

"Who's not going to remember that?" Bob Ferry said. "It'd take a blind man not to be able to remember this damn cartoon buggy and everybody in it."

"Who looks at a fucking van?" Earl Winston said. "I never do. I know that much for sure."

"I'll tell you who looks at it," Bob Ferry said. "The guard at the entrance gate, that's who looks at it. The one who writes down the name of every service vehicle that goes into the Nathan B. Forrest Estates, that's who I'm talking about."

"That's his job," Earl Winston said. "That's why the guard does it. He don't give a shit about what color it is."

"Of course it's his job. Who's arguing about that? And look," Bob Ferry said, pointing to the purple lettering against the green background, "see where it's from? Forrest City, Arkansas, and you think that not's going to be a little extra attention-getter for the guard sitting in the booth of the Nathan B. Forrest Estates?"

"The guard's a Mexican," Earl Winston said, "the time of day we're going in there."

"So fucking what?" Bob Ferry said.

"They used to bright colors and weird-looking shit, Mexicans is. He ain't going to notice nothing. You ever look at the car a Mexican will drive?"

"Racism is eating this country up," Bob Ferry said. "It's making everybody in it as dumb as a fence post."

"You throwing off on me, Buddy-Ro?" Earl Winston said, dropping his voice into the gravelly range. "You looking to get messed up?"

"All right," Tonto Batiste said. "Cut out this crap. Bob's right about the Forrest City sign. We'll put some duct tape on top of that wherever it is on the van. There ain't no reason to ask people to notice stuff."

"That's better," Bob Ferry said. "That's the point I'm trying to make. You're reading it right."

"But," Tonto went on, "we ain't going to be using the damn van long enough to count for much anyway. Now are we?"

"Not long, no," Bob Ferry said. "But I just like to be careful. Details are important. That's all I'm saying."

"Duct tape is good for just about every thing," Coy Bridges said. "They give rolls of it to astronauts when they go up in space. To make repairs and all that shit."

"Let me ask one question more," Bob Ferry said. "Then I'll give up. Where'd you get the van, Earl?"

"At the van getting place, that's where I got it."

"Tell us where you got the fucking van, Earl," Tonto Batiste said. "And let's get this goddamn thing going."

"I got it where you get a plumber's van at night," Earl Winston said. "Parking lot of a titty bar on Winchester, while the old boy from Arkansas driving it was inside getting his rocks off. That's where."

"That s the first thing that makes sense I've heard today," Bob Ferry said. "That makes me feel better. At least you didn't drive to Forrest City, Arkansas, and pick it out special."

"What they say about duct tape was that it was discovered by this old boy that never made dime one off of it," Coy Bridges said. "He got fucked over by the corporate world. Them suits."

"Do tell," Tonto Batiste said. "All right, I'm driving, Coy's in the passenger seat, Bob and Earl in the back out of sight. When do we get started?"

"Any time we want to now," Bob Ferry said. "It's after two o'clock, and that's when Fulgencia says he's in there by himself every weekday."

"None of them damn cowboy assholes are with him then, she says, right?" Tonto said. "We don't have to worry about them showing up. And what about the damn boyfriend? Is he going to be mooning around?"

"The cowboys're never there on weekdays except for Wednesdays, no," Bob Ferry said. "Wednesdays and the weekends he's got to do the worship services and he's getting ready for that. Weekday afternoons he doesn't want anybody around until nighttime."

"Not even that assistant, that Condon guy?" Tonto said. "He won't be there?"

"No," Bob Ferry said. "Middle of the week, Tuesdays through Thursdays, Reynolds has Condon roam around doing his public relations outreach in Arkansas and Mississippi and middle Tennessee."

"What's Reynolds doing then on Wednesday by himself there in that big old house, you reckon?" Coy Bridges said. "Fucking Fulgencia?"

"No, Coy," Bob said. "Jimbo Reynolds is tending to business, the financial side of things, and he doesn't want anybody around to see him doing it or where he's stacking that money up."

"He's fixing to get somebody around to help him with his money," Earl Winston said. "I flat guarantee you he is."

"How do you know Jimbo Reynolds ain't doing Fulgencia?" Coy Bridges said. "They in there in the house by themselves, ain't they?"

"I know he's not because Fulgencia told me he wasn't," Bob Ferry said. "He has no carnal interest in Fulgencia. She's his goddamn housekeeper, Coy. Jesus."

"Why were y'all talking about who she was banging anyway?" Earl Winston said. "If a woman talks about fucking, she is either been doing it or is getting ready to."

"A woman will always lie about who's been fucking her," Coy Bridges said. "The truth ain't in them when it comes to who they been letting get at that hairpie."

"Bullshit," Bob said. "You can't generalize like that about every woman."

"The hell I can't," Coy said. "My first wife was letting my own damn brother fuck her every time I'd leave the house. And I was letting the son of a bitch live there for free. I know the bitches."

"Why was he living with y'all, Coy?" Earl Winston said. "That don't make sense."

"He was between jobs at the time, and he was my own brother, sorry as he was, and I was weak in the head about it."

"How long between jobs?" Earl said.

"Right at two years," Coy said. "The lazy little fuck. He was too sorry to even sell dope to help out with household expenses."

"O.K.," Tonto Batiste said. "Are we going to sit here until sundown talking about Coy's brother fucking his bitch of a wife, or are going to get this thing done?"

"What I want to do," Bob Ferry said, "is wait for us to go until there's a good long line of cars and service vehicles all stopped and waiting at the entrance. Then we'll drive up and take our turn to be checked in by the guard. That way, he'll be less likely to hold us up long or take a hard look at this damn green van."

"Bob's right," Tonto Batiste said. "So get in the van and get ready."

"Me in the passenger seat," Coy Bridges said, "Tonto driving, y'all two in the back, right?"

"Yeah, yeah," Tonto said. "Just like I already said."

Ten minutes passed before Bob Ferry judged the moment was right for Tonto to drive onto the street from where the plumber's van was parked by the rent house. He leaned forward, tapped Tonto on the shoulder, and they eased over the broken curb and the remains of sidewalk which at one point had led past other mansions of cotton brokers and bankers, long vanished from the scene.

Three cars waited in the approach to the guard booth of the Nathan B. Forrest Estates, a Lexus, a blue VW bug, new series, a Lincoln Navigator, and behind them an electric company pickup and a catering service vehicle with a mass of inflated balloons crowding the rear window.

"Reckon it's a kid's party fixing to happen," Coy Bridges said to Tonto as they sat in line. "See all them balloons?"

Tonto lit a cigarette and flipped his match out the window. The line of cars moved up a space as the Lexus won entry and drove ahead.

"How'd you find out your brother was humping your old lady?" Earl Winston said from the back area of the van. "Walk in on them when they was doing it?"

"Naw, not really doing it," Coy said. "David Lynn had done fucked her, I guess, that time, and he was in the bathroom washing his dick off. Tiffany, she was in the bed playing like she was taking a nap. She closed her damn eyes when I walked in the room like she was asleep, but I seen her doing that."

"Heartbreaking," Bob Ferry said.

"It wasn't David Lynn's heart I ended up breaking," Coy said. "I flat ass tell you that."

"Shut the fuck up," Tonto Batiste said, "and sit back real far from the windows. We're next."

The Mexican in the guard booth motioned Tonto forward with a flip of his hand and punched a button somewhere not visible which allowed him to speak over a sound system.

"What residence?" he said.

"I don't know what one it is," Tonto said. "But I got a number here for you to call that they give me back at the office."

"You don't know the name?" the Mexican said, now taking a closer look at the driver of the plumber's van.

"Yessir, I know the name, but they didn't write down the street address on the order form. See, the name is James D. Reynolds, and the street name is Fallen Timbers, but it ain't no street number. Just a telephone one, that's what they give me to work with, that's all."

"No, that's right," the Mexican in the guard booth said. "That's what they always give vendors and service personnel, nothing but the names and telephone. Not no street address. Let me see it, and I'll call."

Tonto handed the form through the window toward the booth, and the guard slid the pane of glass open and took it.

"Particular, ain't they?" Earl Winston said to Bob Ferry in the back of the van. Ferry shook his head and touched his forefinger to his lips, causing Earl to imagine himself rummaging around in the plumber's tool kit riding in the floor of the van until he found just the right sized monkey wrench he would need to tap Bob Ferry across the mouth hard enough to give him some of his own front teeth to eat.

The Mexican guard looked at the number on the plumbing company order that Bob Ferry had worked up back in the rent house on his lap top and printed out for the purpose at hand, and then the guard punched the phone pad before him.

In a few seconds he began speaking in Spanish, and Tonto Batiste felt a little of the tightness in his shoulders and neck ease. Fulgencia was on the job.

"Gracias, senora," the Mexican guard said, hit a button, and handed the order form back to Tonto. "The housekeeper says you are to pull off the street up the driveway and park in behind the house. Don't block the middle garage door none, no."

"All right," Tonto said. "What number is it, and how do I find that street it's on?"

"Go straight on Battery Lane, right on Fallen Timbers to number four, and be sure you ain't got no oil leaking out of the pan to get on the driveway. She said that, not me."

"We ain't," Tonto said. "All our vehicles is well-maintained. I read you."

The guard was wearing shades tinted the color of midnight, so Tonto Batiste couldn't see his eyes, doing both men some good. Tonto didn't have to see the Mexican judging the mealy-mouthing he was having to do, and the guard didn't have to run the risk of being recognized by anybody he cross-examined later on somewhere out on the streets of Memphis. Everything was business, nothing personal, no blow-back.

Fallen Timbers was the third street off Battery Lane, just past Holly Springs and Tupelo. The house at 4 Fallen Timbers, like the others around it, was set well back off the street, surrounded by a headhigh brick wall with shards of multi-colored broken glass cemented on top of its entire length, and the driveway was doublewide and curving, planted profession-ally with flowering shrubs and flower beds.

"High dollar motherfucker, ain't it?" Coy Bridges said, his head swiveling back and forth as he surveyed the scene.

"That's exactly why we're here," Tonto said, pulling the plumber's van in behind the house and parking as close as he could get to the far-left side of the four doored garage.

"I sure hope we don't drip no cheap oil on the preacher's driveway," Coy said, "while this thing's sitting here."

"If we don't, I'm going to find something greasy to pour all over it before we leave," Tonto said. "That I guarantee you."

The back gate through the shard-topped wall was wrought iron, and Fulgencia Villareal as visible through it, her hand lifted to the lock fitting a key into it. She was wearing a maid's uniform, every man in the van could see, her outfit starched and so white it seemed to be projecting a

110

light of its own in the July sun of Memphis. It couldn't hide the depth of her breasts and the swoop of the line in and down from there to her waist and hips, though, Bob Ferry considered as he watched Fulgencia get the gate opened.

"I defy any garment manufacturer to cover that up," Bob Ferry said to Earl Winston, wishing instantly that he hadn't said a word.

"What?" Earl said. "You mean them big old tits?"

"No, forget it," Bob said. "I was talking about how uniforms look on some people, that's all."

Fulgencia beckoned toward the van and opened the gate, stepping back to let Tonto walk past, first out of the van.

"Que pasa?" Tonto said. "Where is he?'

"He's in his office," Fulgencia said as they all moved into the house down a hall, into a room which looked like a kitchen in a display home in East Memphis, "like he always is this time of day."

"Counting his money, huh?" Coy Bridges said. "Suppose he needs himself some help?"

"I don't know what he's doing," Fulgencia said. "He's got his door locked, though. I do know that much. He always does when he's in that room."

"He don't notice people driving up?" Earl Winston said. "Slamming car doors and talking and shit?"

"Mr. Jimbo don't notice nothing when he's in his room," Fulgencia said. "Like I told Bob, it's his safe room, and he can't hear or see nothing outside of it, even if he wanted to, when he's inside of it. That's how he's got it fixed."

"Let's go bust in his door for him," Earl said. "See can we get his attention."

"I hope you're trying to be funny, Earl," Bob Ferry said. "If you are, I'm ready to give you a chuckle or two. But if you're serious, that lets me know you haven't been listening to a word Tonto and I've been saying for the last week."

"Fulgencia," Bob went on, "is everybody and everything where it's supposed to be? Is it business as usual here in the reverend's house?"

"Yes," Fulgencia said. "Pretty much. It's the first week of July, and Jimbo's getting it all together for the transfer to New Orleans like he does every time. It's half a year's worth, he keeps saying to everybody and it's nervous-making, like he always calls it."

"So we'll just wait for him to come out of his hidey-hole, and bring it right to us, then, huh?" Coy Bridges said. "All them old worn-out bills, stacked up in boxes."

"Well," Fulgencia said, looking at Tonto Batiste with her head turned to the side as though she had just remembered something minor and unlikely to be of much interest. "There is one thing that's different, though."

"What?" Tonto said. "Has he got somebody else here with him?"

"Si," Fulgencia said. "El muchacho negro."

"Talk right, girl," Earl Winston said. "Don't jabber that shit. What's she saying?"

"The black boy," Bob Ferry said. "That's what she's saying, right?"

"Yeah," Fulgencia said. "He showed up with Jimbo, and he's in there with him in the room."

"That ain't right, is it?" Coy Bridges said. "That ain't supposed to happen. Who is he? You say black. Is he strapped?"

"He's just a kid," Fulgencia said. "I don't know who he is or where he comes from. But him and Jimbo is been praying together all last night and half of today."

"Praying?" Tonto Batiste said. "Is the reverend believing his own shit?"

"I never knew him to before," Fulgencia said. "I'm just telling you what's been going on, just what I been seeing. I don't know what it means."

"We'll take care of him," Earl Winston said. "Kid or not, no matter what color he is."

"He wears cowboy clothes," Fulgencia said. "Hat, chaps, spurs, the whole enchilada."

"But you saying he's not one of Jimbo's cowboy guards, right? Am I understanding this?" Bob Ferry said. "This muchacho negro is not hired heat?"

"I ain't heard them called negroes in a long time," Earl Winston said. "Hell, they don't even call themselves that no more. That ain't the deal now, is it? They particular about that name shit."

"Naw," Coy Bridges said. "It's African-American now, what they label their own selves these days. I'm talking about right now, understand. Today, I mean. This minute. They likely to change it this afternoon."

"Let's see if we can get this thing back on the road," Tonto Batiste said. "Y'all quit worrying about what to call folks and get ready to do what we come here for. Fulgencia says this little colored cowboy ain't nothing but a kid, and we can handle him if we have to."

"Now you're talking," Bob Ferry said. "Let's get on upstairs and get ready to get the job done. Fulgencia, it's to the left at the top of the landing, right?"

"Just like I draw it for you on the paper, yes," Fulgencia said. "But y'all got to put the duct tape on my hands and feet first before you do anything else upstairs, now. I got to make a living in Memphis after y'all are long gone."

"You not going to take any time off?" Coy Bridges said. "Ain't you planning to use your money to kick back a little bit? Drink you some top shelf Margaritas and eat you some tamales? Quit work? Take your boyfriend on a trip?"

"You don't need to know what I'm going to do," Fulgencia said. "Except that I got plans for my twenty thousand dollars that don't include blowing it or quitting my job."

"What are you going to blow then?" Coy Bridges said, looking around to see if anybody had picked up on what he was saying, grinning a little as he waited for someone to laugh.

"Leave Fulgencia alone," Tonto said. "She ain't got time to fool with you."

"I want to be the one that duct tapes her up," Earl Winston said. "I know just how to do. Let me show you."

"No, you won't," Tonto Batiste said. "You go up with Coy and Bob, and get set up, Earl. I'll do the taping to give Fulgencia the cover she needs. Don't make a lot of racket up yonder."

"I agree completely with Tonto," Bob Ferry said. "I suspect that if a man looks forward to taping a woman's hands behind her back to put her in a posture of bondage then that's exactly the reason he shouldn't be allowed to do it."

On the way up the stairs to the second floor of the big house in the Nathan B. Forrest Estates at 4 Fallen Timbers, Coy Bridges lagged behind

Bob Ferry so he could say something to Earl.

"I'm counting them up, Earl," he said, looking at Bob moving ahead at a good clip up the carpeted stairs. "Ever damn one of them.'

"What? Counting what?"

"Ever word Bob says like suspect and posture and bondage and all like of that shit."

"Why?"

"Time comes when I let myself do just what I been dying to do, I'm going to match up the number of times I bust him with ever one of them words he's throwed at me like that."

"Posture," Earl Winston said. "That's like when you stand up straight, with a book sitting on your head, right?"

"Yeah, that's it, I believe, and walk around," Coy said. "Bob's going to think standing up straight when I turn loose on the motherfucker. He's going to wish he's able to."

17

Colorado was what he'd asked Jimbo Reynolds to call him, putting it in a mild even tone as he said it, that alone making Jimbo realize how important the request was to the kid.

They had been praying together for almost two hours there in the Cathedral of the Big Corral, Bob Condon and all of the boys in the Cowboy Combo of Grace gone except for Arleigh who knew to stay around unless told to leave, and during a breathing spell Jimbo had called to rest for a few minutes, the kid had declared what he wanted to be called now.

It wasn't unusual in Jimbo Reynolds's professional experience as a minister of the gospel, a proclaimer of the crucified and risen Christ, for a man under conviction undergoing a conversion episode to want to rename himself. New body in Christ, new soul in Christ, new name in Christ. So the colored kid saying he wanted to be called by a new label, one more fitting and proper for a man newly joined to the flesh of the Redeemer, was understandable. No big deal, unremarkable in itself. It was like getting a tattoo, Jimbo imagined, the way kids these days will mark themselves to show they belong to something or that something belongs to them. Some rap group logo or football team or computer fantasy game character. A thing to make them feel real.

"Son," Jimbo had said, sipping at a diet cola and dabbing at his forehead with a red bandanna, "I see where you're coming from, and I hope you do, too. You're a new creature now, the Boss has done seen to that. He has slapped His brand on you. That old marking and that old handle, they just don't apply anymore, do they?"

"No sir," the colored kid said. "When I say my old name to myself now, it is just words in the air. They don't mean me now, the way I feel now. They're nothing to me. It's like I'm a chess piece somebody else has won. I'm not what the old sounds say."

"How could they?" Jimbo said, thinking chess piece, what kind of a colored boy is this? "You mighty right when you say that. You're signed on with a new outfit now. You don't work for the old one no more. You know what happens when a cowboy leaves his old spread and signs up with a new outfit?"

"No sir," the kid said. He had refused the diet cola Jimbo had offered him and was drinking from a plastic bottle filled with plain water. That too Jimbo wanted to ask about later. Kids want their sugar, they want their caffeine, they want every manner of drugs percolating through their systems. That's why there's so much money to be made in the street. Any fool but the federal and state governments knows that. You can't keep the young off of and away from dope. They will have it, and they will have it now.

"You don't have to call me sir all the time," Jimbo said. "You can just say range foreman. That's the name I figure fits me best. But let me tell you what happens when that cowpoke leaves the old outfit for a new one."

"Tell me, range foreman. I'd purely like to know."

"He shakes hands with the new boss," Jimbo Reynolds said. "He don't need no paper with writing all over it and a place for names to be signed. That's city dealings. That's what folks do when they're expecting to get cheated. A cowboy don't expect that, to be cheated or hornswoggled or two-timed. He ain't made that way. Understand?"

"I reckon I do, range foreman."

"So what he does after he moves in with a new outfit and they tell cookie to set out an extra plate for him in the bunkhouse, what the cowboy does is he changes the brands on all his gear from the old one to the new one. He will literally take out an old Barlow knife from his kit, and he'll cut off the old brand from his saddle and his boots and his rifle and wherever else he might have carved it to show what was him in the old life. And then you know what he'll do?"

"Put the brand from the new outfit on his gear?"

"You got it, son," Jimbo said. "That's exactly what he'll do. He'll mark his goods just like he's been marked."

Jimbo took the last sip from his diet cola and nodded toward the bottle of water the colored kid was holding.

"You want to palaver with the Boss a little more with me here, before we leave the Cathedral and hit them nasty old Memphis streets?"

"Yes sir, range foreman," the kid said. "But first I want to tell you my new name, and see if it's all right."

"Everybody's name is all right," Jimbo said, "long as it's really his and he can live with it." Looking at the kid's eyes as he waited for him to speak, Jimbo wondered what kind of label he'd come up with. Probably in his case, colored kid he was who'd just been told about black cowboys in the old West, it'd be Ned, or Buffalo Kid or some moniker like that. Derivative, to be expected, worshipful, but hell that was all right. The kid needed to rename himself after the conversion experience he'd been going through, and whatever made him feel whole and a part of the Big Corral would serve. It'd bind him, and this is forevermore a binding game.

"What's your new name here in the outfit the Boss runs?" Jimbo said, casting his voice in the warm and encouraging range the kid now needed to hear, whether he realized it or not. "Tell me, son."

"Colorado," the colored kid had said, holding his bottle of distilled water in his hand there in the steel-sided Cathedral of the Big Corral as though it was a chalice. "Not Randall Eugene McNeill no more, not him, not that one I used to be. He's dead. Colorado, that's who I am now. That's me. Colorado."

"Colorado, huh?" Jimbo Reynolds had said, wishing he had a little bourbon to mix with the dregs of his diet cola to round things out before he left for the house. "That's a new one for me, I got to admit. I've heard plenty of cowpokes called names like Texas Jack or Montana Slim, and handles like of that. There was even one old boy I run into a long time ago that called himself Louisiana Crawfish. But I got to say I never heard of a cowboy with just the name of a state as his handle. You spent a lot of time in Colorado, son?"

"No, range foreman," the colored kid had said. "I never been anywhere but Memphis and over into Arkansas and down into Mississippi a few times."

"You just like the way Colorado sounds, then, I reckon," Jimbo Reynolds said. "Maybe seen pictures of all them pretty mountains and that snow on them."

"I have, all right," the colored kid had said, "but that's not the reason, range foreman, that I want my new name to be Colorado. It comes from a movie I saw on TV once, an old one. Now I watch it every time I can find it."

"Oh, yeah? What's that?"

"It's one with John Wayne in it, and some more old guys, but the one they call Colorado, that's what gave me the idea for my new name."

"Any picture with John Wayne in it has got to be a good one," Jimbo said. "He was a true American, a real cowboy. He saw everything clear and called things exactly what they are. He did not pussyfoot around."

"Ricky Nelson was the one they called Colorado," the colored kid said. "Nobody respected him at first. They all dissed him, but he ended up being the one that made everything come out right in the end."

"Colorado," Jimbo Reynolds had said, "how about letting me introduce you to the Boss by your real name, and then let's mosey on to the ranch house and put on the feedbag."

"To your house? I can go with you to your house?"

"Go with me? Lord, Colorado, you got to see where the ranch foreman lives. Every new hand in the outfit needs to go to the ranch house when he signs on."

The last prayer in the Cathedral with the kid who needed to be called Colorado because of being seized by the idea of some characters in a movie starring that draft-dodger John Wayne had been a good one. And somewhere near the end of the session with the Boss, it came to Jimbo Reynolds that the kid might be useful. He could fetch and carry, he likely had good connections with a black gang or two and with what made them function so well in Memphis, we're talking non-prescription medications, Jimbo said to himself, chuckling at the phrase as he thought it and the colored kid needing to enter a new life as a cowpoke named Colorado was obviously crazy enough to be trusted to do what he was told. He compared himself to a chess piece, and he didn't know anybody in the employ of the Big Corral well enough yet to start plotting against his employer.

That would come with time, Jimbo knew, as it always did with anybody having to depend on somebody else and take orders from above, but there was a window of opportunity when you could get some reliable service out of a new hire for a period. Even a black punk kid from Memphis who thought he had become a cowboy called Colorado.

So on the way to the Nathan B. Forrest Estates, Jimbo Reynolds had stopped at Lil's Western Emporium on Winchester and outfitted the new hand just signed up with the Big Corral from head to toe. Lil herself had overseen the selection of wardrobe, and she had done a bang-up job, no expense spared, smoking one hand rolled cigarette after the other, chuckling and grunting like a bag lady the whole time like she always did. She sounded to Jimbo like a woman fixing to come any minute but in no hurry to get there. Get into it, girl, he thought. Please yourself, and who'd begrudge you.

By the time Jimbo led Colorado into the counting room of the house at 4 Fallen Timbers and locked the reinforced steel door behind them, the black kid was walking in his new boots as though he'd been born to the saddle somewhere west of Yuma. He'd even spoken to Fulgencia when he met her downstairs in a speech pattern a thousand miles removed from the urban mumble of South Memphis, tipping his hat as soon as he saw the lady, scraping at the floor with his new boots, and howdy ma'aming her like a rodeo rider in town for the bull riding competition.

Like always, Fulgencia had looked at the colored kid in his new outfit and treated him as though not a thing out of the ordinary was taking place before her. Damn, Jimbo thought, that is a virtue and a blessing and a side benefit worth gold, the way an illegal will tuck tail, tend to business, and never ask a word about anything that pops up in front of her. I could bring in a kangaroo in a cowboy suit and introduce it to her, and this goodlooking Mexican woman would call him mister and offer to shake hands.

"Colorado," Jimbo Reynolds said, gesturing toward the expanse of the counting room and all it held, "could you give me a hand with some chores here? We got some work to do, if you'd throw in with me on it. The Boss has give us a job that needs tending to. It has to do with children. It's kind of an outreach program."

"I guarantee I can," Colorado had said, slapping his gloves against the palm of one hand, "just show me what needs doing, range foreman."

18

Major Dalbey was asking J.W. Ragsdale to perform a task not in his official job description, but J.W. didn't want to say that to the Major, of course, not even as a joke. Arguing about an assignment on the basis of what category it did or didn't fit into was so damned pencil-necked that the thought of it made J.W. want to break something. Nothing big or worth much, but something. But even breaking some object, say a clock radio, or a water glass, or some kind of a knick knack, that in itself was also pencil-neck behavior, in J.W.'s estimation, and he was disappointed in himself to realize he was thinking about such an action. Going in this direction, the next thing would a crying jag.

So J.W. just kept his mouth shut and looked at the Major, who kept sliding his eyes off to one side and then the other as J.W. stared at him. It's a funny thing, J.W. thought, that when you're in the right you can stand to look full into somebody's eye and when you're shucking and jiving you can't force yourself to stare at a fixed point to save your life.

If you're normal, that is, J.W. amended his observation. If you're a psycho or a sociopath or a politician or a pencil-necked paper-pusher, nothing you ever do can bother you enough to make you look off from somebody else looking at you. I'll have to ask Tyrone about that, J.W. promised himself, see if I can't stir up an argument about the matter.

"Hell, J.W.," Major Dalbey was saying, "I ain't asked you to kill somebody, so why are you sitting there like a bump on a log, not saying a damn word?"

"If you'd asked me to kill somebody," J.W. said, "that wouldn't a surprised me near as much as what you did ask. I might not've accepted the assignment, but I would've admitted it was more in my line of work here in the Memphis police department."

"You ought to take this as a compliment, J.W.," Major Dalbey said, "the fact that your name came to my mind just as soon as the Chief unloaded this mess on me."

"You know, you're right, Major," J.W., "now I think about it. If I turn my head just a little to the side and squint the eye opposite, I can understand and appreciate the honor you trying to pay me. I see I have failed to comprehend it, up until just fifteen seconds ago. It thrills my heart."

"Yeah, yeah, yeah," Major Dalbey said. "Ha ha and all that shit. Here's what it comes down to, like I tried to tell you."

"All right," J.W. said. "Sing that song one more time, Major, and I'll see if I can come up with the words to fit the tune."

"Tell you what, J.W., I will, and I'll tell you this, too. If you can get the lid back on the bottle, I'll send you down into Mississippi to pick up an old boy at the Panola County jail for transfer to Memphis, and I won't look for you back here for three or four days. You can leave for the job that early."

"Why didn't you say that in the first place?" J.W. said. "I can feel my mind beginning to get around this thing already, like the tappets on a eight cylinder Buick starting to smooth out when you pour STP in the crankcase and it running."

"That's something you probably used to do, all right. Here's the deal. Ovetta Bichette has been approached by one of her constituents in her ward all concerned, and so Ovetta's asking for this favor from the Chief."

Major Dalbey paused and looked up at the ceiling of his office, the expression on his face that of a man who's just told somebody the good news that always attends the bad and is now delivering the other part. "No, now let me get it straight. She's demanding this favor from the Chief, and he's of course handed it to me, so I'm coming to you, J.W., hat in hand."

"It do roll downhill, don't it?" J.W. said. "Every time. Who is this constituent of Ovetta's? A landlord in South Memphis? A crack dealer? What? A working girl?"

"No, she is legit, a nice lady who's a licensed practical nurse at Methodist. See, she's got this boy she ain't seen in two, three days. Her name is Marie McNeill, and the boy is a student at Memphis Central High School, name of Randall Eugene McNeill. The mama's afraid something bad's happened to him."

"Oh, so he's the crack dealer," J.W. said. "Not the constituent nurse."

"Nuh uh," Major Dalbey said. "It ain't that easy. The boy is an

121

academic type student, according to the councilwoman, makes straight A's and plays chess on the school team and all that kind of stuff. Intellectual type kid."

"I ain't buying it. I bet he don't even know how to play checkers right."

"All I know is he's a missing person as far as his mama and Ovetta Bichette see it, and the Chief wants us to look into it and give it high priority and not assign it to some uniform who don't know how to do it and will screw it up."

"I ain't handled a missing crackhead kid case since I signed on to this outfit, Major," J.W. said. "Naw, take that back. I never dealt with anything like that, unless there was a killing connected to it."

"I know, I know," the Major said. "But we got to give the Chief something to work with, and I'm asking you to come up with some kind of story to get him off my back. Just, you know, go over there to Central High, talk to the principal or dean or whatever they call them school cops now, poke around a little, and then you can take a little vacation in the Delta."

"Soon as I get that done," J.W. said, "get the chess playing crackhead located and get you told so you can tell the Chief and he can tell Bitchhead, I can take off for Panola County for five or six days. That's the deal?"

"Three or four, I said," Major Dalbey said. "I ain't giving you a furlough, J.W."

"Who's this old boy I pick up for transport to Memphis on the fourth day, then?"

"He just jumped bail when they were fixing to try him for hitting a fellow too hard upside the head with a baseball bat. Nothing to him."

"A real baseball bat?"

"Yeah. This'un's a white power nut. That bunch he runs with call themselves Batboys for Freedom. Some shit like that."

"He'll be interesting to talk to, I do expect," J.W. said. "He'll make that ninety miles to Memphis pass fast, discussing social problems and batting averages and all like that."

"Let me know what you find out soon as you do, J.W.," Major Dalbey said. "Ovetta is just all over the Chief. He tells me it's all he can do not to clock her right in his office, except he'd lose his job."

"And his pension," J.W. said. "Damn, Bitchhead do stay busy, don't she?"

"Don't call her that, goddamn it, J.W. I know you're trying to condition me so I'll get mixed up and say that out loud myself just when I ought not to. But, yeah, Ovetta Bichette stays busy all right. It's a fulltime job being the councilwoman with a conscience, fighting for her people every fucking minute of the day."

"That's the tag she's using now? Councilwoman with a conscience?" J.W. said. "Lord have mercy."

"Yeah, but at least she ain't done what that one up there in St. Louis did."

"You mean the potty thing in the council chambers?" J.W. said. "I read about that in the paper."

"It was little potty, not big," Major Dalbey said. "And they held up quilts and tablecloths and stuff to hide her when she was relieving herself in that waste basket."

"So you really couldn't tell if she was doing it or not there in the council meeting," J.W. said. "Could've been just grandstanding."

"You couldn't see it, no, but you probably could've heard her doing it, if everybody wasn't hollering and stuff when the councilwoman was doing her business in St. Louis."

"St. Louis has always been ahead of Memphis," J.W. said, "in city government matters. I expect it'll be a year or two before some councilperson drops trou in Memphis while they're trying to keep the floor during a council debate."

"They won't be nobody holding up quilts and sheets in Memphis to hide it," Major Dalbey said. "I flat guarantee you it'll be right out in the open."

"Like I said," J.W. said, heading for the door out of Major Dalbey's office, "St. Louis is way yonder ahead of us in government etiquette. I'm going over to Central High School and get my vacation started."

Transporting a prisoner back from Panola County, Mississippi, to Memphis would justify his using a city vehicle for the trip, J.W. considered as he made his way out of the Midtown station, and that was a temptation. There'd be no need to worry about stress on his old Buick or whether the car was up to driving three-hundred miles back and forth and around and about before the visit to the home country was over and done. Anything went wrong, all would be jake.

But using a city police vehicle meant there'd be no reimbursement for mileage like there would be for his old Buick, and that was an advantage not to be lightly given up. He could make money on the deal at 42 cents per mile, J.W. knew, even with a Texas Republican in the White House and gasoline prices out the roof. He'd do the Buick, J.W. told himself, keep good records and earn a few dollars, not push the Century too hard, and it'd probably make it there and back.

J.W. drove to Memphis Central High School whistling the old blues number about the crawling king snake and letting himself think just a little about Nova Hebert. "I'm a crawling king snake," J.W. sang out loud as he pulled into a visitor's parking space at Central High. "And you know I rule my den."

The principal's office was at the end of the hall to the right, and after J.W. Ragsdale had showed his credentials to the guard at the only unchained entrance to Memphis Central High and by doing that avoided having to pass muster on the metal detector, he made his way through a slow-moving stream of young people toward the administrative nerve center of the compound.

The students he worked his way around and through were like all inmates of a correctional facility, he noted, the weaker ones wary and avoiding eye contact with the alpha males, the predators taking up more space than necessary as they looked from side to side, inspecting the herd for possible prey when conditions were right, and the old cons moving in separate bubbles of their own, all hope for release or change long given up, their gazes now permanently set on something in the middle distance only they could see.

The primary difference between the population moving to other various assignments in the halls of Memphis Central High and ones in the state penitentiary in Nashville or in the facility at Brushy Mountain was that the sexual punks at Central High were female. Their dress was more colorful and varied, J.W. considered, but the females of Central High had no edge over the punks in the State of Tennessee's penal system as far as grace of movement and attention to personal appearance.

A woman on display is a woman on display, J.W. judged with genuine satisfaction, no matter what sex she is.

After a couple of minutes sitting on a hard chair in the outer office of the principal's suite, J.W. was told by a hardbitten woman behind the counter, an old hand at controlling miscreants by the looks of her, that he could go into the main office of the warden, though she didn't use that title, naturally.

"Sergeant Ragsdale," the principal said, coming out from behind his desk, hand extended for the obligatory Midsouth handshake, "I'm pleased to meet you."

"Well, thanks," J.W. said. "It's been a long time since I had to go to the principal's office for a conference."

The principal laughed broadly, trained as he was to please, and said something about things being different these days in the public school systems from what they'd been when he and J.W. were working their way through the educational process.

"What can I do for you, Sergeant? I assume it's in reference to one of our Central High students, your visit, of course. Is it a drug or weapon possession charge?"

"No, just a missing person report I've been asked to follow up on, that's all," J.W. said. "I'm from the homicide division, but that don't mean anything this trip. This is all just kind of unofficial, looking to see what you can tell me about one of your kids here at Central who's not showed up at home for a couple of days."

"That's too usual a story, Sergeant," the principal said. "Which young man or woman is this? I can certainly let you know what the attendance records show."

"It's a boy," J.W. said, "name of McNeill. Randall Eugene McNeill. His mama is all worried, and she's got word to us about the situation by means of some folks."

"Randall Eugene," the principal said, beginning to shake his head slowly from side to side to side. He lifted a forefinger to his mouth and tapped sadly at his lips as he looked down at the floor. The principal's manicure, J.W. noticed, was perfect.

"One of our better students, I must say, in the gifted and talented program, and I do know he's not been in attendance for the last day and a half or so, because he missed participating with our chess team in a tournament. He's ranked number two on Central's team, and the coach has been really upset by his absence."

"Chess," J.W. said. "My boss said the boy plays chess."

"He certainly does. He and Gerhard Menzel, an exchange student from Germany, are undefeated this year in the city. Why, Sergeant, they just rolled over the M.U.S. team only last week."

"Memphis University School, huh?" J.W. said. "We kicked their butts in football back in high school. I didn't know M.U.S. was sorry in chess, too."

"Got any idea where the McNeill kid might be, Mr. Templeton?" J.W. went on. "Who does he run with here at Central?"

"He's not really that social," Principal Templeton said, "that I've noticed, but I do see him now and then with some rather surprising companions."

"How's that you mean? Surprising how?'

"Well, we do have, like all schools, an element in the student body we're not too proud of. A few of those are the ones I've seen Randall Eugene with, you understand."

"That's just who I want to talk to, then, I expect," J.W. said, pulling out a notepad and patting his pocket for something to write with. "What's these boys' name? Are they hooked up in a gang?"

"Gang affiliation is not allowed at Central High School, Sergeant Ragsdale," the principal said. "We won't tolerate it."

"I appreciate that attitude," J.W. said. "I ain't got no use for the little gangsters, neither. But tell me something. How do you stop them from forming up? It's been my experience they're like a blood clot. You don't know where it starts from or when it comes together, but it's hell when it shows up and gives you a stroke."

"We work hard on it, Sergeant," the principal said, his voice falling into a tone and pattern familiar to J.W., one he'd experienced on many occasions in meetings and workshops and task force conferences. The speaker was deeply in love with what he was saying, and it was constitutionally impossible for him to keep that emotion out of sight.

"What we've done is to allow a substitute for what the gang-related impulse represents in the maturing adolescent, particularly in summer school with a diverse group. We have honors students and at-risk students in a mix in the summer term."

"Yeah? What's that substitute, then?"

"We allow what we call zones of affiliation among our students. Officially sanctioned groupings of students are allowed to form and are furnished meeting facilities and modest refreshments in the last period of the day on Mondays and Wednesdays."

"Uh huh," J.W. said. "I reckon you're going to tell me this McNeill kid has been taking part in one of these here zone deals."

"That's right, Sergeant," Mr. Templeton said. "You've put your finger on it. Precisely. And that's all to the good, except that unfortunately the zone of affiliation in which Randall Eugene has shown interest does contain some of our rowdier and less academically inclined students."

"Oh, yeah?" J.W. said, looking down at his notepad. "Knuckleheads, huh? What's the names of some of this bunch you talking about and what zone deal are they doing?"

"Antwan Harrell is the leader, and D'Allen Jefferson is prominent in their particular zone. I believe they call themselves the Bones Family."

"Jesus Christ," J.W. Ragsdale said. "They got a meeting room and refreshments two days of the week right here in Central High School? That's what you're telling me, Principal?"

"That's right," Mr. Templeton said. "That's the term of that particular zone of affiliation, and that's what we provide them."

"That's a hell of a zone you got there, Principal," J.W. said. "A junior cell of the Bones Family. I can't wait to tell my partner what an idea y'all have come up with here at Central."

"I have no pride of ownership in the notion," the principal said. "But I must confess this particular concept is my own."

"I like that word confess," J.W. said. "That's one I can't hear enough of. But let me tell you, you have sure helped me out today."

"No problem," Principal Templeton said. "No problem."

"No problem at all," J.W. said. "I reckon not."

"Bullshit," Tyrone Walker was saying to J.W. from across his desk in the Midtown station. "You got to do better than that, J.W., when you try to con me."

"I shit you not," J.W. said. "That zone of affiliation I'm talking about is right there in Memphis Central High, right in among all them chess trophies and debate awards they got on display there in the lobby of the schoolhouse, there in your old high school."

"What you talking about? One of those glass cases full of old bowling statues and shit?"

"That, and cross country shoes and baseball bats and old pennants and all like of that kind of stuff."

"I guess if the Bones Family ever gets an award, it'll be crossed M-9's sitting on a cake of crack," Tyrone said.

"Yeah, or some crossbones and a real skull with an entry hole between the eyes and the whole occipital panel blowed out behind."

"Occipital," Tyrone said. "Who you been talking to, J.W.?"

"Oh, a M.E.," J.W. said. "I've been consulting, see. But what this means is I want you to come with me tonight to visit some of the administrative structure of this zone of affiliation. See what we can learn."

"Go talk to the Bones Family," Tyrone said. "You're saying that."

"Some of the junior partners, yeah," J.W. said. "Share some refreshments with the Antwan Harrell chapter. See can we affiliate with that zone."

"Look at their strategic plan, you're talking about. Blue sky some stuff with them."

"You got it, yeah," J.W. said. "See can the junior chapter pencil us in on their agenda."

19

The first thing that had popped into Randall Eugene McNeill's mind when he knew he was entering a new life surprised him. Why would it be that, he asked himself, a thing so small in the scheme of change that was coming over him and transforming him into a new man that it shouldn't have registered in his thinking at all?

Was he really so limited in his ability to comprehend the implications of events that he would worry about what he should be wearing on his feet? It didn't make sense, and it certainly wasn't a subject he would ever raise with the range foreman. That was a solid fact he knew he could hold on to. If he let the range foreman know that he was wasting the power of his mind by thinking about footwear, he would for certain be pegged as a cowpoke not serious about the real responsibilities of his new life. And he had to have a new life which left behind the old one where Randall Eugene McNeill lived and had done that thing he did. He had to kill the old self and let the new one be born. He was being moved to a new location on the board, and it was his responsibility to understand and accept what the moving hand had done.

But there it was, what he was thinking about, and Randall Eugene couldn't get it out of his mind. Footwear. He was afraid of how wearing cowboy boots would affect him. Would they feel funny on his feet? Would they pinch his toes, the way they came to a point in front? What about the hard high heels, elevated in a way no other shoes he'd ever worn before had been? Would he have the sensation he was always tipping forward as he walked? Would he feel that he was about to fall every step he took? Would having to compensate for a different angle and the lack of a soft cushioned support make him walk funny? Would he have to think too much about himself because of what he was walking around in?

He knew what Air Jordans and Eclipse Supremes had done in the past for his stride and his look as he glided in a controlled step. What had carried him in the old life let him forget some small part of having to think about what it was to be Randall Eugene McNeill.

That was always the hardest thing, the thoughts that wouldn't let him go to sleep at night, and when he finally did, would give him dreams to wake him into the dark place where only he was, no one else to think about, no other thing to put his mind on to give him some relief from being who he was.

They all saw him all the time, and he knew that they were watching, and that made him watch himself, and that was the last thing he wanted to see and have to think about. No more moving on his own, that was what he craved, and that was what the Boss and His range foreman would do for him.

So when the range foreman took him into the store on Winchester filled with the clothes cowboys wore, Randall Eugene was afraid to look at anything the old white woman with the cigarette hanging out of her mouth showed him in any more than short snatches of attention. It seemed that if he let his eyes focus for more than a second or two on any item she put before him, the bright shirts with snap buttons, the jeans with what she called a boot cut, the bandannas to tie around your neck, the leather chaps worked with silver studs and fringes, the cowboy hats with different creases that made them have names like Tulsa and Dallas and High Country any glance that Randall Eugene allowed to linger for a space would pull at him and tug him back into being the man he wanted to escape the mind and body of.

"Give him a Fort Worth roll," the range foreman had said. "That hat crease is just right for him. That hat says Colorado this is you."

And when the range foreman said that, the pressure eased and the things outside Randall Eugene backed off, and their power to pull at him weakened, and the material of the cowboy clothes and their colors and the metal of the fasteners and the leather of the fringes and the belts and the boots became just stuff, and Colorado knew he was Colorado. He adjusted the Stetson so that it set forward a little on his head, and the cowpoke looking back at him from the mirror was inside him and lived there and didn't have to think about doing that. He held on to himself and where he was in the dressing room and in the building and in Memphis, Tennessee, and in the squares of the pattern on the streets he could see all around him and everywhere in the world, and he did all that just by being there.

Colorado took a deep breath and let it ease out as he turned to face his range foreman.

"See what I told you, Lil," the range foreman said. "That cowboy right there with the Fort Worth roll to his headgear is Colorado, and he's looking right at us."

"Yep," the woman had said, stubbing out her cigarette in an ashtray made from a black cooking kettle. "I reckon he is. Now you going to want to try on some boots, I expect. I got some real nice snakeskin dudes over here for y'all to look at. Prime hides."

"No, Lil," the range foreman said. "Colorado ain't looking for no show boots. He wants him some footwear fit for working cattle in brush country. Where's your bullhide selections?"

So the boots themselves made no demands, asked no notice, and from the time Colorado followed the range foreman out of the cowboy store to get into the car for the ride to the spread belonging to the Big Corral, Colorado was at home in his walk, in his garments, in the pattern, and in himself.

"Range Foreman," he said, thinking how to put what he meant in the right words, "I want to thank you for the clothes, and the hat, and the belt."

"Don't thank me, Colorado," Jimbo Reynolds said. "I'm just doing what the Boss said, what he always says. Outfit the new cowboy, that's what He requires of us. Give the new hand what he needs to do his job. That's all the Boss asks, and that's all I'm doing."

"Yessir, Range Foreman," Colorado said. "I'm much obliged."

"Colorado, I tell you what. We all are," Jimbo Reynolds said. "Let's get on to the house. Lord, that Fort Worth roll looks good on your head."

Now in the counting room of the range headquarters of the Big Corral, Colorado moved around inside himself with an ease and thoughtlessness he'd never felt before. Don't think about that, he told himself as he sat before a table covered with roughly stacked piles of currency, most of it crumpled and turned randomly in every direction, ones mixed with fifties, tens, and fives and even an occasional two mingled with hundreds, don't think about not thinking. If you think about something that isn't, then what is can come to life and stick up in your path like a gravestone in the weeds.

Don't think, but don't think that you're not thinking.

"It's a satisfaction to me to see you working here beside me, Colorado," Jimbo Reynolds said. "I purely love to watch a young hand take on a job and just settle into it. You understand what I'm saying?"

"Yessir, Range Foreman," Colorado said, looking at his hands sort through the pile of bills before him, turning each one so that the presidents all looked in the same direction and lay precisely atop the one beneath and the ones his hands placed steadily above. "I believe I do understand you."

Colorado allowed a small tendril of admiration for the way his hands were working curl up from somewhere inside the center of his mind. That should be all right, he told himself, a cowpoke taking pride in what his hands could do. They were his hands, addressing a task given him, and he was a hand himself. That's what the range foreman called him, so his mind could contain the pride he felt and let it grow a little. Just keep it small. Keep it inside the fence it lived in. It's only a hand. It can't think. It can only do.

"A cowpoke doing a job," Jimbo Reynolds said, "tending to his business, giving the Boss a good day's work for his upkeep and his wages, that's one of the prettiest things I believe He gives us in all His creation. We don't need nothing else."

"Yessir," Colorado said, thinking I can even listen to what the range foreman is saying to me and talk back to him myself, and watch my hands still doing their job, and it's all one thing. It's all holding together. "I believe I know what you mean, Range Foreman."

"A course you do, Colorado," Jimbo Reynolds said. "Your inner cowboy is coming out, and he's showing his hand, and it is a full house, not a card lacking. The deal has done favored him."

How does he know that, Colorado asked himself, how does he see what's in my head and how all the parts of me are coming into one thing I can live with? I reckon it's because he's the range foreman, and he knows what he's supposed to know. He's doing what he is.

"You keeping your count, Colorado," Jimbo Reynolds said. "I can tell you are, because you're paying attention, and you're being careful, and you're being dutiful in the performance of your chore. You're cowboying up every minute you're doing your job. You're letting the Boss see what He wants to see in a man."

"Thank you, Range Foreman," Colorado said, observing the true deft movements of his hands among the bills. "I want to do just that. I want to cowboy up all the way."

"You showing me something, Colorado," Jimbo Reynolds said, "and you're showing the Boss, too. Lord, I love the way these love offerings to Him smell. Some just call it the scent of money. To me, it's like sage blossoms in the spring when the wind moves over them. They look like blue bonnets ruffling in the breeze, them bills, the way you're putting them in place in the good old way like the Boss purely wants them."

20

Tyrone Walker was driving, and that was the way J.W. liked it. Being able to look off to both sides of the car at whatever caught his eye, focusing when he felt like it and letting it slide on by when he didn't. Making it all clear up, and then letting it blur. Appreciating a little non-involvement, J.W. considered, was a sign of fully achieved maturity.

"So you think Lo Lo Tedrick is going to know something about a bunch of pissant little Bones claimers at Central High School?" J.W. said. "Be able to give us a little help this evening?"

"He might," Tyrone said. "Lo Lo is likely to, I do expect, for two reasons. One, he styles himself the man these days since he has done worked so hard to get where he is. And you know, the big dog has got to know his puppies and where they den."

"All right, I buy that, I reckon. A rooster that's offed two or three of the competition on his climb to the top of the manure pile is bound to notice things, all right. But why would Lo Lo Tedrick give a shit about a bunch of little fools strutting around a high school claiming they be Bones Family?"

"You got to let me finish my lecture, J.W.," Tyrone said. "You got to be patient when you're in the classroom and the professor's talking."

"All right, Dr. Walker, what?"

"Like I said, number one, as the headknocker of the Bones Family, Lo Lo has got to keep informed, and part of that business is knowing who's being a claimer for Bones."

"And for the Gents and for the Beale Street Boppers and the Jackson Avenue Dump Dogs and all the rest of the little shitheads."

"To use that technical term, yes," Tyrone said, slowing the city car as the light ahead flashed yellow. "And a corollary of that assumption is that Lo Lo has to know who's likely for enrollment in the Bones Family when the time comes."

"Corollary," J.W. said. "Lord, you show me all the time what I missed by not going to Memphis State, Tyrone. But that ain't the second reason Lo Lo might be able to tell about the junior partners of Bones yonder in Memphis Central High School. That's what you mean by corollary, right?"

"Right. And some folks think you're not educable, Sergeant Ragsdale. I always tell them I got faith in you, don't you worry. But, yeah, enrollment planning is part of why Lo Lo would be interested in Bones Family claimers still hanging around high school. That's still reason number one."

"Reason number two comes from the fact that Lo Lo Tedrick is a stone-crazy motherfucker with strong manifestations of obsessive-compulsiveness, and he has got to know everything there is to know about himself and what he thinks belongs to him."

"You got that out of a psychology class back down the line somewhere, didn't you?" J.W. said. "Bringing them theories out of the classroom and into the streets."

"You got it, J.W.," Tyrone said. "Lo Lo is of a kind mentally with lots of aberration. He's like, say, these freaks coming to Memphis by the thousands here during the hottest part of the summer just to be in the place where Elvis first started singing That's All Right fifty years ago come day after tomorrow."

"You mean Lo Lo is nuts."

"Again, Sergeant, you use the technical term to describe the subject, but yes."

"Actually, Tyrone," J.W. said. "Just to set the record straight, Elvis didn't sing it the first time on the fifth of July in 54. Sun just released the record then and Dewey Phillips played it on his radio show that day for the first time. There's your real facts about That's All Right, Mama."

"I suppose you remember it," Tyrone said. "You were probably listening down there in Panola County, all huddled up by the Philco with the whole family while y'all were chopping cotton in the living room."

"Naw, I was barely even born, but I wished I had heard it and known what was going on. It could've saved me some trouble on down the road, that song could."

Tyrone slowed the car again and pointed ahead toward the left side of the street. "Up here's where we got to leave civilization," he said. "Tip toe on down into the jungle."

"Lo Lo be cribbing on Baby Street still?" J. W. said. "Not in the same house where Apple Jefferson used to stay, is it?"

"Not the same house, no. After Apple got done, that shack was torched a couple of years ago by the Gents, and good damn riddance to it. But this whole area is still Bones Family, and Lo Lo ain't about to move out, traditionalist that the little shitass is. That's where we're going to find him cribbing."

"He believes in the old ways, Lo Lo does," J.W. said, shifting in his seat to ease the shoulder holster cutting into his underarm area. "I do respect a man who honors the past."

"Yeah," Tyrone said, hooking a left and slowing the city car to avoid a chug hole in the street big enough to hold a child-sized coffin, "sometimes on a good day when the dope in his head's died down a little, I expect Lo Lo Tedrick can remember the past way back yonder eight or nine hours ago."

Leaving the avenue and moving onto a lesser street plunged the city vehicle almost instantly into a darker region, J.W. noted, like it usually did in particular neighborhoods of Memphis. Ordinarily in these locations, fully half the streetlights were out, some from gunfire, some from well-thrown missiles, some from simple equipment failure which went unattended for months on end.

J.W. understood the reluctance of the city to send work crews in for repair to public property, and he didn't blame anybody for it. After you'd replaced light bulbs in the same socket or support standards or wiring or a combination of all three on a weekly basis for a year or two, thing's got discouraging. That, he considered, and also the fact that as soon as a work crew began attending to the business of repair, they naturally had to take their eyes off their trucks and the equipment carried on them, and that's when the ad hoc work crews of the region would descend.

How many wrenches and spools of wire and plastic pipe and hammers and electronic meters and bulbs and all that went with the job could the city afford to buy weekly? J.W. sympathized with the supervisor who had finally just thrown a sheaf of requisitions and work order forms against the wall and said fuck it, let them live in the dark.

Other than the light from Tyrone's low beams, the only illumination evident the deeper the car moved into the approaches to Baby Street came from inside the houses along the way, and that was muted, coming as it had to from behind closed doors and windows covered with bed sheets and pieces of paper and whatever else residents could come up with to avoid setting themselves up as well-lit targets.

Electrical power was getting to the houses themselves, J.W. knew. It had to be, judging from the bass notes of woofers loud enough to be felt in the viscera of anybody driving by and by the hum of air conditioners in the windows of about every fourth house. The other ones, those not cooled by Freon percolation and forced air, were generally the last residences of old women and a few old men now and then, huddling behind all the locks and barriers they could afford to erect against what might be moving outside through the Memphis night.

"Been a lot of old folks suffocated by the heat this summer, Tyrone?" J.W. said. "You hearing of many?"

"Not so many this summer as last," Tyrone said, steering carefully as he focused on the moonscape of roadbed before him. "But hell it's early still. Wait'll August gets here. That'll bring a spike in the mortality rate among the old folks in the less upscale neighborhoods of Memphis."

"Damn a closed window," J.W. said. "I purely hate being boxed up."

"You got to choose what box you want, J.W.," Tyrone said, hitting his high beams for a couple of seconds "That's the choice these old folks got. Look up yonder at that collection of SUV's."

"Looks like either a fundraiser for soccer moms, or a convention of the Bones Family," J.W. said. "Kill your lights, and let's pull in behind that Navigator. You don't suppose they're all in the same house, do you?"

"No," Tyrone said. "There's not but three cars in all, and I bet the titles of every machine up there's in Lo Lo Tedrick's name."

"You don't figure Lo Lo messes with car titles?"

"I know he does," Tyrone said. "I've had occasion to look into that matter, and I can tell you Lo Lo's a law-abiding citizen as far as his property rights are concerned."

"Let's walk up on his porch, then," J.W. said. "Say howdy to the landowner."

"Yeah," Tyrone said. "Let's test out his knowledge of the sub-contractors operating under Lo Lo's trademark. See how well he keeps up with the help."

The house the two detectives headed for had begun its existence as a small bungalow, built as a unit in a subdivision of cheap housing during the postwar boom of the late 40's and 50's and financed mainly by VA loans. It had been added to over the years, and its ill-planned sprawl reminded J.W. of the architectural genius he had often seen cropping up in sections of towns in North Mississippi Holly Springs, Batesville, Senatobia, even Oxford of its time and going down fast.

"What do you think the old boy that added that garage to the side of the house thought he was doing, Tyrone?" J.W. said, picking his way around a discarded mattress on the curb next to the shell of a Kenmore washer from which the salvageable parts had been pulled, leaving only rust marks to show they'd ever been there.

"Looking for space for all them children, I expect," Tyrone said. "Just like he was when he built that lean-to or whatever you call it on the other side of his residence."

Much of the porch to the bungalow had rotted away, but a poured cement set of steps led up to the front door, wide enough for J.W. and Tyrone to climb abreast.

"You want me to knock on Lo Lo's door and you stand off to the side, or do you want to do it?" Tyrone said.

"The way you're gathering yourself I know you're dying to do it," J.W. said. "You knock, and I'll be unlimbered off to the side here." He unsnapped the strap on the holster of his Glock 9 and moved to the end of the cement platform to give Tyrone room to operate.

Tyrone Walker set his feet, reared back and began hammering on a panel of the door to the house on Baby Street with the flat of his hand, creating a series of booms loud enough to rival the bass notes of a good midlevel-quality sound system.

After the first three or four strokes from Tyrone's hammering resounded, the only lights in the area visible, those from windows of two houses across the street, went off, and true darkness descended on Baby Street.

"What you want?" somebody said from the other side of the door Tyrone was working on. "Who the fuck beating on my door?"

"Open up," Tyrone said. "Memphis police officers are standing out here in the cold. We need to talk to Lo Lo."

"Lo Lo ain't here," the voice said. "He gone."

"Open the goddamn door, Lo Lo," Tyrone said. "Or I'll let a police officer try out his hello hammer on it. It's a brand new one, and he's just aching to see how many licks it'll take to bust a door down."

A lock turned, the door opened a crack, and J.W. shined the beam of a flashlight at eye-level at the opening.

"Damn, get that light out of my face. I can't see nothing."

"Come outside and talk to us, then," Tyrone said, "or we'll light up your hidey-hole like a Christmas tree."

"Let me get the chain first. I got to push the door close first."

"Officer," Tyrone said. "Step up here with the hello hammer. We got resistance to a lawful police request and reason to believe a felony has been committed on these premises."

"Naw," the door opener said, yielding the point. "It's done open. Don't be busting my front door up none."

"Lo Lo, turn on your lights and step aside. This ain't going to take long if you don't act the fool with us."

Tyrone Walker was first to step through the door, J.W. close behind with the flashlight, and by the time both men were inside the room, Lo Lo Tedrick had flipped the wall switch.

"Damn, Lo Lo," Tyrone said. "Why you so afraid of the light? You making me think you're half vampire or something."

"What y'all blue knockers want?" Lo Lo said, backing up from the door, both hands held out to the side, clearly visible to both detectives.

"Look at that, Sergeant Ragsdale," Tyrone said. "I told you Lo Lo would know how to do. See how pretty he's acting? He understands just how to stand when he's talking to officers of the law."

"He's had plenty of practice, what I think," J.W. said. "I'd be surprised if he didn't remember how to act, all them times he's been bent over, having people feel of his ass. I bet you half of Memphis would know blindfolded it was Lo Lo the way his buns is been patted down and pawed over time and time again."

"I ain't done nothing for y'all to come here in the middle of the night," Lo Lo said. "I be trying to sleep. You ain't got no paper on me. It ain't none out there now."

"We don't need no fucking papers when a man asks us to come inside his house, Lo Lo," Tyrone said. "You did the polite and nice thing, said come on in, and we did."

"Here we are," J.W. said, "right in the parlor of your house, and Lord God, ain't it a sight? You never heard of picking things up off the floor and at least laying them on top of each other, so it looks like something's been put somewhere and not just throwed at the wall and let stay where it hits? Damn, Lo Lo, that's the first housekeeping trick you learn when you start living indoors. Read your ladies' section of the Commercial Appeal and learn something. Shit, Lo Lo."

"I don't prescribe to the newspaper," Lo Lo Tedrick said, backing further into the room, his open hands still extended to the side. J.W. noted that Lo Lo stepped adroitly over the piles of clothing, pizza boxes, beer cans, used paper plates, DVD boxes and CD sleeves, and what looked like the innards of a fuel-injection system from a General Motors product, and he did so without a falter or a look down behind him.

"Lo Lo," J.W. said. "I see I owe you an apology, and I take back what I been saying about your housekeeping. You do know your layout here, because I see you ain't falling down or catching your feet in any of this shit. You just happen to use a different organizing plan than most housekeepers do. But it is a plan here. I'm man enough to say I'm wrong when I see that I am."

"No," Tyrone Walker said. "You're wrong when you say you're wrong, Sergeant Ragsdale. Lo Lo hadn't got a plan here, no more than a house cat does when he's using his litter box. He just knows by instinct where the shit's buried, and he won't step in it himself. Anybody else, it's their tough fucking luck. Right, Lo Lo?"

"Them two bitches back in yonder's supposed to pick stuff up and wash around and all, but they too sorry to do it," Lo Lo Tedrick said, gesturing over his shoulder toward a hall that led out of the front room. "I can't do everything myself around here."

"Ain't it the goddamn truth?" Tyrone said, shaking his head as though in deep sorrow. "You can't get good bitches no more. All they want to do is lie up in the bed, watch TV, and snort blow all day. But what you going to do, right?"

Lo Lo nodded, but didn't say anything, beginning now to let his arms drop to his side.

"Yeah," J.W. said. "You can relax a little, Mr. Tedrick. We all see you're used to doing just that very thing here in your den, and like Sergeant Walker said, we ain't here for nothing more than a little talk."

"This won't take no more than two minutes of your valuable time, Lo Lo," Tyrone said. "Provided you give us just that little bit of information we need."

"I ain't been doing nothing," Lo Lo said. "Just trying to make a living and get my GED diploma done finished."

"Don't get me started to laughing," Tyrone said. "I ain't got time for it, and we didn't come here to Baby Street for the entertainment value you trying to give us. I want to ask you about a Bones Family claimer, get you to give us his name and location. That's all we interested in, period."

"Listen here," Lo Lo Tedrick said. "I don't know nothing about no Bones Family business. I ain't in that no more, see."

Stepping forward on his right foot and pivoting, Tyrone Walker backhanded Lo Lo across the face hard enough to rattle the windows in the living room of the house on Baby Street.

"You can't do that," Lo Lo said, rubbing his face with both hands. "Goddamn."

"Don't never say listen here to me, motherfucker," Tyrone said. "Only one says that to me's my wife, and she ain't here."

Lo Lo blinked and backed up, this time upsetting a stack of something behind him.

"See what you made Sergeant Walker do?" J.W. said. "Now you done ruined your own floorplan."

"The punk's at Central High School," Tyrone said, leaning forward as though a harness was fastened to his shoulders with its fibers strained to the breaking point as it held him. "His name is Antwan Harrell, and he's running with a kid named Randall McNeill. He's the one we looking for, McNeill."

"Antwan," Lo Lo said. "Yeah, he Double Lunch's brother, but I don't care what he claim. He ain't Bones."

"You know what I recommend?" J.W. said. "Not to be sticking my nose in here between y'all, but I think if you got word to Antwan to give us a call when the sun comes up this morning, let us know where Randall

McNeill might happen to be, why, hell we'd just go on about our business. Wouldn't we, Sergeant Walker?"

Tyrone said nothing but leaned a little stronger into the harness that nobody but him could see, his eyes fixed on Lo Lo's face.

"Damn, Mr. Officer," Lo Lo said. "I ain't done nothing to you. I'm just a working man trying to get his rest before he has to get up in the morning and be back out on the job."

"I believe," J.W. said in a thoughtful tone, "that ain't the way to try to play this thing, Lo Lo, with Sergeant Walker. See, he just naturally hates and despises having to listen to bullshit. It gives him some kind of indigestion or something. I don't know exactly what it is, since I ain't no medical doctor. But let me tell you what I've noticed over the years of observing him in the kind of condition you putting him into. He gets plumb dyspeptic. Rolaids nor Tums won't touch it. What you say? You want my advice, or do you want me to go outside and wait in the car while y'all work on through this thing?"

"No sir," Lo Lo said, still rubbing the side of his face. "Don't be going outside none. Y'all want me to get ahold of Antwan and see where Do Run Run is, right? And then let y'all know asap."

"Do Run Run?" J.W. said. "Randall McNeill got him a street name, huh? He been broke yet?"

"I don't know what you mean, Officer," Lo Lo said. "When you say that about broke. But I'll surely find out what Antwan knows about Do Run Run quick as I can."

"You standing there with that crooked little finger on your hand," Tyrone Walker said, "and you're trying to tell us you don't know what getting broke means? You still lying and shucking and expecting us to believe your bullshit."

"Naw, naw," Lo Lo said, lifting his left hand up as though for inspection by a government official at a border crossing in a hot climate. "I got this pinkie caught in a fan belt when I was working on my car. That's what mess it up."

"Setting the timing, I suppose," J.W. said. "It was misfiring and all, I reckon. And you're a crack mechanic, right?"

"Sergeant Ragsdale," Tyrone said, "this asshole is lying to us again, and I will not stand for him to keep on acting like we as dumb as he is. I will not bear it."

"I understand," J.W. said. "But I'll tell you what. If we ain't got the true word on Do Run Run by the time we start the morning shift at the Midtown station, I promise you we'll catch up with Lo Lo before sundown and reason further with him. How about that?"

"All right," Tyrone said. "I got to get out of this house and draw me a breath of clean air or I don't know what I might do. My lungs is about to bust from holding back."

"Y'all's phone will be ringing before nine o'clock," Lo Lo Tedrick said. "I flat guarantee you I'm going to find out what Antwan knows about Do Run Run just as soon as I get my shoes on."

"Well," J.W. said, winking at Lo Lo and putting out a hand gingerly toward his partner as though to coax him into a neutral corner, "I'll take that as a promise, Lo Lo, and I'll be sitting right by that phone waiting for it to ring."

Outside in the car, as Tyrone fired up the engine, he looked over at J.W. in the passenger seat and began to laugh.

"That went pretty well, J.W., damn if it didn't."

"You put on a hell of an act, Tyrone," J.W. said. "You had me believing you for a minute or two there."

"I really don't think I was acting," Tyrone said, "and I know you don't believe but half of what you literally see, J.W."

"I believe in the International House of Pancakes, for one thing," J.W. said. "I'm a keeper of the carbohydrate faith. Let's go eat."

21

"How long you think we going to have to wait, Tonto?" Coy Bridges said, leaning forward in a leather wingback chair in the anteroom area of the second floor of Jimbo Reynolds's big house in the Nathan B. Forrest Estates, just outside the counting room.

"How do I know?" Tonto said, without opening his eyes to speak. "We'll wait as long as it takes for the preacher to get his business done and come out of there."

"It's taking a long time to get her done, ain't it?" Coy said. "We been here what? An hour anyway."

"He'll be out when he's ready to roll," Tonto said, "and we'll relieve him of all that burden of toting that money out of here."

"I wish now we hadn't put that duct tape on Fulgencia before we came up here," Bob Ferry said. "It's got to be damned uncomfortable for her sitting there all this time."

"From what she says, it'd be a lot more bother to her later on if she wasn't taped up," Tonto said. "That's the way she wants it. Fulgencia is thinking long term. She is one to hedge her bets, and she doesn't want to have to leave here before she wants to. She's been tied up before a lot worse than this, I do imagine. She's probably enjoying a nap about now."

"I think I might go down there to the kitchen and see if the tape's bothering her mouth or anything. Might be too tight on her somewhere, cutting off circulation and shit," Coy Bridges said, standing up from the leather chair and beginning to stretch, getting a lot of motion in it as he twisted from side to side and bounced up and down on his toes.

"You ain't going anywhere," Tonto Batiste said. "And you're sure not going to be checking on Fulgencia. Set your ass down."

"Why the fuck not?" Coy Bridges said. "I might have to piss, you don't know."

"And I might have to bust your head wide open, too," Tonto said, opening his eyes now and beginning to lean forward on the sofa where he sat beside Bob Ferry. "You want to try me?"

Coy looked out a window for fully half a minute and then sat back down. "The sun's going down," he said.

"I hope it don't get dark while we're in this house," Earl Winston said. "I want to be out of here while it's still light outside."

"Why's that, Earl?" Bob Ferry said. "You got an appointment somewhere?"

"Thing is, see," Earl said. "I know about old houses like this one is, and I just as soon be gone on about my business before it gets night time around here."

Nobody spoke, and nobody looked at anybody else, their eyes all fixed on their own private space just in front of their faces.

"Old houses like this one is," Earl Winston said, "is liable to be spooky after dark, if you get what I mean."

"This house is not old," Bob Ferry said. "This whole estate, all these places in the Nathan B. Forrest development, every one of them was built in the last four or five years. It's all brand new here, from the foundations all the way up."

"That may be," Earl Winston said, "but let me ask you something, Bob. What was here before all these new places was put up? You tell me that."

"What was here was the equivalent of that old mansion we rented over there across the street. Just an old neighborhood of mansions and big houses where cotton factors and plantation owners and timber barons and bankers lived the good life a hundred years ago in Memphis. That's what was here."

"All right," Earl Winston said. "That's what I'm talking about. What used to be here where this new house is standing now? What's it built on top of, huh? That's what I want to know."

"Probably on top of the location of some wonderful old Victorian or turn-of-the-century home just full of great hardwood floors and stair cases and moldings," Bob Ferry said. "Most likely. So what? It's gone now, like they always say, with the wind."

"That's what I mean," Earl Winston said, "and that why I want out of here before it gets dark. After the sun goes down every night, I flat-ass promise you this place is just eat up with ghosts."

Gerald Duff

"Jesus Christ," Bob Ferry said. "Ghosts? What're you talking about?"

"If you ain't had experience with one of them boogers kicking up a fuss, you ain't got a damn bit of room to talk, Bob," Earl Winston said. "I have lived with the fuckers in more than one old house place over in Middle Tennessee, and it is nerve-wracking to be around the sons of bitches. Ever one of them in that country was a goddamn consequence, much less what you're liable to get in a big town like Memphis. They'll be hell here, the goddamn ghosts will. They've had time to fester in Memphis."

"What would they do to you, Earl?" Coy Bridges said. "Kind of mess with you at night?"

"Mainly at night, yeah," Earl said. "You know, when I was by myself, but you'd get some in the daytime, too, now and then. The women ones, that's the ones that's active when the sun's up."

"Why is there that gender difference, do you think?" Bob Ferry said. "You suppose it breaks down along work-role distinctions, Earl? That'd make sense, now that I think about it."

"Oh, yeah?" Earl Winston said. "Why you figure that?"

"Well, the duties of a female, particularly back when women were so place-bound, would center about the house, and women would be most active in the daytime. Males would be out and about, no matter what their line of work would be, but the women would be home all day. So if any kind of female supernatural manifestations would occur after death, it's only logical they'd be active in the ordinary work day, maintaining the household and all."

"And the men ghosts," Earl Winston said, "they'd be doing their shit at night because that's when they was used to being at home when they was alive, right? After dark, when they got home from work. Sure, that makes sense. I believe I learned something today, sitting here talking to you."

"That's a new development which I'm glad to be a part of, Earl," Bob Ferry said, looking around the ante-room for signs of appreciation for what he'd just allowed.

"Would they poke at you when you was asleep, Earl?" Coy Bridges said, "them ghosts in them old houses? Touch you and all?"

"Naw, not usually," Earl said, putting a hand to his chin as though

146

to aid the progress of memory. "They'd most of the time just pop up at you or duck around a corner or something when they knew you'd seen them. It wasn't no real touching or nothing. I don't believe a ghost is got fingers, has he? He's just usually head and shoulders floating when he's moving around and all."

"Would you silly bastards shut the fuck up?" Tonto Batiste said. "Talking about ghosts and shit. Next thing you'll be remembering how one day you met the Easter bunny."

Bob Ferry began to laugh in the way he always did, a dry chuckle which included rolling his eyes from one man to the next as he measured to what degree everybody understood how smart he was to be recognizing something was funny that they didn't. The less other people laughed when he did seemed to give Bob great satisfaction, and that was another reason Coy Bridges added to the ones he was storing up for when he would get the chance to get way up on tiptoe and bust the living shit out of Bob. Let that time come, Lord, soon.

"All I'm saying, Tonto," Earl Winston said, "is that I'll be damn glad when this deal is done, and I'm long gone out of this kind of place where it might be a ghost hanging around, waiting to fuck with me."

"I believe you've explained that to my satisfaction, Earl," Tonto Batiste said, "and I don't want to hear another goddamn word about it."

"I like to be in new buildings, put up on a piece of property where there ain't been nobody ever lived before, that's what I mean," Earl Winston said. "What I really like is a trailer house put up on cement blocks out in a pasture somewhere. Then I know it's just me and live people around. Not no spirits. Nothing ever been there before but cattle."

"You mean a unit of manufactured housing," Bob Ferry said. "Not really a mobile home that's portable. We aren't talking an RV."

"I don't make no distinction," Earl Winston said. "Just as long as it ain't no goddamn ghost slinking around the place."

"Why don't we just go knock on the door of the room where the preacher's getting his money together?" Coy Bridges said. "Just cut to the chase? Answer me that."

"Because," Tonto Batiste said, "like Bob and me have told you, that counting room Jimbo Reynolds is in is a fortress. He built it that way, and if he suspects there's anybody waiting on him, he is prepared to pick up a cell phone and have cops swarming all over the place in two minutes."

"Tonto's right," Bob Ferry said. "The only way to get to the reverend is to wait on him right here, just like Fulgencia's told us, and we have to be patient."

"What if he sees us out here waiting?" Earl said. "What's going to stop that phone call then?"

"We have reconnected the security system for him, Earl, like we told you. Fulgencia let us in to do it while he was preaching and praying at his big cowboy warehouse church. All he sees in there on the monitor is a continuous loop of this room as empty as Jesus's tomb. As far as he can tell, it's just another end of a fiscal year, business as usual, and Fulgencia's down in the kitchen making quesadillas and shit like she always does."

"What if he just pops out the door on us while we're sitting here bullshitting?" Coy Bridges said. "And he jumps back inside before we can grab his ass?"

"As soon as he touches that inside release, this little buzzer vibrates and the light goes on," Bob Ferry said, holding up for inspection an electronic device the size of a deck of cards. "Tonto's got one too, and when the reverend announces his coming out party, we're ready to welcome him home."

"It sure is getting dark outside," Earl Winston said, looking out the window. "That damn sun is about sunk all the way into Arkansas, all the way to hell and gone. Look at them shadows how long they are."

"You think they'll be cranking up, Earl?" Coy Bridges said. "About now?"

"I expect they will, if it's any of them around this part of Memphis," Earl said. "From my experience.'

"Shit," said Coy, drawing out the word like a moan.

"Say one more word about ghosts," Tonto Batiste said, "and I swear I'll kick the crap out of both of you."

22

"You can take it to the bank," J.W. Ragsdale was saying to Major Dalbey, "what I just told you. I got it on the best authority."

"And that's Lo Lo Tedrick's best intelligence," Major Dalbey said, rearing back in his office chair and peering over the top of his reading glasses. J.W. could see that Dalbey had loosened his collar but kept his tie cinched all the way up to his Adam's apple. It made him look on both the edge of relaxation and in imminent danger of an explosion of the carotid artery, and seeing that caused J.W. to consider the compromises a middle-aged man must constantly face in day to day existence. You want to look good, goddamn it, J.W. thought, but you got to be able to draw a breath while you're wearing your work clothes. It is a quandary. And quandary is a damn good word I'm glad I just came up with, one I'll use on Tyrone the first chance I get.

"Well, if you can say Lo Lo Tedrick's name and intelligence in the same breath, yeah," J.W. said. "That's what Lo Lo's turned up and called into me this morning and asked me to relay it to Sergeant Walker."

"Why didn't he tell Tyrone himself?" Dalbey said. "I been seeing him at his desk all morning doing paper work."

"Lo Lo don't want to talk to Tyrone, best way I can figure it, Major. That's why."

"Uh huh, and why's that, you think?" Major Dalbey said. "Has Tyrone been being rude to Lo Lo Tedrick?"

"Not exactly, no," J.W. said. "Lo Lo just recognizes me to be of a more sympathetic and understanding nature than Tyrone, that's all. But he wants Tyrone to know he did call up."

"Yeah," Dalbey said. "You known for that, J.W. Sympathetic is your middle name. So anyway, this here kid, this Randall Eugene McNeill, he ain't in no real trouble, far as Lo Lo can tell us."

"That's right," J.W. said. "Lo Lo's informant, a young man of real substance there at Memphis Central High, Antwan Harrell his name is, wouldn't tell Tedrick anything but the truth. See, he looks up to Lo Lo as a kind of role model. What they call a positive mentor in these workshops we're always having the opportunity to attend here as officers of the law."

"Bones claimer, huh?" Major Dalbey said. "Been broke yet? I guess not, since he's still hanging around the schoolyard part of the time."

"Naw, Antwan ain't broke, but he'd love to be. He's in training for it, and what he says is Do Run Run's been acting funny the last few days."

"Do Run Run?"

"Randall Eugene McNeill," J.W. said. "That's the street name he's trying to live up to. Or down to. Do Run Run."

"So what can I tell Ovetta Bichette to get her the fuck off my back for a day or two about this here Do Run Run? His mama is just dying to know where the little shit's got off to, and Bitchhead is worrying that question like a dog with a bone."

"Antwan Harrell says that Randall Eugene McNeill AKA Do Run Run has been heavy in his mind," J.W. said, looking down at the notes he'd made on the call from Lo Lo Tedrick which had come well before nine o'clock that morning. "Says he's been talking about Jesus and cowboys."

"Jesus and cowboys?" Dalbey said, sitting up straight in his chair. "He's nuts, huh? Is he fixing to off himself or something?"

"Now, Major," J.W. said. "We don't use terms like that no more in the helping professions. You not supposed to say nut or off himself, terms like that. What you mean, see, is self-destructive tendencies and emotionally challenged. You got to learn how to express yourself in a less aggressive manner."

"J.W.," Major Dalbey said. "They made me send y'all to that workshop. It wasn't my idea, it was the chief's and and the city council's and the mayor's, so you ought to quit throwing it up in my face all the time."

"You got me wrong," J.W. said. "I learned all kind of coping strategies in them workshops, and I appreciate what you've done for me, Major. I speak for all of Homicide."

"Oh, fuck you, J.W.," Dalbey said. "So I can tell Ovetta Bichette to let the worried mother know that Do Run Run is OK and will show up in a day or two here."

"Yeah," J.W. said. "That you can tell her, but don't call him Do Run

Run. That'll run up what they call red flags for the concerned parent. You can tell her his Central High School buddies feel like Randall Eugene is just fine, trying to get a closer relationship with his savior, see, and that they will let him know it's time to check in with mom."

"All right, J.W.," Major Dalbey said. "I'll try slinging some of that and see if any of it sticks. But I'd sure like to be able to say something encouraging too to the good councilwoman about that lady that got done there at Montgomery and Peach. You ain't got nothing more on that yet at all? Beulahdene Jackson, I believe her name is. I hear it enough to remember it, by God."

"I have consulted closely with the Medical Examiner," J.W. said, pausing and looking toward the ceiling of Dalbey's office as though attempting to call up a name. "Hebert. That's it. And we are going over blood evidence and some other stuff. Hope to fill in some blanks here soon."

"Well, all right. Keep me posted. I appreciate what you did with this Bones claimer kid, J.W. Good response. I know it wasn't your business to tend to."

"It wasn't me," J.W. said. "It was Tyrone that got that job of communication done. Him and Lo Lo Tedrick."

"Tyrone carried the load, huh? That's why Lo Lo's afraid to talk to him on the phone."

"Lo Lo Tedrick ain't afraid, Major. He ain't afraid of nothing. He be Bones Family."

"Yeah," Dalbey said. "So when are you leaving to go pick up Perry Lester down yonder in Batesville? And when you getting back? A couple of days?"

"Four days after I leave Memphis to go get him, Major. That's what we said, wasn't it?"

"Two," Dalbey said.

"Three, wasn't it? I mean I'm on police business and all, right? Hauling that dangerous white supremacist back up to Tennessee to face justice and all. Putting myself in jeopardy just to be in the same vehicle with him."

"J.W.," Dalbey said, "Perry Lester's going to be about as dangerous as them ugly tattoos he has all over his face and neck. You got to do better than that."

"Perry Lester and his Batboys have done declared war against the government of these United States. Why, he's liable to bear a grudge against me for being a Mississippian that's sold out like I have. He's just going to radiate contempt for me from where he'll be sitting in the back seat of my Buick."

"Oh, hell, let's say three, then, counting all parts of it. When you leave, what you do in Panola County, transporting him back and checking him in at the Moron's Hotel, showing up back here at work."

"All right," J.W. said. "There ain't no rush on getting him, is there? I mean I don't have to leave Memphis until I think I'm able to."

"Not as long as it's in the next day or two. Perry Lester ain't going nowhere. I expect Sheriff Seay has got him fastened to the floor there in Batesville with a log chain. Just don't put it off until the boy starts growing mushrooms on his feet."

"Let me know," Major Dalbey went on, "when you're going. Be sure to keep that cell phone close to you, turned on, too."

"Quick as I can break loose," J.W. said. "I can hear Mississippi calling."

"I don't think I'd admit that," Major Dalbey said, but J.W. was out the door before he had finished the statement.

* * *

J.W. was supposed to be meeting Nova Hebert a little after six o'clock at some bar on South Main she said she liked and thought he might enjoy, too. He was suspicious, though, not only about the bar but a couple of other things. The drinking establishment had a name which was not only cute, but clever, and that, J.W. had learned over the years, was generally a bad sign.

There ought to be a necessary and logical link between what function a place was intended to serve and what it was called, he believed. When that connection was hazy or non-existent or too damn much of an insider's game the rules of which could be understood only by people with college backgrounds in professions which required certifications and licenses, the establishment usually sucked big time.

The Owl on Central Avenue now, the bar where off-duty and retired cops and the random road-running woman or two gathered to get untwisted or twisted, whatever the need may be, was in J.W.'s opinion well and appropriately named. It hadn't been labeled the Owl because anybody meant anything by the name, like wisdom as in wise old owl or late night because that's when owls hunt down what they kill and eat.

No, somewhere early in the bar's existence, the owner had stuck a cement statue of an owl up on the roof to scare off the pigeons which inhabited Midtown Memphis like flying rats, and the name of the bar became the Owl. It made sense to one and all, particularly to cops and ex-cops and the hangers-on, all needing to have their nerve centers hammered into or out of balance.

Over the years of his time in Memphis, J.W. had made it his practice not to know certain things or keep current with new cultural developments in the entertainment aspects of the city. It made life simpler for him, it allowed him to focus on what served him well during his time in the Bluff City, and it did not encourage elevation in his blood pressure level.

So when Nova Hebert had suggested they meet for drinks at the Metronome on South Main, J.W. had felt a twinge kick up just below his breastbone, a definite clinch in the stomach area. He made no external sign of the response, and said sure he knew where the Metronome was. He didn't, but one of the young uniformed cops in the Midtown station would certainly be eager to tell him the bar's location and brag about what he'd done among the women there.

Nova Hebert was a good ten or twelve years younger than he was, J.W. estimated, she probably had guys her age all over her all the time trying to get her pants off, and he would be a fool this early in the game to show her how he really felt about anything. Nova was not likely to be amused or attracted by the fact that trendy new places gave J.W. heartburn. What was a metronome anyway? Something like a pendulum in a grandfather's clock? That name for a bar was probably real funny to a bunch of young lawyers and stock brokers and pharmaceutical executives, but it left J.W. cold.

It sounded French to him, and he imagined that the drinks favored by the clientele of the Metronome would come in oversized wine glasses with names not one graduate in a hundred of the Batesville, Mississippi

High School would even attempt to pronounce, much less be in the habit of chugging down.

It was early in the first quarter for him and the female medical examiner, too, early enough that she had said she'd meet him at the bar on South Main. That meant, naturally, that she wanted her own car available for a graceful exit if she decided she ought to make one, and that precaution taken by Nova Hebert J.W. respected. He wanted the same out himself, if need be.

What if some Rhodes College graduate with an executive position at FedEx came bopping up to the table where J.W. and Nova sat, the woman sipping away at a half-filled glass of chardonnay or merlot or some such concoction and him knocking back a double tumbler of house gin, and said, "Why, hello, Nova. So good to see you again. How's Terence or Cameron or Jennings blah blah blah?"

The Rhodes graduate would be named something like Randall Holaday, but he'd be called Ran by all his old fraternity brothers, and his eyes would be dancing because he'd be looking at Nova Hebert and thinking about how he'd already had her in bed in some high-dollar condo on the Bluff. Then, according to how many of the double house gins J.W. had taken on by that point, he would probably say something witty to Ran Holaday like "fuck off, dipshit" or worse, get up from his chair and put a violent hand on the paper-shuffling, white-toothing little junior executive asshole.

So all in all, at this point, separate cars for him and Nova Hebert, a white shirt on J.W. buttoned at the neck with one of his three wearable ties hanging from it, and his blue jacket worn tight and smooth over the Glock 9 in his shoulder holster, and J.W. set to be civilized, cool, and laid back.

As soon as J.W. stepped through the front door into the chilled air of the Metronome, he could see a long bar to the left, the gleam of polished metal fixtures bright against the deep mahogany expanse of wood before the shelves of bottles and glassware, and he instantly felt better at the sight. Do what they could to a drinking place to gussy up the look, there was no way they could hide its purpose and reason for being. To get that feeling going in the base of the neck, the pit of the stomach, and the big muscles of the back and thighs that only a couple of shots of alcohol can bring.

This place might not be exactly a home to your taste, but it is a home, by God, it says. Come on in.

J.W. took a deep breath of the air of the Metronome, looked deeper into the bar area, and caught the sight of Nova Hebert about two people down the way, her hair an announcement in its curl and its thrash as she leaned forward to say something to the bartender.

She's here, it said, right here and now, no mistake. J.W. moved toward her, thinking act lively now, but don't show you're straining. Be cool.

Nova Hebert looked up just as J.W. arrived at the bar, then back at the bartender. "Hey," she said to J.W. "I got this gentleman's attention, so you better jump on in while he's focused."

The bartender nodded, white-toothing, looking from Nova to J.W. and then despite himself back at her. "What can I get you, sir?" he said. "Same as the lady?"

"What're you drinking?" J.W. said. "Some kind of wine, I bet."

"Yeah," Nova Hebert said. "It's not bad, but you probably wouldn't like it much. It's a tad too impudent for your taste, I imagine."

"Give me a double gin on the rocks," J.W. said to the bartender. "I done had my wine today. Whatever brand you're pouring will do me fine."

"House gin is Schenley's," the bartender said, then going into his pitch, "We've got two for one on the Bombay Sapphire this time of day, though. It is so smooth, let me tell you."

"Naw," J.W. said, not doing the arithmetic in his head, but knowing the numbers would be against him as always on special deals. "Just squeeze a couple of slices of lime in the Schenley's. I'll see can I worry it on down."

Fifteen minutes later, J.W. was into the first drink of the second round, the world was looking more level, and he and Nova Hebert were sitting at a small table at the edge of the bar area of the Metronome, the roar of the crowd at the bar itself having now reached a sustained pitch which promised to last for a while. Young attorneys were beginning to throw caution to the wind and work more aggressively on administrative assistants, junior bankers were arguing points of contention about Allen Greenspan, and commercial real estate brokers were trying out new sets of lies about investment possibilities in the Memphis metropolitan area.

"Seems to me," Nova Hebert said, "you watch baseball kind of funny."

"How's that?" J.W. said, rattling the ice in his third drink of Schenley's gin, the clink a true and friendly sound at the edge of the feeding frenzy in the Metronome's bar area. "You mean I don't pay attention to what's going on?"

"You paid attention all right," Nova said, "the other night at the Redbirds' game, but it didn't seem like you focused on what most people did."

"Yeah?"

"What was the final score, for one thing?"

"I don't remember. Eight to five?"

"No," Nova said. "It wasn't."

"Oh."

"Do you want to know what it was?"

"Not really, no, " J.W. said. "I don't mind knowing, though. What was it?"

"I'm not going to tell you, Sergeant Ragsdale," Nova said. "You got to do your own research, if you want to know."

"I don't, though."

"I know you don't."

"You still working on that glass of wine?" J.W. said. "You ready for some more of it?"

"In a minute. Why did you want to sit so close to first base? To watch if the runners were safe or not, coming from home?"

"Naw, let the umpire worry about that," J.W. said, feeling the gin beginning to move in the tops of his thighs, a gradual process and then a jump. "I ain't going to do his job for him."

"Why, then?"

"Oh, I like to listen to what the first baseman's saying to the pitcher and catcher. That's what I like about that ballpark. You're close enough you can hear what they're saying most of the time, at least when the damn crowd ain't hollering too loud."

"What does the first baseman say?" Nova Hebert said. "I'm ready for some wine now. See can you catch Elvin's eye."

"Elvin?"

"The bartender. I don't know his real name. That's what I call all bartenders. Elvin."

"Why Elvin?"

"That's what they like to be called. They might not know it until I say it, but once I do, they come to recognize that's the name they've been wanting to be called all their lives. So I do it."

"I imagine most men would like to be called any name by you," J.W. said, thinking that was a damn good comeback for a man in midlife to come up with on the spur of the moment while his legs were being put to sleep by three double gins.

"Some names no man wants to be called, though," Nova Hebert said. "No matter who says it to them."

"What name would you not call a man? What one could you say he wouldn't want to answer to?"

"Harold," Nova said. "For one. Or Shirald. Any name that rhymes with that."

"Yeah, I guess you're right," J.W. said. "You put it that way, I wouldn't want to argue."

"What does the first baseman say that you want to hear, J.W.?"

"Well," J.W. said, "the other night, the best thing the Redbirds first baseman said was when that shortstop for Nashville kept taking a long lead because he figured he could run on that right hander for Memphis. Remember that?"

"No, I don't. What did he say?"

"He said," J.W. said, taking the first drink from his fourth gin and lifting a hand in the air for Elvin to see, "after the third time the pitcher'd thrown over to first base to hold the runner, he said there he goes.'"

"That was it?"

"Yeah. I liked the way he said it. The first baseman didn't say there,' he said something like thar.' And he said the same way a cotton farmer in picking season says it when he looks out at the goddamn rain coming just when it's right to start picking the crop. He ain't surprised, he ain't whining about it, but he's damn sorry to see happening what he knew was going to happen all day. Thar it goes,' he says. He ain't complaining, he's just telling what he sees, what he knew was coming, and there ain't a damn thing he can do about it but let folks know."

"I believe I understand that, J.W.," Nova Hebert said. "Here comes Elvin with my wine. Are you getting hungry?'

"I sure am," J.W. said, the bar gin at full blossom in his legs. "Yes, ma'am, I am ready to eat."

Later in the night after steaks at the Butcher Block, where patrons cook their own meat if they feel like it, and Nova and J.W. had, J.W. heard Nova beside him in her bed in her apartment on Fondren Street say something.

"What was that you just said?" J.W. said. "I was halfway dozed off here."

"I said thar he goes.'" Nova said. "That's all."

"Why?"

"I knew that damn runner was going to take off and steal that base, but there wasn't a thing I could do about it. But I had to make a statement."

"Yeah," J.W. said. "See, when the first baseman does that, it don't stop a single thing from happening, but at least it gives him some relief."

"It shows he's in the game," Nova Hebert said, moving her head to a more comfortable position on her pillow.

"It does that, for sure," J.W. said and carefully buried his face in the mass of curls of Nova's hair there beside him on her bed.

23

Counting bills, putting them in neat stacks, slipping a paper band around each of these, placing the same number of stacks in separate boxes all this work was not the usual chores for a cowhand, Colorado knew. What he'd like and expected to be doing after he'd signed on with the Big Corral outfit was a far cry from the first thing the range foreman had set him to do.

But Colorado was a cowpoke belonging to an outfit that gave him a bed in the bunkhouse, grub three times a day, payroll every month, and work that helped make the enterprise go, and what that meant, Colorado told himself as he worked away at the job at hand, was that he was to undertake what he was assigned to do, he was to do it to the satisfaction of the range foreman, and it wasn't part of the arrangement for him to worry about what it was he was told and set to do.

You like that, Colorado heard a voice say in the middle of his head. You know you do. You do what you're told, the range foreman picks out for you what chore he needs to have taken care of, and at the end of the day, you take off your cowboy work clothes and go to bed to get your rest so you can do what you got to tomorrow when the sun comes up over the mesa like it always does and the air smells clean and new.

And if you've worked hard and done what the range foreman set for you to do, you won't dream a thing in the night, and you won't have to wake up and lie looking into the dark all around you. You'll be too tired to do that, and if you happen to wake up because maybe a coyote's howled and got the cattle to milling around, why you'll drop right back off to sleep. And you'll be dead to the world, and nothing will be working in your head to remind you of what you don't want to be thinking about. Nothing will be behind you. It's all in front, waiting for you to be there. And the square shapes all in lines and patterns won't be pulling at you to stay where you've been put and wait until the hand moves you to the place it wants you to be. You haven't got time for that. The range foreman has set you to a task that needs doing.

Do this job here in the counting room of the ranch house, don't mess up your numbers, don't forget to keep your head down and your mind focused, and next thing you know you'll be in the bunkhouse asleep.

In the morning maybe the range foreman will have you tending to a different chore out riding fence, maybe, or rounding up some strays that have got off from the herd on their own and need to be brought back to where they belong, or mending something's that broke and won't work right. But whatever it is, even if it's just the same thing you're doing right now in the counting room, you'll do it, and do it right, and you won't complain, and you won't have to think about anything but what you're doing.

You're Colorado, a new hand just signed on with the outfit, a good one, the Big Corral, and you're doing the Boss's work, and the range foreman shows you what part of that work to tackle next.

"Colorado," the range foreman said, "I see we're getting down close to the end of what we're doing here. These stacks of offerings have done shrunk up to a lot littler pile. Way we're going here, it won't be long until these offerings'll be doing the Boss's work like they're ordained to do."

"Yessir," Colorado said, watching his hands tend to the chore without him having even to think about it or what to tell them to do, "it's a lot bigger bunch of the ones that've been done than the ones that're not yet finished."

"And you know what, Colorado?" Jimbo Reynolds said, pausing to stretch and rotate his head from side to side to get a crick out of his neck, "I give you the credit for most of that. I never seen a hand take to the work right off the way you have. If I didn't know better, I'd say you used to work in a clearing house bank."

"No sir," Colorado said. "I never have handled offerings before."

"But you like it, don't you? I can tell you do."

"I do," Colorado said. "But I reckon I'd like any chore you give to me to do, range foreman."

God Almighty, Jimbo Reynolds said to himself. I have found me a jewel here. Weird as he is, this colored kid is a working machine. I wonder how long it'll be before he starts getting sticky fingers and that itchy neck, though, starts scratching that itch and letting green stuff fall down his collar and catch in his clothes. It ain't long before the infection hits them, that's for damn sure, not that I mind a little skimming during a count. But trust our African-American friends to steal more goods than they can tote off without their knees buckling. That'll happen with this one, too. Matter of time is all it is, but that's the burden I have to bear. You can't find true loyalty no more. There ain't a honest one in a trainload of the thieving bastards.

"What makes a hand relish his work, Colorado," Jimbo Reynolds said, "I've learned during my time of serving the Boss, is this one thing. If all that a cowboy wants out of his work is a way to fill his belly and a place to lay his head and enough money to throw away at the saloons in town, then it all turns to ashes in his mouth. I hope you're learning that same thing here today taking on the first job I asked you to do for the Boss."

"I aim to, range foreman," Colorado said. "I want that more than anything."

"We about to finish here, and then we're going to go see what Fulgencia's cooked for supper," Jimbo Reynolds said. "Then we're going to take these processed offerings to the Boss down to the bank where it'll be put into service to His work. But first I want to give you a little test, see how you're progressing here in your first day in the outfit. What I'm trying to get a notion about is what this first chore is doing for you. Ready?"

"I hope I am," Colorado said, looking up from the box into which he was stacking the counted packages of currency. "I'll try, range foreman."

"All right, then. When you're working with all this money, all these hundreds and fifties and twenties, what does it seem like to you you're handling? Is it just paper?"

Colorado told his hands to stop what they were doing for a spell, so he could look directly at the range foreman as he answered the question put to him, but they didn't want to rest. They kept lifting, turning, placing, arranging, settling the stacks of bills. Nothing to do but let them go on about their business, he realized, and tell the range foreman what was in his heart as best he could.

"It's not just paper, no," Colorado said, "any more than a saddle is just leather or a rope is just string wound all up together or a sixgun is just steel. This money here that belongs to the Boss, I figure it's not what it is. It's what it does. It's the good the Boss puts it to."

"That's the time, Colorado," Jimbo Reynolds said. "I ain't never heard it put better," thinking as he spoke, I expect this one might last two or three more countings before I have to run him off or he leaves on his own with a backpack full of my money. He is as nutty as a boar hog drunk on rotten peaches.

"Colorado, let me take a look here at the monitor, see how things are looking around the spread before we open up the door and go downstairs. I expect you been wondering what all these little TV screens are, while you been working away here."

Colorado looked at the bank of monitors against one wall of the counting room at which the range foreman was pointing, seeing them for the first time since he'd come through the door. Each of them framed a scene of a room, a doorway, a hall, a window, a parking lot, an expanse of lawn, and all were absent of any movement or human figures, not even a flicker.

"I hadn't noticed them, range foreman," Colorado said. "No sir, I hadn't."

"I'll tell you what they are, Colorado, what job these here machines are doing for the Boss. See, they are today's equivalent of a whole outfit of cowpokes keeping an eye on the herd every minute of the day. Back in the old West, see, the range foreman used his top cowboys to make sure none of the stock strayed off and no varmint came creeping in to take off a new calf, or a heifer walked off too far from the herd. But you don't have to guess what the real danger was, do you, Colorado? I expect you done figured that out while you were counting these offerings for the Boss's work. Tell me what that is."

"You mean the thing to be most scared of?"

"Not scared, Colorado. But on guard. The cowboy ain't never what you could call scared. He ain't built that way. He's just watchful. He ain't to be fooled. But yeah, what?"

"Rustlers?" Colorado said, noticing that his hands had finished placing the final stack of counted bills in the last box he'd been working on. "Cattle thieves?"

"You got it, Colorado," Jimbo Reynolds said. "I knew you'd figure that out by yourself. You wouldn't need no help."

Jimbo moved toward the bank of monitors, pointing directly toward one in the upper right quadrant of the display, labeled C Room A. "Looky here, Colorado," he said. "What you looking at yonder is all there is to see outside the door of this room we in. What you see in it?"

"Nothing but some furniture," Colorado said, stepping toward the bank of monitors for a better look. "That and some pictures on the wall."

"Nobody there, right? No prairie wolves, no mountain lions, no stray Indians out on a hunting party, no strangers on horseback or afoot, nothing to raise the hairs on the back of your neck?"

"No sir."

"Let's get out there, then. See what Fulgencia's got waiting for us to eat down yonder, and then get this chore finished for the Boss. We got to mosey on down to First American where the Boss keeps his money. They going to be open special for us, as a favor, see."

Jimbo Reynolds flipped a switch on the door of the counting room, punched in four numbers on a pad set into the wall, waited until a buzz sounded and pulled the door open, stepping out into the anteroom with Colorado close behind him.

It wasn't until both of them were fully through the door that Tonto Batiste put the muzzle of the .357 to the point on Jimbo's face where the lower jaw hinges to the skull and took a tight grip on Jimbo's right arm just above the elbow.

"Come right out, preacher," Tonto Batiste said. "Damn, we been waiting a long time on you. What you been doing back in there? Holding a prayer meeting?"

"Here you go, Slick," Earl Winston said, grabbing Colorado's new cowhand work-belt just beside the buckle and pulling him to the side of the door facing. "You got to move so my buddy can get that chair stuck there in the door."

"Gentlemen," Jimbo Reynolds said, "that door has already been open long enough for the alarm to sound at the headquarters of the security firm. So your enterprise is doomed to failure even as I speak. Our consultants tell us not to warn you like that, but I always figure it's better to be friendly and upfront. You know, let a man reconsider the merits of what he's getting himself into. Give him room to back up."

"You do?" Tonto said. "That's mighty white of you, preacher."

"Yeah," Jimbo said, as Tonto led him toward one of the leather chairs in the ante-room, the revolver tight enough against his jaw to leave an impression, "so I'll call up the security people and report the mistake I made in exiting the safe room, and everything will be just like it was before. Nobody hurt, all forgiven, you're on your way out of here headed for wherever it is you're going, and nobody's the wiser. Not a soul will know or follow up on this. It didn't happen."

"He's a talking son of a bitch, idn't he?" Coy Bridges said. "Just like you said he was going to be, Bob."

"Naturally," Bob Ferry said. "The Reverend Reynolds is a minister of the gospel. That's the way he makes his living. Explaining things and pointing out the right directions for people to take."

"You want me to shut him up?" Earl Winston said. "Soon as I get this colored cowboy set down and cuffed to his chair?"

"No," Tonto Batiste said. "I don't. He'll stop preaching in a minute or two here, all on his own. I'll lay you odds he does, just like a wind-up clock running down."

"What do you say to my offer, gentlemen?" Jimbo Reynolds said. "It's getting a little late now. I got to let the security people know it's a matter of human error, that alarm that's gone off, or they'll be here in less time than it'll take you to get out of the house and back on the road. The time is now."

"Preacher," Tonto Batiste said. "I'm going to tell you one thing, and then I want you to shut the fuck up. If you don't, I'm about ready to turn that man there with the two-pound .45 loose on you and let him do to you what he is the guaranteed best at doing. So tune in and listen."

Jimbo Reynolds sat forward on the edge of the leather chair, not speaking now and beginning to pluck at the turquoise and silver watchband on his left arm, as though it was binding him.

"All that you're saying about Guardsmark Security Service of Memphis would be right on the money," Tonto Batiste said, "if you were dealing with your typical dumbshits from around here. But you ain't, see. We have made some adjustments to your technological set-up here in this big old house, you understand. So we're not worried about alarms going off in headquarters somewhere and people hauling ass over here in security vehicles and shit like that."

"Your system's subverted," Bob Ferry said. "Turned inside out electronically. Every signal coming into Guardsmark from this location is reading situation normal."

"That's enough, Bob," Tonto Batiste said. "The preacher don't want to know another fucking thing. He's heard enough. Hadn't you, reverend?"

Jimbo Reynolds opened his mouth to speak, closed it, and nodded his head, holding out his wrists for the cuffs Tonto had pulled out of a black bag.

"You want to know anything else, or want to talk some more," Earl Winston said, "just say it to me, that's what Tonto's talking about."

"Set to your seat, Earl," Tonto said, "and just watch these two cowboys while we see what's waiting for us in yonder."

"You ain't got to worry about me," Earl said. "I'm going to set here like an old mother hen guarding her eggs."

"You do that, and that's all you do. Hear me now."

The cuffs on Colorado's left wrist fastening him to the arm of the chair where they'd made him sit were the first real ones he'd ever seen. They were heavier than they looked, not really that tight, and cold enough to the touch in the air-conditioned room to make him shiver a little when he first felt them clamp around his arm.

The man who'd put them on him was the one the others called Bob, and he had looked directly into Colorado's eyes as he pushed him back into the chair, trying by that to scare him, Colorado figured.

Bob was the boss of the outfit, Colorado guessed, or at least equal to the Indian, who was maybe a half-breed, a renegade certainly, separated from his own tribe and now part of an outcast band of white outlaws.

The Indian wasn't wearing any feather stuck in his hair, though, and that was what surprised Colorado a little, causing him to think half-breed rather than full-blood as he tried to figure out what tribe the Indian was from. Too bad he didn't have a headband holding his hair in place, since markings on a leather strap might help place him. Apaches would have lightning bolt representations worked into the leather, done by scarrings with an instrument, and Comanches would be likely to have some beadwork done by women, usually, to decorate the headgear of a warrior.

Colorado closed his eyes and tried to remember what patterns of design a Comanche brave might have worked through the arrangement of beads, but he couldn't come up with anything. He ought to have paid more attention to the Comanches he'd seen before, the ones hanging around the reservations in the winter, eating the white man's beef in the cold time now that the buffalo herds were so few.

A cowboy ought to pay attention to everything he runs into, Colorado told himself, whether he thinks some detail is worth knowing at the time or not. That's what separates a real hand from one just drawing his pay, having enough sense and presence of mind to store up what he runs across, not for just now but for later. That's what can keep a cowboy alive, especially a black cowboy, paying heed and learning what you're supposed to learn, for later on down the trail.

One thing I do know, Colorado thought, speaking to that part of his mind deep inside his head where he was the only one able to visit, the man to worry about here is the Indian, not the other ones, not even Bob. They were drifters, smalltime, undirected frontier trash, on the move from failed lives behind them somewhere in the East. They would take your goods, they would cut out a few head of steers from a herd that didn't belong to the outfit, they would get drunk in a low sorry saloon, and they might even shoot you if they thought they could get the drop on you from behind.

But they wouldn't be thinking about what they were doing, they wouldn't plan to do it, and they wouldn't even present much danger to a real hombre as a stray rattlesnake or a sudden sandstorm or a stampede might do.

The Indian was different, especially if he had some white blood in him from somewhere along the way. That made him unpredictable, that made him crazy, that made him dangerous. Mixed blood was bad medicine.

Colorado opened his eyes and leaned forward a little in his chair, enough so that the cuff bit into the flesh of his wrist, causing him to increase the pressure until the length of chain tightened against the arm of the chair where it was fastened. The chair arm gave a little.

"Be sure they don't see you doing that," somebody said.

He was standing in the corner farthest from the door to the room that three of the outlaws had entered. He was in the shadows, leaning against a wall, one leg bent so the heel of his boot rested against the dark wood facing. His hat was pulled low, causing him to peer from underneath the brim, and Colorado could see the whites of his eyes.

He was wearing gloves, and he lifted one hand and pointed a finger at Colorado in greeting, as though saying by the gesture you're here, I see you, you're a consequence.

"Ricky," Colorado said. "Ricky Nelson. It's you. Howdy."

"Colorado," the man said, shifting his weight forward as he nodded, the leather of his chaps and gunbelt creaking a little at the movement. "Howdy."

"You're the real Colorado," Colorado said, pulling again at the cuff holding him to the chair arm. "I know that."

"Not any more," the man in the shadows said. "I reckon you're Colorado now."

"No, I'm not. I know I'm not."

"Oh, I reckon we'll see, here in a little while. I expect you might be Colorado after all, whether you know it right now or not."

"Can he hear you?" Colorado said, cutting his eye toward the man they called Earl Winston, sitting on the leather sofa and doing something to the .45 automatic he held.

"I don't reckon so, but I believe he might hear you pulling at them cuffs, if you're not careful."

"Oh," Colorado said. "Thanks, Colorado. I'll watch it close."

"Call me Ricky for now," the young cowboy in the shadows said, his eyes more visible now as he smiled at Colorado. "We're going to see who gets to be called Colorado here in a while. We're going to see directly who cowboys up and who doesn't."

24

The telephone on Tyrone Walker's desk blinked its light at him, and Tyrone looked at it as though it was announcing news that no man in his right mind would want to hear, not picking it up until it began to ring as well as blink.

"Why'd you make it do that, Myra?" Tyrone said. "You didn't need to set the dogs on me."

"If you'd pick up quicker or activate your voice mail to begin with, I wouldn't have to let it ring, too, Sergeant Walker," Myra said. "I ain't the one designed the system. I just know how to make it do."

"It ain't your job to do anything else, right? Is that what you telling me?"

"You took the words right out of my mouth," Myra said. "You got a call here."

"You just trying to drive me crazy, talking about your mouth, Myra," Tyrone Walker said. "You know that's cruel to a man, getting him all worked up."

"It's some clerk two's would give you up for sexual harassment, saying stuff like that to a woman in the work environment, Tyrone. You going to take this call or not?"

"Yeah, anything to get my mind off what you just said. Put it through."

"Yo," somebody said after a pause and a couple of electronic clicks and tones, "this here that homicide detective be named Tyrone Walker?"

"Yo back at you, my brother," Tyrone Walker said, dropping his voice into the lower range and rhythm often heard on the streets of South Memphis, North Memphis, Downtown Memphis, but definitely not East Memphis.

"You talking to him. Who's this on my phone?"

"This Lo Lo, the man you and that cracker sergeant done talked to in the middle of the night."

"You could've fooled me, Lo Lo," Tyrone said. "I thought it was Denzel Washington calling, wanting to play me in one of these here thriller movies. Now I'm all disappointed."

"Naw, it's Lo Lo Tedrick, that's who. Not who you just said."

"Don't go putting yourself down now, Lo Lo. Denzell ain't nothing up beside you, the way you sound on the phone. And I tell you what. I won't even say a word to Sergeant Ragsdale about that name you just called him. Now what's on your mind?"

"I figure I do something for you, you do something for me."

"That's the way it works sometimes, all right," Tyrone said. "Long as you got something I want. What you got, Lo Lo?"

"Well, er uh," Lo Lo said. "First, what you got for me, Sergeant Walker, if I tell you something about a thing y'all been wanting to know yonder in the homicide place? That's what I'm talking about."

"Let me put it this way, Lo Lo," Tyrone said. "I got stuff to do, so if you got something to tell me that'll do me some good, I might forget where you stay. Maybe I won't be seeing you on any more nice little visits, unless I just have to. Maybe I plumb forget how to get to Baby Street, I don't know."

"All right, then. See, I'm trying to live a quiet life now, kick back, take care of my kids and all. Visit with my babies's mamas. Smell the roses, you understand."

"Aw," Tyrone said. "Ain't that nice. But what you got for me, Lo Lo?"

"That old lady that got done in her house on Montgomery, you know? I got a name for you."

"You talking about Mrs. Beulahdene Jackson now," Tyrone said, beginning to write on the corner of a piece of paper on his desk. "I'm very interested in hearing a name from you, Lo Lo."

"The name I'm giving you ain't Bones Family now," Lo Lo Tedrick said. "Bones ain't in this shit."

"I got you."

"Do Run Run," Lo Lo said. "He ain't Bones, remember, no matter what he been saying, but that's the name I been give."

"Do Run Run? That's Randall Eugene McNeill, right?" Tyrone said. "We been looking for that young scholar. His mama's all worried to death about him."

169

"I know y'all are," Lo Lo said. "You done told me that."

"All right, Lo Lo," Tyrone Walker said. "I ain't going to ask you where you come up with this name, if it's the right one, you understand. I give you that much slack. I do appreciate your nice little call this morning."

"I ain't said nothing to you," Lo Lo said. "I ain't on this phone."

"No, you sure ain't," Tyrone said. "And I won't be coming out to Baby Street neither, if what you're not on the phone to me about does give me some help. But if it don't, you know, well shit, I just have to look in on old friends, see how they're making out and all. Maybe meet the kids and all like that, you know."

"I'm gone," Lo Lo Tedrick said and broke the connection.

Tyrone Walker hung up the phone, looked at the wall across from his desk, the one lined with badly framed photographs of past award-winning officers in the Memphis Homicide Division, and then began to write on a new sheet of paper. Where was J.W. Ragsdale when you needed him, he asked himself, and then answered his own question. In the fucking Mississippi Delta, of course, wandering through his past with a barbecue sandwich in one hand and a strange woman in the other. I do predict and know that for a fact. I'll give him a call on his cell phone, see if he can figure out which button to push to make it work.

25

It had been a good trip to Panola County. J.W. Ragsdale had got in a full day's fishing on Sardis Lake in a bass boat he'd borrowed from Leon Butler, once the slowest linebacker ever to play for Batesville High School and now co-owner of Butler Chevrolet, he'd eaten the vegetable plate twice at the Cottage Caf, he'd drunk most of a pint of Heaven Hill as he drove around every street he could remember in Batesville, and he'd avoided running into a single one of his cousins, aunts, and uncles during all his activities in his home country.

So as he walked into the front office of Sheriff Jimmy Seay in the government building to which was attached the Panola County jail, J.W. felt pretty good. No, he thought as he approached the receptionist's desk with his Memphis Police Department ID out for inspection, he felt damn good, or at least good enough to face riding the ninety miles back to Memphis with a white supremacist baseball bat swinger in transport and chained to the D clamp welded to the frame of his '92 Buick Century.

Maybe one of these days he'd invite Nova Hebert to accompany him on a road trip back down here, just as soon as he could face again the notion of re-entry into the Panola County version of reality in the Deep South. Nova was scientific and might take an interest in the specimens at large where J.W. was raised. Some of them might even raise up from the mud and let her take a close look at them.

"Do you want to talk to the Sheriff, Sergeant Ragsdale?" the receptionist asked him, looking up from the ID which J.W. had flipped open for her to read. "Or just have one of the deputies bring the prisoner for transport on out here?

Sheriff Seay was hiring him a better quality representative to the public these days, J.W. noted, as he looked at the one behind the desk, a dark-haired woman with eyes that didn't appear to need makeup, though that hadn't stopped her from doing a paint job worthy of a Hollywood cosmetics expert on them. She didn't look to be older than fourteen, in

J.W.'s estimation, but during the last several years, he had reached the point that he couldn't tie a number to a woman any more exact than ten years plus or minus. Hell, they all look the same now, he told himself, and that's too damn young for me to think about messing with.

"Well, if Sheriff Seay's not too busy to talk to me a minute or two, I'd like to say hello," J.W. said. "If it's not any trouble."

"I don't expect it would be," the teenager or newly married woman or Cub Scout organizer or soccer mom or whatever the hell age lady she was said with a perky smile. "I'll just tell him you're here."

Both statements she made ended with what sounded like a question mark, J.W. noticed, and that let him know she was not anywhere close to the upper range of the age category he had estimated for her. She probably was fourteen, working on an internship out of Batesville High School. Go Bulldogs.

"I'd appreciate it if you did that," J.W. said, and in a minute or two he was sitting in Jimmy Seay's office, ready for some hoorawing before he had to load up his sociopath for the trip to Memphis.

"Goddamn, J.W.," Sheriff Seay said, rearing back in his leather office chair, "how long has it been since I had the chance to talk to you?"

"I don't know exactly, Jimmy, but I expect it was when your receptionist out yonder was still sucking on a baby bottle."

"Dawn? Hell, J.W., she's older than she looks. She's been working here for two or three years."

"They all older than they look to me nowadays," J.W. said. "Damn it to hell."

"I know what you mean, J.W. I purely do. Why, I ain't had nothing to do with a woman other than Myrlie so long, I wouldn't know which way to turn her if I got hold of one."

"She'd show you, Jimmy. They ain't shy about that no more. These young'uns scare me to death. They know exactly what they want and if you can't give it to them, they will flat tell you about it."

"You still between wives then, huh?" Jimmy Seay said. "Not took the big step again."

"I done took that big step twice, Jimmy, and I tell you I stubbed my toe both times I done it and about broke my neck. You still married to Myrlie Putnam, huh?"

"Hell, yeah. Sometimes it seems like I was born married, like everything before then never happened I just dreamed it."

"Tell me about it," J.W. said. "I started feeling that way the third day of my second honeymoon."

"You still catching them bad boys up in Memphis?" Sheriff Seay said, after laughing politely a little too long at what J.W. had just said. "Getting them straightened out and put on the road to moral rehab?"

"Homicide work in Memphis is like picking fleas off a redbone hound, Jimmy," J.W. said. "You know you ain't going to do no final good, but you keep popping them on your thumbnail just to watch the blood fly."

"This old boy you carting back to Memphis is a damn good argument for that, J.W.," the sheriff said. "I'll be glad to see the backside of that little son of a bitch for good."

"He's a bad'un, huh?"

"Let me put it this way. He don't belong in Batesville. His rightful home is Memphis, Tennessee. He was born for the city life."

"Urban shithead, you're saying," J.W. said. "I understand he swings a mean baseball bat."

"Perry Lester does that all right, or used to before we relieved the little bastard of his Louisville Slugger."

"How'd y'all get him here in Panola County? So dumb he ran here to hide out?"

"He's plenty of dumb, all right. But it's family connections, of course, like always, that brought him here after he killed that black kid up in Memphis."

"Is this Perry one of them Lesters from out close to Drew? Leonard and Byron Lee and Junius and that bunch?"

"Perry is the grandson of old man Leonard Lester himself. His mama is that youngest daughter of Leonard, Estelle I believe she's named."

"Yeah, that's Estelle. I used to ride the school bus with her when I was in the lower grades. She was half grown then. But tell me something, why is her son got the last name of Lester if she's a Lester?"

"Shit, J.W., why not? It's easy enough to tell who his mama was, but there's no way to pin down the daddy's identity. When you back into a spinning buzz saw, how can you tell which particular tooth bit you? So Perry is just another Lester, that's all."

"Not to put too fine a point on it," J.W. said. "I got you. So Perry got in with the Batboys For Freedom up in Memphis, once he'd reached escape velocity from Panola County."

"He did, and up yonder they tell me, he got too damn enthusiastic with his 32 ounce bat and killed some colored kid outright."

"Major Dalbey tells me it was Perry Lester's first at bat, Jimmy. It was his initiation run he was on when he knocked that boy in the head. Perry had something to prove to the assholes he was working to join up with."

"I reckon so," Sheriff Seay said. "He was sure easy to find, I tell you that much, after we got the call from y'all up there in Homicide that Perry was likely to be here in Panola County. Soon as I heard his last name, I piled in the car with one of the deputies and we run out there to Drew to pick him up."

"Didn't put up much of a fight, Perry didn't, huh?" J.W. said. "Saw the game was up and threw his hands up in the air."

"It wasn't even that much to it, J.W. We got to the house, the old Vance place it is, you remember, and Perry was asleep in one of the backrooms. Denned up in there with old clothes and rags and cardboard boxes and busted video game sets and empty cans and junk throwed everywhere. Time he woke up, the deputy had the cuffs on him, and I was holding the muzzle of my .44 in his ear."

"You still carrying that .44, Jimmy? That ain't regulation, not even here in Panola County, is it?"

"No, I imagine it don't meet the specs, but a man who's looking in the end of that barrel tends to just get real quiet and stand there waiting to be told what to do next."

"I know I would," J.W. said. "But tell me something. What's Perry Lester got against black folks that'd cause him to join up with the Batboys once he got to Memphis? Did black kids whip his ass regular when he was little or something?"

"When does a Lester need a reason for anything, J.W.?" Sheriff Seay said. "Perry doesn't know why he does a single damn thing he does do, and if you was to ask him why he did something, it'd just piss him off."

"You know something? Here entering my declining years, I have just lost all patience with that kind of shit. I got plumb sick of that behavior."

"I go along with that, J.W.," Sheriff Seay said. "Makes me want to pick up my own baseball bat is what it does. You ready to meet Perry?"

"Yeah," J.W. said. "I got him a nice little seat fixed up in my Buick. Let's go get the young man situated."

When Perry Lester arrived from where he was being housed in the Panola County jail, he was led by a deputy holding a thick leather belt ringed with chains attached to the inmate's wrists. He was also fastened at the ankles with shackles and a chain leading upward to the belt, causing him to shuffle along the hall and keep his eyes focused on where he was stepping.

"Hey, Perry," J.W. said. "You sound like one of Santa Claus's reindeer trotting along with those chains on you. I bet you just stay in a holiday mood, listening to your jingle bells working out."

Perry Lester lifted his gaze at that statement and stared at the man before him, his eyes as dead as he could make them and his face as blank as a slab of sheetrock wall board.

"Not too perky this morning, I see," J.W. said. "Well, that's understandable, a man of your substance having to be led on a leash by a little bitty woman in a uniform. Damn, that must be embarrassing."

"I don't know you," Perry Lester said, "and she ain't no woman. She's a nigger whore."

"Lord, you talk rough and mean," J.W. said, then turning his attention to the deputy with the prisoner in tow, "I reckon Perry here has got you about scared half to death."

"He don't scare me none, Sergeant," the deputy said. "Perry is just as sweet as he can be once you get to know him. He just act nasty."

"My goodness," J.W. said. "Ain't that nice, Sheriff? Who would've thought that?"

"Why Janelle says that is because she caught old Perry crying yesterday in his cell," Sheriff Seay said, "when he thought nobody'd catch him at it. Just boohooing, wasn't he, Janelle?"

"Yeah, he's just a big old fat teddy bear wanting his mama, Perry is," the deputy said. "Don't let his rough outside fool you none."

"Well, I'm so glad to hear that," J.W. said. "Maybe on the way to Memphis, Perry and me can share our feelings with one another. Get, you know, connected as one human being to another one, like it says all the time on TV."

"Just don't let Perry come back down here to Panola County no more, Sergeant Ragsdale, " the sheriff said. "We don't appreciate the air pollution he takes with him everywhere he goes."

"All right, Perry," J.W. said, taking the handle on the restraint belt from the deputy and beginning to move toward the door. "Come on, Slick, time to go to the big old jail in Memphis, see can we introduce you to some nice roommates."

On the way out of Batesville, Perry Lester fastened to the D ring welded to the Buick's frame, J.W. pointed out what he considered interesting sights and landmarks of the town in which he'd grown up, noting in particular what wasn't there any more.

"See that store where you can rent videos and computer games and shit, Perry? That used to be a pool hall. Yonder across the street, that was an ice cream place, there where it's empty. I ain't talking about soft-serve now. I mean the old fashioned dip ice cream, hard as a rock when it's froze up good."

Pery said nothing, staring straight before him and now and then moving his head in a tight circle as though to work out a crick in his neck.

"What's wrong, Perry?" J.W. said. "Here we are, two white men riding along in Panola County, Mississippi, and you ain't said a word to me. Are you just going to sit there and stink all the way to Memphis? Don't you know this is probably your last time ever to be by yourself with just one white man in the car with you? Why, son, Memphis is a majority African-American city now. Has been for I don't know how long. You just going to be right in among black folks from now on out everywhere you look."

"Majority?" Perry said.

"Yeah, you know what that word means? Run across it in your extensive reading? It means more than half, majority does."

"I know what majority means," Perry Lester said. "I know my words."

"Why that makes me proud of the educational system of my home county to hear you say that, Perry. And I bet it didn't take long for you to learn all your words, did it? When did you get all that schooling could give you? Third or fourth grade?"

"I went to high school," Perry said.

"Why, hell, I went to France one time," J.W. said. "But that don't mean I'm a Frenchman. Let me ask you another word. Do you know the word barbecue?"

"Yeah."

"You want some?"

"I could eat me a sandwich," Perry said. "Yeah, I could."

"I'm going to do you a favor then," J.W. said. "Give you a present, one white man to another before the state of Tennessee puts you in that room with the lifetime lease. I'm going to buy you the best barbecue sandwich to be had in Mississippi, and of course that means the whole wide world. I'm taking you to Big Daddy's Dreamland, out yonder where Sunflower Road crosses Bumblebee."

"I heard of that," Perry Lester said, shifting in his seat until his chains rattled. "It's a nigger place, ain't it?"

"Son, you ain't been listening to me," J.W. said. "What all I been trying to tell you. Get focused now. From now on out for you, everything you see and everywhere you go is going to be a nigger place."

"I got your voice mail on my cell phone," J.W. Ragsdale said to Tyrone Walker back in the Midtown station. "And I believe we ought to go pay a little visit to this here Jimbo Reynolds, preacher man. See who's staying with him."

"You just now concluding that, J.W.?" Tyrone said. "You're slowing in your reflexes. I left that message for you three or four hours ago, and you're just answering it now."

"Well," J.W. said, looking down at the pile of pink slips of paper left on his desk for call backs, "I just now listened to what you said."

"You didn't know how to retrieve your messages, did you, until somebody showed you the way to do it?"

"What it was, Tyrone, was that there wasn't a ten-year old kid around in Panola County to do it for me, so I had to wait until I got back to Memphis to find me a nerd to take care of it. I drove here fast as I could."

"On that model you just punch the button marked" Tyrone started to say and then stopped. "I ain't got time to do a seminar right now, J.W.

Let's just go see the Major and tell him what we're fixing to do."

"That'll work. Major Dalbey will light up like a Christmas tree when he hears we might be getting Ovetta Bichette off his back."

"At least for a while," Tyrone said. "Until some other member of the councilwoman's constituency's got something that needs doing by the poh-lice force."

On the way to Major Dalbey's office, Tyrone asked if J.W. had gotten his Batboy delivered to the Shelby County Hilton for Criminals, as many of the taxpayers of Memphis called the justice complex located downtown near the river.

"Oh, yeah," J.W. said, beginning to laugh, "I wanted to swing by here to introduce Perry Lester to you before I deposited his sorry ass, but I was running late. My fellow Panola Countian has a thing about African-American citizens of this great nation, and I wanted to show you to him. Here's a sample of your perfect bunkmate, I was going to tell him. I hope you got you a lifetime supply of lubricant, Batboy."

"You are a nasty-talking white man, J.W.," Tyrone said. "All you do is deal in stereotypes. I expect this Lester fellow is going to meet the love of his life any day now, and then you'll be sorry you jumped to all these perverted conclusions."

"How you think we ought to handle picking up this Randall Eugene McNeill kid?" J.W. said. "Just the two of us, right?"

"Yeah, let's low-profile it. And let's not give the Major time to think about it. He does, and he's likely to want to put on a show for Ovetta. Get word out to the TV people and call in the SWAT assholes and all that bunch, just to pick up one little murdering shitass."

"Right," J.W. said. "You tell him we ain't got time to get nothing organized but a quick little in and out. Say Lo Lo Tedrick gave you the word this kid's fixing to go somewhere with the preacher's show or something."

"I'll tell Dalbey if we don't do it quick, it'll look real bad when the kid ain't there by the time we show up. I'll say response time a lot."

"That'll do it," J.W. said. "The Major does hate it when somebody promises him some candy and then takes it back."

26

Two of them were rummaging around in the secure room, the Indian and the most intelligent looking of the white men, the one they called Bob, and Jimbo Reynolds sat back in one of the leather chairs in the ante-room, considering how dumb and smug he'd been to let conditions favor and allow this kind of bullshit robbery to take place.

It was always a balancing act, trying to come up with an optimum plan for any contingency. A man was fucked if he did, and he was fucked if he didn't. It would have been easy enough to hire enough muscle to hang around the house heavily armed, eating up every damn thing in the kitchen, half-drunk most of the time and high as a kite on enough dope to stock a drugstore the rest of the day. You can find those moral retards all over Memphis.

That was the problem, of course, Jimbo knew, and he had made a conscious and informed decision not to take that option. Best case scenario, if you went with that choice, they'd be steadily stealing all they could lay their damn hands on, forcing you to spend half the time worrying about how to maintain a decent share of the inventory for yourself. You'd have to be thinking about that every minute of the day, worse than a mama cat having to move the kittens every two hours to keep the coons from eating them.

Worst scenario would be having that much trash all together all the time, watching what was coming in the door until finally one of the dummies would come up with the genius idea of taking all of it and offing the boss in the process.

So Jimbo had opted to be daring, to take the road less traveled, to do it all himself with a good strong safe room and a foolproof electronic monitoring system and only one or two harmless nuts crazy enough to buy into the Cowboy Jesus concept and see themselves as servant-leaders to the Range Foreman and the big Boss in the sky.

Shit and motherfuck, Jimbo thought, fastened to his leather chair by handcuffs and looking from one of the conscienceless misfits before him to the other as he listened to a full fiscal quarter's worth of counted and boxed cash being scooped up by the two others in his safe room. Shit and motherfuck, it has come to this.

And it's my fault because I made a wrong decision, let myself be swayed by greed, thought I could eat the whole goddamn pie myself. I have got to learn to share, he told himself as he looked across the room to the colored kid all dressed up in his cowboy suit. Any business has got to allow for shrinkage and be content not to keep it all. That is the lesson to be learned from the event, and should I get to the other side of it at the end of the day, I swear I will hire me an army of protection and let them feed as they will, and I will take my regular fucking like a man.

Two questions I need answered, he announced to himself. How did this collection of inbred and evil-minded, thieving sons of bitches get onto what I've got here and to the flaws in the system? Who in my employ gave them the word?

Second question, and the big one, for me and the darky cowboy over yonder in the corner looking as goggle-eyed as a goose knocked in the head, but fuck him, I got myself to worry about, why are these people calling each other openly by name and why have they made no attempt to disguise their looks? Not a mask, not a beard, not a hat pulled low over an eye among them.

Bottom line, are they going to leave my brains splattered all over the wall of this ante-room when they take off with every damn cent of this quarter's worth of my money?

"Friend," Jimbo said to the one sitting in the chair closest to him, the rangy narrow-headed one studying the weapon in his hand as though it was a D cup full of titty, "we're all businessmen here, don't you think?"

"You talking to me, preacher?" the man said, Earl as Jimbo remembered him being called by the Indian-looking one. "The fuck you mean by saying that?"

"I just mean we all suffer gains and losses as we're trying to make a living," Jimbo said. "Just a thing I've noticed about how we have to make a go of it. It's nothing personal about any of it, is it? I may make a good payday today, I don't tomorrow. People buy what I'm selling sometimes. Sometimes I can't give it away. I win a little here. I lose a lot there. And you know what?"

Let him answer that, Jimbo prayed deep inside his head where nobody but him ever reached, let him talk back some, please, let him give a shit, Lord God.

"What?" the man called Earl said, shifting his attention from the automatic to Jimbo's face.

"I just forget about it the next day. Win or lose, make money or lose money, get there or get lost looking, I just put all that behind me, and go on with my life. What comes next is what interests me. It's got to. You can't change what's happened. I know you believe that way, too, from just sitting here looking at you."

"Huh," the retard said. "I don't know what I believe about that, what you just said. I don't give a shit about none of it."

"You got that right," Jimbo Reynolds said, leaning forward in his chair until the handcuffs bit his wrist, "that's exactly the way I see it. I don't give a shit about what's happened. Hell, that's over and done with. Done with, I tell you. I'm just thinking about tomorrow. You know what I mean?"

"Tomorrow is that Elvis day doings, ain't it?" Earl said. "That mama business, right?"

"I do believe that's right," Jimbo said. "A global moment in time, I hear they're calling it. You an Elvis fan, sir?"

"Me? Naw, I don't listen to music on the radio none. Not no more."

"A man grows up, his musical tastes change," Jimbo said. "I know what you mean. I purely do. There was a time I might've listened to a few of Elvis's records, back when there was records, but not anymore, no unh uh. I'm just like you on that subject."

"The one thing I did like about Elvis," Earl Winston said, "was he didn't sing this rap shit the niggers is all into now. When he was singing something, you could tell it was a song."

"Amen," Jimbo Reynolds said. "I heard that."

"Another thing," Earl Winston said, laying the .45 down on the floor by his chair, "I always respected about Elvis Presley. He liked his pussy, no matter how much he dressed like a queer sometimes."

"He did," Jimbo Reynolds said, nodding his head in affirmation and praying for further psychic connection with this tattooed retard reared back in one of Jimbo's Moroccan leather chairs. "You got to give the man credit and just due for that. He would get after that tail, from all accounts I've heard."

"Yeah, a old boy I run into in California one time got to talking to me about me being from Mississippi and all, and he told me he had worked on the sets of some of them pictures Elvis made in Hollywood."

"No kidding?"

"He said Elvis would have them young girls brought in by the carload so he could hem them up in a corner and pick out one to fuck. Prime stuff."

"No shit?"

"Yeah, that's what he claimed, this old boy, and he didn't have no reason to lie about it. I wasn't asking him nothing."

"Well, that's good to hear, and I'm proud of Elvis for that. Them was the good old days, back when a man that had a chance at good-looking young pussy would take advantage of it. Not just, you know, do like they do these days, just play around the edges of it."

"By God, that's the way I believe," Earl Winston said. "You see something worth nailing, you go after it, if you got any sense. It might not never come back again, that chance."

"Praise Jesus," Jimbo Reynolds said. "Amen and amen."

"What the fuck're you doing, Earl?" the big Indian said, coming into the ante-room carrying two 30 gallon black garbage bags under one arm and holding one in his other hand. He had a revolver in the waistline of his pants, Jimbo could see.

"It sounds like a goddamn prayer meeting in here," the Indian said.

"No," Earl Winston said, "we just talking about normal pussy, me and the preacher, that's all."

"Normal pussy? What do you know about normal pussy, Earl? What the fuck does that mean, normal pussy?"

"Well," Earl Winston said, "see, he was saying about Elvis Presley having a thing for women."

"Don't tell me what the preacher's been saying," Tonto Batiste said. "Pick up your piece off the floor, and go see what Bob wants you to carry. We got a little over three more minutes to get this deal done, and here you are talking about normal pussy with a goddamned Jesus-jumper."

"He ain't like most of them," Earl Winston said. "That's why I was talking to him."

"He is exactly like most of them, Earl. Exactly. Get in there with Bob."

Jimbo Reynolds shifted his feet to the side to allow the tattooed retard to get by his chair without having to touch him, hoping that the Indian would see he was being cooperative, and Earl went through the door into the counting room.

"We were just passing the time of day," Jimbo said to the Indian, "me and Earl. Nothing more than that, you know, sitting here waiting for y'all to finish in the counting room."

"You and Earl are on a first name basis, huh? See if you can pass this, preacher," the Indian said. "Put it somewhere in your notes so you can get at it if you need help remembering. Shut the fuck up."

"I got you, sir," Jimbo said. The Indian hadn't noticed yet that Earl had left the .45 automatic still lying beside his chair, and Jimbo quickly looked away from it. What if the Indian saw him eying it and thought he was having notions about making a grab for the gun? He probably wouldn't apply logic and realize Jimbo couldn't reach the weapon, fastened as he was to the arm of the chair he was sitting in, and he might just slap Jimbo up beside the head with the revolver stuck in his belt just on general principles. The Indian was likely to be Old Testament in his take on the world and would judge the appearance of sin to be as much a cause for punishment as an accomplished act of transgression.

What if he mentioned the fact that Earl had not listened closely to the Indian and had forgotten to take his weapon with him? Would that gain Jimbo any credit, or would the Indian just run roughshod over any rational way of acting? Jesus, what was a man to do when dealing with ethnics, especially what they called Native Americans these days? Blacks, that was different. If you could show one that there was a material gain to be made by taking some action, he was likely not to move beyond the present moment and the literal fact before him. He wouldn't give a shit about proving something, most of the time. He'd just grab up the cash or the dope or the car keys and be on his way. Unless he had a new pistol in his hand which he hadn't tried out yet. Then he might pop you just to see how it worked. That was the chance you always took with one of them, of course. That was the nigger way of doing.

With this overgrown savage who let people call him Tonto, there was no predicting what he might do. Still, shit, you had to roll the dice, when that was all you had to work with. Throw something out and see will it stick.

"I believe Earl has forgot to take something with him, sir," Jimbo said, holding his head up and away from the back of the chair, thinking that if Tonto decided to backhand him it would be better to leave some give in his posture. You wouldn't want to be jammed right up against the back of the chair and be held firmly in place in the event of somebody slapping the shit out of you. You wanted some slack in your neck.

"I see he has, preacher," Tonto said. "You want me to let you hold it? See if you got the balls to pull trigger on me?"

"No sir, I don't," Jimbo Reynolds said, shaking his head back and forth with great resolution. "I'm a man of peace and a child of God. Praise Jesus."

"I expect you are," Tonto said. "That's what makes me not likely to give you the chance. Don't say another word, Reverend, like I told you. You've done reached your limit on talk."

Well, I tried, Jimbo said to that part of his brain which he trusted for non-rational hints and indications, and now I'll just leave it to the Lord to get me through this. If He will. If He can. If He gives a damn about a faithful servant just trying to get by and do the best he can to advance His work. Lord, I want to curse and blaspheme and howl, but it won't help unless I can give it public utterance, and this heathen Indian has taken away any room for me to do that.

A movement of the colored kid in the cowboy suit across the room caught Jimbo's eye and was a fleer and a mockery to him. There the young punk sat, likely without a thought in his head, just glad to be inside a house with air conditioning in Memphis in July, his brand-new boots extended before him as though he was studying the way they looked on his feet, knowing without realizing he knew it that he was perfectly safe from what this gang of redneck and Indian thieves might do. They wouldn't even bother to notice him in comparison to Jimbo Reynolds, and that grated Jimbo like a dull knife sawing into the palm of his hand. If I live through this, Jimbo promised himself, that darky there will be one fired motherfucker, no matter what kind of a job he can do counting and stacking money.

Randall Eugene could see that the Range Foreman was looking at him now, and he had been doing that off and on since the members of the outlaw outfit had fastened the two of them into chairs with handcuffs. Maybe he was trying to give him a signal about what his plans were for getting them out of the fix they were in, but if that was true, Randall Eugene couldn't figure out what it was the Range Foreman was trying to tell him. The things he was saying to the renegade Indian didn't seem to make sense, and if Randall Eugene didn't know better, he would have thought from what he heard the Range Foreman saying that he was afraid of the renegade Indian and was trying to suck up to him.

Most likely the Range Foreman had something working, though, and all he was doing with the Indian was setting up a situation which he would use to advantage later when the time was right. Still, though, it was disturbing to hear the tone of voice the Range Foreman was using as he talked to the Indian. It sounded exactly like the way Randall Eugene's mother told him to talk to white people, and that was the way he did use to talk to them before he learned who he really was, back in the dead time before that thing he did and talked to Dr. King about it and then met the Range Foreman and learned about the Boss and the Big Corral.

Back in the corner of the room in the shadows where only Randall Eugene knew he was observing things happen, Ricky made a noise with his mouth, something like a little smack and an expulsion of breath. That meant something. Everything that Colorado did meant something, and he didn't have to use words to get his meaning across, the way Randall Eugene had been told to do since the time he first realized he was separate from other people and things and what went on around him and that there was no connection to be made with anything and anybody else.

Here is what Colorado meant when he made the little sound with his mouth. Here is what he is saying, Randall Eugene told himself. The first part of it, the smacking noise Colorado made with his lips said he was impatient and dissatisfied with the way things were going there in the room where the range foreman and Randall Eugene had been surprised and were now shamefully fastened by chains to pieces of furniture. The renegade Indian and the trash cowboys he controlled were in charge, they were taking the proceeds of the Big Corral away from the range foreman, and they were showing every sign of disrespect for the range foreman and what he stood for that they could come up with.

That was what Colorado meant with the first sound he made with his mouth, the smacking noise, tiny in the room to anyone who didn't know how to listen but speaking clearly to Randall Eugene. He heard what Colorado said.

The expulsion of breath, a sound something like puh, that was the noise that mattered most, Randall Eugene knew, and he looked over now at Colorado in the shadows of the corner of the room, slouching against the wall with one leg crossed over the other and his hat pulled low over his eyes. He looked back at Randall Eugene, Colorado did, from under the brim of his hat, and it was too dark to see his eyes, but Randall Eugene understood what had been communicated by Colorado when he made the little sound by expelling a puff of air from his mouth.

All right, partner, he was saying, it's getting close to the time to do something. We've waited long enough on these hombres, don't you think? What say we let them know what it's gonna cost them to mess with Colorado and Randall Eugene McNeill? Ain't it time they understand that if they fuck with the bull they going to get a horn up their ass?

"Colorado," Randall Eugene said in a low voice, "I hear you, partner, but I ain't exactly right in my head about what to do next. I reckon I need to palaver with you some first."

"Who you calling Colorado? Are you talking to yourself?"

"I appreciate what you saying to me, partner," Randall Eugene said, hearing the smile in Colorado's voice and knowing how it would look to see him if there weren't the shadows to hide his face. Colorado's smile would begin slowly, and it would grow like the light gathers as the sun comes close to setting across the Mississippi River in the late summer afternoons in Memphis, and the smile would mean without words having to be said, and it would mean strong and true. Randall Eugene, the smile from Colorado would say, we're partners on the trail together, but we don't have to brag about it or make signs to say it or call each other anything. We know who we are. We depend on each other, but we don't have to say that in words they teach in school.

"Ain't we getting a little restless with what's going on here?"

Colorado said, his voice low in the room but clear to Randall Eugene. "You figuring it's about time to throw in together on this thing? What you hankering to do about it?"

"Well, partner," Randall Eugene said, "I see a piece on the floor over yonder. Nobody seems to be using it."

"You mean that .45 automatic by the chair leg? Don't call it a piece. That ain't the way for a cowboy to talk about a firearm. It ain't nothing but a tool, like a hackamore or a bit or a wire-stretcher or a horseshoe. It ain't no magic in it. It just helps a hand do his job, that's all it's good for."

"You're right, Colorado. I'm sorry for miscalling it."

"There you go, talking to yourself again, calling out your own name," Ricky said, and Randall Eugene knew the smile was there on his face again, though he couldn't see it in the shadows. That was all right, though. If you believed a thing was there and knew, you didn't have to be checking on it all the time to see if what you knew was true was true. You could depend on it, if you believed it, and you could count on yourself to know what was real.

"Well," Randall Eugene said, "I'll try to keep that in my mind, from now on when I'm talking to you."

"Partner, when you and me are talking, you don't have to worry about who's who, now do you? We think just alike, most of the time. Ain't that right? "

"I reckon it is," Randall Eugene said, "except for when we might get into an argument about something. You know, get to jawing at each other in the bunkhouse."

Ricky Nelson laughed at that, and Randall Eugene joined in a little, keeping it low, so nobody from the outlaw bunch would hear him and start looking around to see who he was talking to. They didn't seem to notice much of what was going on around them, not even the renegade Indian, and that was strange, given who he was and where he was comng from, Randall Eugene thought, but still, there was no use to draw attention to himself and his partner in the shadows just yet.

"We might holler at each other some time, all right," he said to Ricky, over in the corner being Colorado, "even get into a tussle now and then. I got to admit."

"That don't mean nothing, Colorado," Ricky said, "and you know it, partner. You and me, we stay the same we ever was. Hollering and fighting a little don't change that. But back to this firearm that hombre left lying over there on the floor. What you figure to do about it?"

"Damn, Colorado," Randall Eugene said, "I don't know. They got me hog-tied here in this fancy chair. I reckon I could drag it over there, carry it or something, but it'd make noise, and they about to come out of that counting room anyway in a minute or two here."

"You don't think the range foreman could give you a hand with it?" Ricky Nelson said. "Do something to help out, I don't know. Distract them while you take care of that little chore? What you reckon?"

"I don't know," Randall Eugene said, looking at the range foreman across the room, sitting slumped in his chair now with his eyes closed. His lips were moving as though he was speaking to himself. "Appears to me he's talking to the Boss right now."

"Praying?"

"Yeah, I believe so," Randall Eugene said. "Like the range foreman says, the Boss's telephone is never busy when you call Him up."

"I don't doubt that," Ricky Nelson said, "but there comes a time, partner, when a cowhand's got to do the Boss's work here on the ranch. He ain't going to do it for you, Colorado. When's the last time the Boss showed up directly to ride fence for you or to round up a lost yearling and get him out of harm's way? Tell me that."

"Well, never, Colorado," Randall Eugene said. "I reckon He depends on me to do what He wants done here at the Big Corral."

"You ain't just a wolfing about that, partner. So what you going to do? You know I can't help you myself, much as I'd love to fling in with you and do it."

"Just having you with me is help enough, Colorado," Randall Eugene said. "I don't have to tell you that, Bud."

"Naw, you don't," Ricky Nelson said. "So what's the plan?"

"Did you ever take a look at my wrists, Colorado?" Randall Eugene said. "Close up? They mighty small to belong to a working cowhand."

"I never did notice that before," Ricky Nelson said. "But you're right. Show me what you about to do. Let's get this thing started up."

"I'm fixing to, Colorado," Randall Eugene said, beginning to move the fingers on his cuffed hand as close to each other as he could make them be. "Let's see where the trail's headed, up around that next bend. Looky here what I'm about to do."

"Damn, Colorado," Ricky Nelson said from the shadows, "I sure ain't never seen such a little wrist on a cowhand before. You're getting it done. Now remember, that firearm ain't a revolver. It's an automatic with a slide action, but I reckon you know how to handle it just fine."

"Thanks for reminding me, partner. I believe I do."

27

"The major hated to turn us loose by ourselves, didn't he?" J.W. Ragsdale was saying to Tyrone Walker as they turned left off Union onto South Main headed toward the series of high-dollar residential developments lining the Memphis bluff. "He wanted to get himself something going big enough to get Ovetta Bichette's attention. Make her know he's about to deliver big time."

"You can't blame him, I guess," Tyrone said, "but sending a whole bunch out there to pick up one little murdering shitass wouldn't make sense. Even Major Dalbey could see that."

"He couldn't see it until you poked your bottom lip out and looked all hurt about it, though."

"I hated to do that to the Major, but I was down to my last card, J.W."

"That wouldn't be the race card you talking about, would it?" J.W. said. "You wouldn't a been dealing that one, would you?"

"Call it what you want to," Tyrone said. "I don't believe in using it except when I have to, and that has to be in a good cause."

"See, Tyrone, that was just the argument that Mr. Perry Lester was making to me. That's what he fears most from our African-American citizens here in this great nation. People trying to get by on being a certain color rather than on their own individual merits, like he's always having to do."

"Norvel wouldn't know a merit if it jumped up and bit him in the ass," Tyrone said. "Merit ain't nothing but a cigarette to that retard."

"Today is Sunday," J. W. said after watching a couple of abandoned warehouses and some upscale dwellings pass by the car window. "You reckon that's going to influence the afternoon's activities for this cowboy preacher that Randall Eugene McNeill is staying with? We going to find them at home, you think?"

"I do know one thing about preachers on Sunday, J.W.," Tyrone said, "and what happens after they preach a sermon in the morning. They eat them a big meal of fried chicken and mashed potatoes and pies and ice tea and shit, and then they go lie down for a good long nap."

"Sounds to me like what a sane man does after getting him a piece of pussy," J.W. said, "that and smoking a cigarette or two."

"They are exactly the same thing, J.W., the religious experience and the sexual, and they require some downtime after an episode."

"Lord, I hope God don't hear you saying that," J.W. said. "He does not like everything getting all mixed up like that in people's heads. It confuses them and makes openings for Satan to claw his way into the works. Your wasted years at Memphis State have led you down strange and wrong paths. They have twisted your head around, Sergeant Walker, and I pity you in the afterlife."

"He leaves me alone, and I leave Him alone, J.W."

"Don't get me wrong, Tyrone," J.W. said. "You handle your sex life, and I'll handle mine, but just don't stand too close to me in a thunderstorm, that's all I'm saying."

"Good," Tyrone said. "I'm glad you're willing to let me handle my sex life, whatever the hell that is, and I'm going to hold you to that promise."

After turning the unmarked police car to the right, Tyrone pointed ahead to the gate opening into the Nathan Bedford Forrest Estates, and pulled over to the curb. "We're here. How do you want to play it once we get to the preacher's house? You knock, and I walk around to the back, or vice versa?"

"No, you knock. Whoever's answering the door'll take less time to open up to a man all spiffed up the way you are. They'll take you for a dude who's been to church and is acting under conviction or something. Maybe got some spiritual business that needs tending to. I'll slip around back."

"You forget this is a cowboy church deal, J.W. I ought to be wearing a sombrero or something, following that thinking."

"They sure ain't going to take me for a cowboy," J.W. said. "I know that much. They liable to think you're Lash Larue on vacation or something. Let's go introduce ourselves to that guard and tell him not to be making no calls after he lets us through the gate."

As soon as the guard saw the badge holder Tyrone showed him, he sat up from his slump in his chair and assumed a more military posture, even tugging the Confederate gray cap he was wearing into a more serious angle. J.W. noted this fact and approved. Maybe the man had thrown a hitch in the Mexican militaria before he had broke and run for the border and the steady paychecks it promised. Or maybe he was just concerned about the status of his green card. Whatever the reason, the guard had made a gesture toward recognizing at least one organizing principle still operating in the world, and J.W. drew some solace and satisfaction from that.

"You can't miss the house Reverend Reynolds lives in," the guard told Tyrone. "It's the last one on the left side of the court, and it'll have that plumbing van parked in the driveway, the one from Forrest City, Arkansas."

"A plumber from Arkansas come in there today?" J.W. said. "I guess the preacher's got something backing up on him, not wanting to take its ordained trip down the pipes."

"Some kind of a leak, I guess," the guard said. "I remember the sign on the truck because of what it said, you know. Forrest City, Arkansas, just like Nathan B. Forrest Estates, what the name is here."

"Named for the same man," J.W. said. "I wonder why the preacher would call all the way to Forrest City for a plumber to take care of his sewage needs."

"You don't know it's sewage, J.W.," Tyrone Walker said, beginning to pull away from the guard booth. "Could be intake problems the cowboys are having today, not sewage."

"I predict sewage," J.W. said. "I feel it in my bones."

"You always assume the worse, every time something comes up. You are bound and determined to look on the dark side."

"That way I am seldom disappointed," J.W. said. "There's the number we're looking for, but I don't see a plumber's van."

"I do," Tyrone said, turning into the driveway off Battery Lane, "it's pulled up behind the house. You can see just the rear end of it."

Tyrone killed the engine, and both men alighted, pausing to check their Glock 9's before separating to go to the front and back of the house.

"What you showing to whoever answers the door?" J.W. said.

"My smiling face, and my badge holder," Tyrone said. "That's the way you supposed to act on a Sunday afternoon in Memphis, ain't it?"

"Yeah, you do that, but I got a feeling about this place. Something's not right here, I don't think. I believe I'm going to put my training into operation back yonder behind the house."

"Oh, Lord," Tyrone said. "What you won't do to inject a little excitement into your day. Go on ahead, and do that. But I think what you're feeling is just plumbing anxiety. I'll just step up to the door and ask about our wandering schoolboy."

"Give me a holler if you need to."

The front door was massive, Tyrone noted, appearing at first glance to have been hewn from one huge section of a single tree, but as he leaned hard on the bell he could see the structure was an illusion crafted from metal. That's reassuring, he thought, as he listened to the chimes working somewhere deep within the house. I'd hate to run into something real here at a cowboy preacher's ranch house. It'd mix stuff up too much, even for Memphis.

When no sign of response came after a couple of minutes of pushing the button and hearing the bells go off inside over and over, Tyrone began to bang on the textured steel door with the flat of his hand, setting up a series of booms that he knew would wake even the dedicated deaf. Even J.W. will hear that, way around the back of the house, Tyrone was telling himself, when he saw a movement to his right just beyond a set of reddish colored ornamental bushes.

"Tyrone," J.W. said. "We got something you got to come see, round behind the house there."

"What? Is somebody trying to exit the rear?" Tyrone said, slamming his hand against the door one more time, and then turning to face J.W. "They heard me, huh?"

"Nope, no sign of anybody trying to leave the premises, but there's a good-looking Mexican woman taped to a chair in the kitchen, wearing a uniform and all. She don't look like she's tied too tight, either."

"She looks nuts?" Tyrone said, coming off the porch.

"No, I don't mean that. What it is she looks like she could stand up anytime she feels like it and cook me a mess of enchiladas without a damn bit of hindrance from that tape."

"Where's the fucking plumber?" Tyrone said as he followed J.W. to the back of the house. "Is he the one that taped her up?"

"There is some duct tape stuck on the side of the van, too, all right. But if the plumber did the taping of the senorita, he is now tending to the sewage backup. There ain't a sign of nobody else I can see. Let's go bust in there and see what's going on."

"That's a go," Tyrone said. "We got imminent danger."

"We got imminent horseshit, it appears to me," J.W. said, lifting his Glock to tap at one of the side windows framing the door into the kitchen. "Watch out for your eyes."

28

Upstairs, the figure in the corner shadows of the ante-room leaned far enough forward for Randall Eugene to see the brim of his hat reflect light from a lamp near a side table. Ricky Nelson was trying to see what was happening with the handcuffs, Randall Eugene figured, interested to gauge how well things were going as his hand worked from side to side in the cuff.

"What's all that pounding on the door down there, Colorado?" Ricky said. "Reckon it's another one of this bunch of outlaws trying to get them to let him in?"

"If it is, he's going to be as surprised as the rest of them if he ever gets up here," Randall Eugene said, lifting his hand for Ricky to see that he had slipped the cuffs. "Look at what I just did."

"You told me you'd do it," Ricky said, "and I see you're a cowboy who don't say nothing he ain't going to back up."

"I appreciate that, Colorado," Randall Eugene said, rubbing his wrist as he took a step toward the chair where the badman they called Earl had been sitting before the Indian called him into the counting room. "You're the one give me the idea to get loose and pick up this piece."

"Call it a firearm," Ricky said. "A man should always call a thing by its right name."

"This firearm," Randall Eugene said. "That's what I meant, Colorado. I just forgot the right thing to say."

"What the fuck are you doing, kid?" the Range Foreman said, sitting up straight in his leather chair, not praying now, his eyes wide open. "Get back where they put you, goddamn it. You going to get me killed when they come out of there and catch you with that .45 in your hand."

"Colorado and I have done come up with a plan, Range Foreman," Randall Eugene said. "You just keep your head down, and we'll get this chore wrapped up."

Ricky had stepped back again, farther into the shadows, and he was grinning now, Randall could see, his teeth a white blur as he lifted his head to laugh. "I do believe you have thrown a scare into the Range Foreman," he said to Randall Eugene. "He don't want no part of what you fixing to do. He ain't got sand enough for it."

"He's not used to having to deal with varmints like these, Colorado," Randall Eugene said. "That's all. He'll be all right once things get started up. He'll remember what a cowboy's got to do. You'll see."

"I admire a cowhand that won't hear nothing bad said against his boss," Ricky said, "I purely do. But the Range Foreman's done showed me you ain't going to be able to count on him. You got it all to do yourself."

"Now, Colorado, that ain't right, and you know it. I got help coming."

"Who from?" Ricky Nelson said, sounding interested but not sure Randall Eugene was making sense. Ricky was standing out away from the wall now, a little closer to where the circle of light from the lamp was falling. The way he moved as he leaned forward looked perfect to Randall Eugene in its grace and balance.

"I'm talking about you, partner, of course. That's who," Randall Eugene said, pulling the slide back on the automatic until a sound told him a cartridge was chambered. "Me and you. You and me, Colorado."

"What're you saying?" the range foreman said. "What you talking about Colorado for? Get hold of yourself and sit back down in that fucking chair. Who's that knocking on the front door? What in the name of Christ Jesus is going on?"

The one named Earl was the first one to start to come out of the counting room as the door swung inward and gave him room to swing the black garbage bag past it. It was heavy, and what was in it poked up into the sides of the bag and made points and lines and marks of strain in the plastic. What could that be, Randall Eugene asked himself, and even as he put the question to himself knew its answer. It was what he had been counting, it was the Boss's money, and that sorry sidewinder with the untidy hair and sideburns was taking it out of the room where it belonged.

"Hold up there, partner," Randall Eugene said, telling himself he wasn't really saying the word partner to mean it the way he would if he was talking to Ricky Nelson. The right label for the piece of trash carrying off the Boss's money in the saddlebags had nothing to do with being a cowpoke's partner, but speaking the word to him now pointed out how unfit it was. Not that the outlaw scum would know that, as underbred and ignorant as he was. He might even take it as a compliment, and that made saying it even better.

"Where you headed with the Boss's property, partner?" Randall Eugene said, using the word again and wanting to smile but not letting himself do that, because that would be a waste and a tip-off. Say things to trash like the man called Earl without him knowing what was really being said, and never let him know you're meaning anything but the surface of what he thinks he's hearing. It would be good now to be able to see the look Ricky would have on his face, hearing Randall Eugene call the man that word partner, and Randall Eugene could feel on the back of his head a little weight, a pressure so light it was a feather touching him, as Ricky watched what was going on.

Don't look around, Randall Eugene told himself, no matter how much good it would do you to see the way Ricky is looking at you. Keep it inside yourself, let it stay there to look at later, don't waver in what you're doing, hold it together. Cowboy up.

"You little punk-ass motherfucker," the man with the saddlebags full of the Boss's money said, "what the fuck do you think you're doing? Hand me that piece, and sit your skinny ass back down in that chair."

"It's not a piece, partner," Randall Eugene said and shot Earl Winston in the chest. "It's a firearm, see. You're supposed to call a thing what it is. Always."

Earl let the black plastic garbage bag slide out of his hand, as he began to fall back against the door facing, lifting his hand to his chest and patting at the place where the .45 slug had entered, but he couldn't seem to find the right spot. He looked down at his shirt front as though by seeing it closer he'd be able to do a better job of locating where everything seemed to be happening all at once. The door facing stopped him from falling all the way back, letting him slide toward the floor where the black plastic bag had landed and tilted to one side as the stacks of bills inside it shifted.

Earl looked up at Randall Eugene, opening his mouth as though to say something, and that was neat, Randall Eugene thought as he saw it happening, but he didn't expect the outlaw to actually be able to make any statement as he died. If he had been more of a main character, sure, he could've said a few words, tried to brag or be the big man or something, maybe even confess to something he'd done, show he was sorry he had taken the hoot owl trail all those years ago. But, no, not this one, and Randall Eugene knew if he himself didn't speak up fast, the moment to sum up the meaning of the misdeeds Earl had done would slip away unremarked.

"See, partner," Randall Eugene said, loud enough for Ricky to hear him from where he stood in the shadows, "if you don't call a thing by the handle that belongs to it, you'll never know what's true and what's a lie."

Probably Earl didn't hear all of that, judging by the way his eyes were all rolled back in his head, showing only their whites now, and he was so relaxed looking that whatever was inside of him had shifted to the side just like the money in the saddlebags had done. Everything lying on the floor was on its own now, nothing was controlled by anything outside of itself, and that included Earl with all that blood running down the front of his shirt, onto his pants, and soaking into the carpet of the anteroom of the house belonging to the Big Corral outfit.

It made no real difference, though, Earl not hearing all of what Randall Eugene had said because he was too busy dying. Randall Eugene knew that Ricky Nelson had heard it and that later on they'd talk about it, somewhere by themselves as they stared into the embers of a fire before they threw the dregs from their cups of coffee into the ashes right before bunking down.

He couldn't hear Ricky saying anything right now, though somebody was talking, yelling really, and Randall Eugene wished whoever it was would shut up so he could hear what Ricky had to say if he decided to talk at all now.

"It wasn't me," the voice was saying. "I just been sitting here praying and waiting for y'all to leave. I didn't have a thing to do with it."

Randall Eugene had heard the voice before, he knew he had, and he was just about ready to say the name his brain was fixing to furnish him, when Ricky Nelson spoke behind him. "Colorado," he said, his voice low but carrying well from the shadows in the corner of the room. "The half-breed. Keep an eye out for him."

What would I do without my partner, Randall Eugene said to himself as he dropped to one knee and moved to take cover. Later on when we got time, we'll laugh about him having to tell me to watch out for the Indian, Ricky and me will. He'll give me a real hoorawing about being a tenderfoot, and I'll act like I'm sulling up about it. I really won't be, naturally, but you got to play along and do the way you're supposed to act around a bunch of cowboys. Everybody knows you're just putting on a show, but that's part of the fun of it, a way of knowing they'll never let you get a big head, but they'll all be right there with you if you get into a scrape. And you're going to get into that. They ain't no doubt about it. It's a hard country and a hard life and a hard bed at night, and that's why having a partner like Colorado means so much to a cowboy.

But don't talk about that to him, Randall Eugene told himself as he leveled the sights of the .45 at a point on the open door about the height of where a big Indian's head would be if it appeared in the opening. When you talk and talk and talk about a thing that makes you feel a certain way, good or bad, the way I used to with the Bones Family standing on a street somewhere when I was somebody not me, it kills it. The more talk about what you think about a thing, the less you really think about it and the more it all seems to bleed out and die.

Ricky just sat there in that sheriff's office and didn't say a word to John Wayne when he asked him if he could help out with all the Clantons coming to get the young one, the wild drunk one of the bunch, out of the cell. He didn't even nod, Ricky didn't, he just lifted the shotgun up a few inches to show he'd heard what John Wayne had asked him, and when he did that, old Walter Brennan just cackled like he always would do. Then he said something like, "Colorado ain't got nothing to say. I reckon he'll let that shotgun do his palavering."

Those words were not exactly the ones Walter Brennan used, Randall Eugene knew, and he felt the real ones somewhere just out of his reach, and he lifted the hand that wasn't holding the .45 automatic as though to touch something floating past his eyes in a slow drift, something like a dandelion thistle. That was when the Indian's head showed for just an instant in the open door, and the breeze took the dandelion thistle just past Randall Eugene's eye close enough to affect his aim. The slug from the .45 must have hit the metal door facing and ricocheted because instead of falling down the Indian jerked his head back, and paint flecks and dust jumped up into the air of the room and someone was yelling about Jesus and making crying noises.

"Don't let it bother you one bit, Colorado," Ricky said to Randall Eugene from behind. "I wish I had me two bits for every time I've missed what I drawed down on."

"I wasn't watching what I was doing," Randall Eugene said. "That big buck Indian was going to be hard to hit, and I ought to've been allowing for that."

"You'll get another chance," Ricky Nelson said. "I guarantee you that, Colorado. And you'll be ready next time, too. You'll put one right between his eyes."

"Son, son," the Range Foreman was saying. "All you're going to do is get us both killed. Lay down that gun and beg these fellows to let us live. Use your goddamn head, boy. Quit that jabbering to yourself, please, son, and listen to me."

I'm not going to answer him when he talks like that, Randall Eugene thought. If I don't make any sign I'm recognizing what kind of a fool he's making of himself, he won't have to try to explain it to me and Ricky later and we won't have to say anything back to the Range Foreman. Ricky won't listen to him anyway. He'll just turn away and look way off across the prairie toward where the mountains begin. Sangre de Christo, that's what they're called, those mountains. That means blood of Christ.

29

The good-looking Hispanic woman taped to the kitchen chair had started to cry as soon as J.W. Ragsdale broke out the small window next to the door lock and stuck his hand through to turn the deadbolt. She turned her eyes on him, beginning to roll them around as though trying to tell him something, stretching her jaw beneath the duct tape across her mouth as though she was trying to warn him about whatever it was that was causing her to toss her head around and jerk it to the right in a gesture directing attention over her shoulder. Shit, J.W. thought, you trying way too hard, child.

When he reached her and began to pull the tape away from her mouth, the woman dropped her chin toward her chest, groaning as though the removal of the silver tape across her lips was costing her dearly.

"I can breathe now," she said, closing her eyes into a tight grimace as she sobbed out the words. "I thought I was going to choke to death."

"Couldn't draw in no air, huh?" J.W. said. "I guess you're a mouth breather, like I am half the time. It helps if you throw your head back. That way you get yourself a clear passage through all your pipes. Where is everybody? Where's the plumber?"

"The plumber?" the woman said, relaxing her face and opening her eyes, as dry as he figured they'd be despite all her groaning, J.W. noted. "Who?"

"The one that taped you to your chair," J.W. said. "He didn't know what he was doing, did he? Looks like he forgot to snug things up nice and tight here."

"It wasn't no plumber," the woman said. "It was some men I never seen before, sir. I don't know nothing about them."

"Are they all in the house still? How many of them's here?"

"I don't know. Four, maybe. They must be upstairs where Mr. Jimbo works, him and the boy."

"What boy?"

"El muchacho negro," the woman said. "I don't know his name. Mr. Jimbo didn't tell me. I been cooking lunch for him and the boy. That's what I was doing when the men come in here and abused me like you see here."

"Don't start up that crying again," J.W. said. "I ain't got time for you to get it going right. A black boy, you say. How old is he?"

"I don't know. He was wearing a cowboy sombrero too big for him. He's new to here. He's pretty little, but he looks grown. That's all I noticed."

"I got to go let a man in the house," J.W. said. "You can get up if you want to, but after you do, I think you ought to go on outside and sit in the shade. It's hot out there."

"You not going to take off these tapes?" the woman said, lifting her hands up and letting her head fall back toward the chair, her eyes closing. Damn, that is a nice curve her throat makes when she does that, J.W. thought. Looks like a picture you'd see hanging up in the Brooks Museum of a Mexican beauty about to do some business with her boyfriend. Her amigo.

"I ain't got time to play out this scene just the way you want it done, senorita," J.W. said. "I couldn't do it any real justice. I ain't got the right dramatic training for it. You going to have to do what you think you have to do to close it out on your own. Just don't make any noise doing it, and everything'll be jake."

Tyrone had stopped hammering on the door before J.W. got to it to let him in, but that was no real advantage, J.W. considered. It would probably work better if he'd kept on doing it. That way the four or six or two or whatever number of people it was upstairs would think nobody had gained entrance yet, and they might not be moving around much.

Passing through a hall off the kitchen, J.W. could see the foot of a wide set of stairs and a landing halfway up. Being where he was at the bottom of the stairs was like sitting in the stands at a baseball game on the third base side. Everything is going to be coming toward you, he considered, from first and second base and down those stairs. You just had to wait for the first hard hit ball to get through the infield by the shortstop, and then all hell would start breaking loose.

"Tyrone," J.W. said, opening the front door to Jimbo Reynolds's house and finding his partner standing to the side with his Glock 9 out and ready, "I believe we may have a situation here at the ranch. Better call for them to send some back-up."

"How quick is stuff going to happen?" Tyrone said, then both of them hearing the deep cough of a .45 come from upstairs. "Oh, that quick, huh?"

"Shit," J.W. said. "We probably going to have to do all this by ourselves. They ain't going to get here fast enough to pitch in and help."

"The cavalry always shows up at the ranch in time, partner," Tyrone said, thumbing his cell phone. "You seen enough John Wayne flicks to know that."

"I always go to sleep before they get there, though," J.W. said. "Every fucking time."

"That was a heavy round," Tyrone said, the last word he said immediately followed by the sound of another shot from upstairs.

"So was that one," J.W. said. "It sure ain't no .22."

"They got to come downstairs," Tyrone said, looking about him at the configuration of the entrance hall, "unless they decide to jump out a window."

"They'll be coming sooner rather than later, what's left of them, don't you reckon? Who's popping a cap on who's is what's going to decide it."

"There is a disagreement going on, all right, among some parties," Tyrone said. "What did that good-looking woman in the kitchen tell you?"

"She didn't tell me shit, Tyrone. She's in on it somehow. Sitting there with tape no tighter on her than I wear my house shoes. Said there there was four men up there that did her so nasty and taped her all up like that. I reckon they're here to make the preacher and our Bones claimer cough up the church proceeds or the deed to the ranch or the horses and cattle or something."

"She said the kid was here?"

"Yeah, she did. Dressed up like a cowboy, big hat and everything, she said. Chaps, boots, you name it."

"And she's part of it, you're saying, this ranch invasion."

"I wouldn't believe a word said by anybody tied up loose the way she was," J.W. said. "She let them in, the way I figure it, but butter wouldn't melt in her mouth how she's telling it."

"Quit talking about her mouth, J.W.," Tyrone said as he moved from one side to the other of the bottom of the staircase, looking up at the landing that led to where the gunshots had come from. "I'm trying to work here."

"You suppose they finished doing whoever they're doing?"

"If they have, they'll be coming down here directly," Tyrone said. "From what you say about what the Mexican lady told you, these boys will know their window of opportunity is closing fast. They ain't going to wait around to see who else shows up at their party before they leave. They'll be coming."

J.W. and Tyrone looked at each other. From the kitchen they could hear the sound of the door to the outside closing as the woman left the house. J.W. spoke first. "I'm going to do it," he said. "You get to be hindcatcher this time."

"You sure your knees'll still let you climb stairs, J.W.?" Tyrone said. "Old as they are?"

"I ain't seen no elevator to the top, much as I'd prefer a ride," J.W. said. "I'll see what I can sneak up on."

"Keep your head down, Old Folks."

"Yessir, Boss," J.W. said and headed for the stairs.

Fulgencia had just started for the street, walking beside the driveway behind the row of ornamentals and thinking she should stay on the cement but she couldn't seem to make her feet go that direction, they would not do it—when she saw the gray-green VW Phaeton pull over and stop. Then when that happened, her feet suddenly let her change the way she was going, her sandals making a slapping sound as she ran down the driveway.

"What's going on?" Don Condon said, standing outside the car now, still between the opened door and the Phaeton itself. "You're not inside the house like we said."

"No, I'm not inside. They're killing people upstairs. And the cops have already got here, two of them."

"Killing people? How do you know? Are they doing Reynolds?

"I don't know who they're doing, but I heard the shots. Open this goddamn door."

"Did you get the money?" Condon said, hitting a switch which let

Fulgencia open the door and climb into the car. "Did you get any of it?"

"No, I didn't get the fucking money. I got what you see. Let's go."

"You didn't get the money, that's what you're saying. That's what you're telling me."

"It went all wrong, chinga," Fulgencia said. "It all went wrong. It was that damn kid, I just know it."

"Randall Eugene?"

"El muchacho negro," Fulgencia said, leaning forward in her seat as though she intended to crawl up on the dashboard and was trying to figure out a way how to begin doing it. "I knew he was bad medicine as soon as I saw him. Muy malo, the little bastard."

"Does Jimbo know what's going on?" Don Condon said, putting the Phaeton into gear and beginning to move toward the end of the circle on which the headquarters of the Big Corral was located. "What're we going to do?"

"I don't know what the preacher knows. He may be dead by now. But I know one thing."

"What?"

"You're taking me to Little Rock today. Now ."

"Why?" Don Condon said.

"So I can get public transportation out of this fucking country, and I can't do it in Memphis without them knowing it. That s why."

"Oh, Sugar, no," Don Condon said, looking at Fulgencia. "No."

"Sugar, my ass," Fulgencia said. "Move this fucker."

In his Moroccan leather chair in the anteroom to the counting chamber, Jimbo Reynolds was imagining himself suddenly able by an act of will to shrink his body into an exact copy of itself, reduced in scale by at least ten to one. That way his wrist would instantly slip out of the cuffs which held him, and he could then force himself to crawl back into the shelter of the chair arm and be out of sight.

No. That wasn't good enough. Let's say twenty to one, that would be twice as good, twice as small, little enough that Jimbo could actually crawl into the space between the seat cushion and the back of the chair, slide down into the crack and be completely hidden from view.

That way, the redneck misfits in the counting room and the Indian

205

chief who ran them would forget all about him and focus on the crazy colored kid and the hole he'd put in the chest of the one leaning up against the door facing. Jimbo could see that he was still leaking, that faraway and long-ago look on his face they always get when it happens, but the pumping action had stopped, so that meant he was likely meeting his maker on the other side, even as we speak. If I was front of a congregation, Jimbo thought, I could be talking about the divine act of judgment working right now at the Gates of Paradise, as the angelic guards listen to him whine and beg before they get ready to kick his redneck ass to where he belongs in Hell.

But, shit, I'm not, and that crazy kid is rolling his eyes and jabbering nonsense into the air about Colorado and somebody named Ricky, and that Indian-looking bastard is about to come out of that door blazing away at everybody he sees. Oh, Lord, bless my tongue with eloquence now in the hour of Thy servant's need, and let the arrows of Thy enemy fall harmless against the breastplates of Thy righteousness.

And, oh, Jesus, Gentle Savior, make me real little and hard to hit.

"Son," Jimbo Reynolds said to the colored punk with the .45 automatic hanging from his right hand, "put down your weapon, and tell these folks you're ready to call it quits. Let them know you're sorry for what you've done to their departed comrade and that you'll stop shooting at them. Please, son. Think of your sweet mother. You're breaking her heart, son."

Jimbo stopped to think of what else he might say to influence the maniac before him, listening at the same time for any sounds coming from the scum in the counting room and pulling at the cuff fastening him to the chair arm. Goddamn a chair made so sturdy you couldn't break the arm loose from the back of it. What had the bastards made it of? Stainless steel?

"Range Foreman," the kid said, smiling as he spoke. Smiling, goddamn it to Hell. Smiling. "Me and Colorado believe you might be onto something there. I told him when the real nut-cutting started that you'd cowboy up."

"Cowboy up?" Jimbo said, feeling something beginning to happen at the back of his throat, something fighting to break loose from deep inside his chest and belly, something connected with a whole shitload of

trail songs and western clothes and boots and word pictures of sunsets and herds of cattle grazing on purple hills. "What the fuck are you talking about, you crazy little shit? You're going to get me killed here in a minute."

"Range Foreman," the kid said, that smile stuck on his face like a tattoo, "let's get this chore done for the Boss. Listen now to what Colorado's saying."

"Lord," Jimbo said, giving up all notions of persuading the punk-ass little fucker to let the rednecks come out of the counting room and kill him and leave Jimbo alone, "I know I've fallen short. I have sinned against the light. But give me one more chance. I'll work with the homeless. I'll comfort the sick. I'll get politically involved on the grassroots level. You name it, Jesus, Sweet Infant Child of God, and I'll do it, I swear I will. I shit you not, Lord."

"That's what I'm talking about, Colorado," the kid said, looking behind him into an empty corner of the anteroom. "See, I told you. He's fixing to cowboy up."

"What're you looking at?" Jimbo said, leaning forward to see where the crazed punk kid was focused, his voice crawling higher in his throat. "There's not anybody there. There ain't nobody in this room but you and me and the man you killed."

"Oh, sure, there is, Range Foreman," the kid said. "Ricky is here, and Jesus is here, and the Boss is always here. All we got to do is tend to our chores with everybody pitching in, and things'll turn out fine. Cowboy up, Range Foreman."

"Don't leave me out of the picture, Randall Eugene," someone said. "I'm right here with you, too."

The first question coming to Jimbo's mind was whether this new one was a look-out who had been staying downstairs and was now showing up because he has heard the shooting. All he could see of the man was his head as he looked around the half-wall separating the anteroom from the hall. That and the weapon he held in his right hand pointed toward the floor, some kind of automatic it appeared to be, like the one the crazy colored kid had killed the first redneck with. He wasn't dressed as well as the rest of the bunch was, and he seemed a lot less in a hurry than they were, except for the Indian misfit in charge. What this new one had just said had been delivered in a low voice, flat and uninterested in the words he was speaking. He sounded bored to Jimbo, in fact.

Oh, Jesus, this one is the stone killer of the bunch. He would drop a man without even getting his pulse rate up. Look at his fucking eyes. Pale and washed-out and not an ounce of compassion or humanity in them. Sweet Infant Child of God, hold my hand in Thine.

"Sir," Jimbo said, "I had nothing to do with the slaughter of this poor fellow beside me. I witnessed what happened to him, and I have been praying every second as a minister of the Gospel of our Lord Jesus Christ for the eternal salvation of his soul. That little murdering bastard there in the cowboy duds shot him down just as cold-blooded as an Arab terrorist."

"Yeah," the pale-eyed man standing halfway behind the wall said. "Didn't take Randall Eugene but the one shot, neither, did it? He bored that fucker right through the pump. But cut the shit, preacher, and tell me something."

"What?" Jimbo said, thinking shit it's going to be worse than I thought. You believe you've imagined the worst that can happen, and then you find out that cancer ain't a consideration for what's turning up next. "What?"

"That door there to that room. What's it made out of?"

"Steel, tempered steel," Jimbo said. "That's my safe room. Nothing can get in there."

"That means no other way out, then, I reckon," J.W. Ragsdale said. "They'll be coming out of there in a minute or two. What do you think, Randall Eugene? We going to be able to reason with them or are they ready to sell all the way out?"

"My name is Colorado," Randall Eugene said and then moved his head in a gesture directed behind him. "My partner over yonder is Ricky Nelson."

"That right?" J. W. said. "The traveling man himself, huh? I ain't seen Ricky since he was in Tom Lea Park must've been twenty years ago. He was wearing a pink sportcoat, hot as it was that day. He was looking good."

"He's in the clothes he wore in Rio Bravo today," Randall Eugene said. "Have you seen that one?"

"Not in a long time. John Wayne and Walter Brennan in it with Ricky?"

"That's the one," Randall Eugene said, then turning to look behind it. "He remembers you in that one, Ricky."

"He had a shotgun," J.W. said, "laying across his lap there in the jailhouse."

"Yeah, that's right."

In his Moroccan leather chair, Jimbo Reynolds let his wrist relax in the cuff holding him in place and dropped his head. Thy will be done, Father, he prayed. Both these fuckers are crazy, and my life is in Your hands. There is no help in this world. But Lord, please do consider letting this cup pass from me.

"Thing we got to do, Colorado," J.W. said, "is take up good positions so when they come out we do the surprising. How many are in that room? Three, I reckon, not counting this one."

"Two white men and the big Indian. I think he might be a half-breed renegade."

"Worst kind," J.W. said. "Name wouldn't be Tonto, would it?"

"Yeah, that's it, partner," Randall Eugene said. "How'd you know?"

"I've had some dealings with him, me and my partner have."

"It's good to have a partner," Randall Eugene said. "I never had one before Ricky. What's your partner's handle?"

"Tyrone Walker."

"He's a brother, then."

"Yeah, he is," J.W. said. "A Memphis style brother, and he acts like a real one sometimes, too. The knucklehead."

"Ricky liked what you just said," Randall Eugene said. "Hear him laughing?"

"Yeah, I guess I do, but I'll tell y'all what. Don't you let on to Tyrone Walker I called him a knucklehead behind his back. He's liable to take that serious."

"Ricky's really laughing now," Randall Eugene said. "Just listen at my partner."

Inside the counting room, Bob Ferry stood with his ear up against the steel door, trying to hold his breath to listen. The problem he was having was with his heart rate and respiration, and all he could pick up was the sound of their function, sucking in air and hammering away as though his lungs were about to break through the wall of his chest cavity.

"Stand away from that fucking door," Coy Bridges was saying. "Unless you want to get in the way of my nine. I'm fixing to punch me some holes in some motherfuckers."

"You're not going to do shit shooting at the door, Coy," Tonto said. "All we'll get out of that in here is ricochets."

"That door ain't wood?" Coy said. "Let me try it and see."

Tonto didn't bother to answer, reaching instead into his pocket for a cigarette and lighting up. At the first whiff of smoke, the ventilating system in the ceiling of Jimbo Reynolds's counting room kicked on, making it even harder for Bob Ferry to listen for sounds on the other side of the steel door.

"What're we going to do, then?" Coy Bridges said. "Just sit here and wait that jig cowboy out?"

"He's not the one to worry about," Bob Ferry said. "Is he, Tonto?"

"Nope, he's not," Tonto said, taking one more puff and stubbing his cigarette out on a table next to him, one still covered with stacks of bills. "They'll be here in a couple of minutes, if they're not outside there already."

"Who?" Coy Bridges said. "You don't mean Memphis cops, do you?"

"Duh," Bob Ferry said, stepping back from the door and shaking his hands before him as though they were wet and he couldn't find a towel to dry them.

Taking a quick step to put himself in range, Coy Bridges slapped Bob Ferry on the left side of his head with the flat of the Sig Sauer, not getting a lot into it but enough to cause Bob to drop to his knees.

"Shit," Bob said, holding his head with both hands and looking up at Coy. "Why'd you do that?"

"Because I been wanting to ever since I first laid eyes on your candy ass," Coy said. "And you know what? It felt even better than I thought it was going to."

"Get up, Bob," Tonto Batiste said, "and get the fuck out of the way. Coy, you swing that door open when I tell you. I'm going out first, and I'm going to be as low to the floor as I can make it. You come right behind me, and don't get excited and shoot me in the back, motherfucker. You do, and I swear I'll gut you if it's the last thing I do."

"No," Bob Ferry said, up now and propping himself on the edge of the heavy oak table where the cigarette butt was still smoking. "All we got to do is stay where we are, and when the cops get here they won't let that kid shoot any more of us."

"One thing you don't seem to understand, Bob," Tonto Batiste said. "I'm not going back inside again. I'm not waiting another minute to get through that door. Get ready, Coy."

"Wait," Bob Ferry said, taking his hand away from the side of his head and looking with surprise at the blood covering his palm. "We won't have to do that much time in Tennessee. It's still just a home invasion. Use your head, Tonto."

"Coy," Tonto said. "Shoot this motherfucker."

Coy did, twice in the face, then stepped over Bob Ferry where he'd fallen, and put his hand on the door handle.

"Now?" he said.

30

In the anteroom, Randall Eugene could feel the time coming, it was on the way, and he took a deep breath to steady himself, being careful not to let Colorado see him show any signs of nerves now that it was getting here. Hoss, he said to himself deep inside his head where nobody but him could hear, it's coming like a blue norther working its way across the plains. Nobody can see it yet, but the cattle can feel a storm coming before any man is able to know it, and they're restless and milling around and showing signs of wanting to run, maybe even stampede. You know your job, you've rode the range before, there ain't nothing or nobody but you that can do the job. It's about time. The hemming and hawing and bullshitting's over. You got it to do, hoss. You fixing to have to cowboy up.

Colorado's got your back, though, and you know that, and if he doesn't have to lift a hand to help you do what you got to do, that doesn't mean he wouldn't when the nut cutting starts. He ain't going to leave you on your own. Colorado ain't built that way, but he doesn't have to say that to you. He's there, he's your partner, and you feel it down to the bone without a bunch of palavering about it.

The old cowpoke who's just showed up is right there, too. You don't know where he's come from, and you ain't going to ask him that. If there's a reason to tell you that, he'll tell you. But he's like Colorado. He ain't going to waste time talking and bragging and strutting and explaining what he's liable to do. He'll just do it when the time comes, and there won't have to be no talk, no words, no posing and styling and putting somebody else down to make himself look big.

He's long in the tooth, and he's dressed wrong, and he acts like he doesn't give a shit about anything, but all that that means is that he's still around after all the years that put the traildust on him and the lines in his face and the gray in his hair. The old dude has made it to where he is right now by knowing when to act and when not to, and Randall Eugene could feel the respect for the old cowpoke rising in him as he looked over at him out of the corner of his eye.

Later, after the storm has come and gone and the cattle have settled down again, we'll all sit around with each other, me and Colorado and the old cowpoke, and we won't have to say much about what took place and how it got that way. We'll hooraw each other some, I imagine, and we'll look into the fire at the shapes the flames are making, and we'll know we depended on each other without having to ask for a hand or justify why we need it. It'll have been there, and that's all we'll need to know, and we won't have to spend a bunch of words on it and waste breath doing it. We can put out the fire, call in the dogs, go to sleep, and not dream about anything.

The old cowpoke was saying something now, and Randall Eugene leaned his head toward him to let him know he was listening. No reason to say anything. Ricky Nelson wasn't saying anything, but that didn't mean he wasn't there in the corner of the room, the shotgun laid across his lap and him ready to do whatever he would have to when the time came.

The Range Foreman, though, seemed to have gone to sleep, his head dropped to his chest and his eyes closed. He was talking to himself or maybe to the Boss, but he wasn't looking up to do it. He wasn't meeting anybody's eyes.

"Colorado," the old cowboy said. "I need to ask you to do something for me. I hate to, but I don't see no way around it."

"What's that, partner?" Randall Eugene said, hearing Ricky move a little where he was sitting in the shadows. He wanted to hear what the old boy had to say, too, but he sure wasn't going to waste any words letting people know about it. "What you need?"

"Well, here's what it is. I expect that bunch in that room there is going to be coming out here in a minute or two, and I don't how they'll be doing it or what they're minded to do. If you know what I mean."

"I believe I do," Randall Eugene said.

"My partner I told you about, Tyrone Walker, is downstairs there waiting, and he needs to be told what's going on. I'd like to ask you to go down there and let him know what's going on and what I just told you."

"I'd purely like to help you out, but if I leave now, that outfit is liable to come out with just you and Ricky to face them," Randall Eugene said. "I don't want to leave you shorthanded. I don't expect the Range

213

Foreman's going to be any help, even if he wasn't hogtied to that chair. He's acting real discouraged."

"I appreciate that. I see what you're saying, but Tyrone's got to be told what's happening, don't you see. A man doesn't want to leave his partner in the dark, you understand."

"I savvy," Randall Eugene said. "But I'm sort of between a rock and a hard place. I don't want to leave Ricky outgunned here."

"Yeah," the old cowboy said. "I wonder what Ricky thinks. Why don't we ask him?"

"We don't need to ask him. He's been listening to everything we been saying. He don't talk a lot, but he don't miss nothing going on. If he's got anything to say, he'll tell us," Randall Eugene said. Then, "Won't you, Ricky?" Waiting then to hear what Ricky would come back at him with.

"All right then," the old boy said. "What's Ricky say?"

Randall Eugene couldn't keep from laughing a little, not loud or long, but the way Ricky Nelson put it struck him as funny.

"I'll tell you," Randall Eugene said. "Ricky says to go on and help you out, but be sure not to make the same mistake this fool lying over yonder against the wall did. Ricky says to me not to lay my firearm down and wander off without my tools."

"That makes sense all right, but you know what?"

"What's that, old timer?"

"If you go down there with that weapon in your hand, my partner might mistake you for somebody he ought to be shooting at. Tyrone, see, is kind of on a hair trigger when he sees somebody coming up to him strapped."

"Strapped," Randall Eugene said. "I despise that kind of language. It's a trashy way of talking."

"I'm with you on that. I just get lazy in the way I express my ideas sometime. I ought to watch closer how I talk. What do you say, though? Ready to do what Ricky says and help me out?"

"I tell you, friend," Randall Eugene said. "I don't question what Ricky Nelson tells me to do. He is the original Colorado."

"That's my way of thinking, too," the old cowboy said. "But I tell you what, Colorado. Why don't you just let me hold your weapon for you while you go down and talk to Tyrone Walker. You know, fill him in on what's fixing to come down up here. I'll keep it ready for you."

"All right," Randall Eugene said, beginning to hand the .45 butt first to J.W. Ragsdale. "I rather you call it a firearm, though, not a weapon. It ain't nothing but a tool to a cowboy, same as a saddle or a set of spurs. He don't set no special store by it."

"Firearm, right, I got you," J.W. said, taking the handgun and sliding it under the armchair he was crouched behind. "See where I'm putting it? When Tyrone sends you back up here, you can just reach up underneath here and pick it up."

If he will just go on and get down the goddamn stairs, J.W. said to himself, crazy as he is, he'll say enough to Tyrone for him to key in a call for some help, maybe change the odds a little bit in our favor. Otherwise, it's fixing to smell more like a shooting gallery in here in a minute or two than it does already.

"Preacher," J.W. said, watching the brim of the kid's hat vanish as he moved down the stairs and thinking that Tyrone would have him laid down on his face and trussed up like a Christmas present in no time at all now. "Yo, man of the cloth, cowboy. Tune in here and listen at me."

"I have put aside childish things," the man handcuffed to the overstuffed leather chair said. "It's not in my hands anymore. I give it up to the Lord God of Hosts. Let him sort through the works of man, separating the wheat from the chaff."

"Tell that to Ricky Nelson. He probably got the time to listen," J.W. said. "I want you to tumble that chair over and get down under it the best way you can. It's fixing to be a shit-storm here in a minute, and I don't see no bulletproof umbrella over your head."

"Bullets?" Jimbo Reynolds said, "Ain't there been enough shooting off of guns in my house? It's already one thief lying here shot all to pieces. Oh Sweet Jesus, Infant Child of God. Don't let them harm me, Savior."

Doing what he was told, Jimbo tipped his chair up on two legs and began a slow tumble to his right, groaning as he followed the piece of furniture in its arc. When he hit the floor, air forced its way through his throat and mouth with a sound which put J.W. in mind of a large shoat in its last tumble at slaughtering time in North Mississippi. He didn't have time to dwell on the details of the memory teased up by Jimbo's expulsion of breath, though, because at the same instant it arrived J.W. heard two shots come from behind the steel door closing off the counting room of the Big Corral. Muffled and close enough together to be almost one though they were, the reports were unmistakably nine millimeter.

Wait long enough and maybe they'll all kill each other, he told himself, moving to a little better angle with reference to the door beyond which the shots had come. Yeah, and maybe Ricky Nelson will pitch on in from behind me with that double barrel ten gauge and take out the first fucker coming through that door, too.

Not likely, J.W. thought bitterly, either possibility. And just when I do a favor for that little cowboy-nut kid and send him out of the line of fire to save to put in jail later, here comes the time when I'd love to see him blasting away with that .45 at anything that moves.

The preacher on the floor was scuffling to get as much of himself under the upended chair as possible, and he had set up a steady mooing as he worked at the job, alternating that sound with pleas for mercy to his own personal Savior, reminding the deity that He had an obligation to fulfill his promises to Jimbo Reynolds.

"You said You would, Jesus," Jimbo said. "You know You did. You are bound to Your promise, Sweet Infant Child of God, bound by hoops of steel. There is no way to void the reconciliation and the covenant of blood."

If he doesn't shut the fuck up in the next minute, J.W. made his own promise to himself, I'll save that bunch the trouble and shoot this fucker myself. That would be the easy way and it would be wrong, as Dick Nixon always used to say, but I could live with it.

Jimbo Reynolds fell silent for a space, probably thinking up new arguments to make Jesus realize He couldn't weasel out of the contract He'd made with the leader of the Big Corral all those years ago. Once saved, always saved, J.W. thought as he focused on the handle on the steel door and reminded himself not to hold his breath as he aimed and the tastefully painted door of Jimbo Reynolds's counting room jumped back from its facing as though a charge of dynamite had just knocked it loose from its lock and back into the room it guarded.

The big Indian, identified by Tyrone Walker as Tonto Batiste that early morning in the International House of Pancakes, was the first man through and out of the door, coming low, straight, and hard like a linebacker blitzing a quarterback who hadn't expected it and was about to have the ball crammed down his throat before he could get rid of it. Look, I ain't got it, why you picking on me, shit, there's the man you ought to be mad at, all that alibi running through his head and announced in his eyes in the instant before the wrong-colored helmet would take him in the throat.

The Indian was holding the Glock 9 in both hands, the conventional grip for doing straight-up business, as he came through the door, but something on the hardwood floor of Jimbo's anteroom caused his left foot to slip, only a little, but enough to make him drop his left hand to the floor, bent as low as he was, and he dipped to that side.

"Police," J.W. said, loud enough for a man to hear if he was listening for it, thinking, Ricky I wish you would put a load of buckshot in this motherfucker, and then squeezed off two rounds. The first one missed completely, because of the slippage Tonto had suffered, and took out a China lamp with its base in the shape of a lamb being watched by a smiling shepherd with a crook in his hand. The second slug hit high on the Indian's left bicep, blooming like a flower and turning him in his charge a bit toward J.W.'s right, enough so that the Indian saw who'd just shot him from behind the overturned chair.

Somebody was screaming in a loud voice, and J.W. wondered if it was himself, wishing if it was that he'd be at least a little less high-pitched than what he was hearing. The Indian began to pull the Glock around in the direction from which he'd been shot, his eyes now fixed on J.W., and it was happening slowly as it always does when you see the hit coming and are waiting for it, J.W. thought, wondering that he had time to think about what was happening so fast that if you watched it on tape you wouldn't be able to believe it had even taken place at all it was so quick and over and done with, and J.W. shot Tonto Batiste in the throat and just beneath the left eye, both wounds simple black holes still with nothing liquid showing yet, but causing Tonto to get a thoughtful look on his face as though he'd stopped seeing any further than a foot in front of him and he was trying to understand why everything was getting so close up to him and why his focus was sharp only when he brought his field of vision to a point just at the tip of his nose, and then that stopped working, too.

Tonto heard a bird call outside somewhere, and he was walking through the kitchen of the government reservation house to try to see what kind it was, a cardinal maybe or a mockingbird doing a good job of imitating a cardinal, but his mother told him to go to bed now, there still wasn't anything to eat, and he did that, and felt the pillow against his face, rough and then smooth, and then nothing because he was asleep and he knew he needed that: a long, deep nap that would last him.

"Put that weapon down," J.W. Ragsdale said to the man standing in the doorway with his hands up before his face, a Sig Sauer in the right one, turned so that the flat of it was toward the direction he was facing and the other hand palm out, clear enough in the light of the anteroom for J.W. to see its creases. How long's his lifeline, J.W. wondered, and then, "I'm on a roll here, friend. Do it or it's still rock and roll time in Memphis."

"I'm through," Coy Bridges said. "I'm putting it down. Don't cut down on me, officer."

"Are they all dead?" Jimbo Reynolds said, peeking from beneath the overturned chair. "Is that all of them?"

"Well, preacher," J.W. said, moving to put cuffs on Coy Bridges who had laid his Sig Sauer on a sidetable, hit the floor face first, and put both hands behind his head. "I believe between me and Colorado and whoever offed the other shithead lying yonder on the floor, we've done all reached a state of peaceful equilibrium."

"Equilibrium?" Tyrone Walker said from where he was standing on the next-to-top step of the staircase, weapon in hand. "You been reading again, haven't you, J.W.? Have you joined some woman's book club when I wasn't looking?"

"You finally decided to come give me a hand once all the noise stopped, huh?" J.W. said. "I wish you would look at how nice this man is laying down yonder waiting to be restrained. I do believe he's had experience in his chosen line of work."

"I wanted to give you the opportunity to do something on your own, partner." Tyrone said. "But I was waiting in the wings case you fucked up and fell off your tricycle. You needn't've worried."

"Praise Jesus for the victory," Jimbo Reynolds said, standing almost all the way up now but for the wrist still fastened to the leg of the leather chair. "I prayed for the salvation of all of us, but I give Him the glory. Bless His sacred name."

"Praise Sergeant Ragsdale's nine is a better way to put it," Tyrone

Walker said. "That, and Randall Eugene McNeill's .45."

"Where is the young cowpuncher?" J.W. said. "I expect Ricky Nelson's worried about him."

"You didn't see Ricky go by you on his way down the stairs?" Tyrone said. "He's been down there carrying on a conversation with Randall Eugene for a couple of minutes now. Hear Colorado talking?"

"Ricky slipped by me, I reckon," J.W. said, "while I was tending to mine and your business up here, Tyrone. I didn't notice him, busy as I was in the middle of this Indian war."

"Who's Ricky Nelson?" Jimbo Reynolds said. "Who's Colorado? Where's that little colored boy that shot this poor fellow that's still bleeding all over my wall here?"

"You don't know much, do you, preacher?" Tyrone said.

"The preacher," J.W. Ragsdale said, "don't know shit."

31

They were coming now in large clots, three and four and five to the bunch, stepping in time to the music nearest them, some of them, while others listened to a tune originating farther off, matching their steps to that. A few made their way alone, heads held higher up than the ones bunched together, the music of the loners coming from their own portable CD players or in some cases from nowhere and anywhere, the nostrils of the loners flared as though they were smelling the vibrations in the air rather than hearing them in the late Monday afternoon funk of Memphis.

J.W. had pulled his chair around so that he was facing the front of the building rather than the expanse of Madison working its way into, within, through, of, and out of Overton Square. That way he could get away with not having to watch each and every freak tripping down the asphalt. People around him would let him know when to look, he figured, by their ooing and ahhing and carrying on, and he hated to feel like his head was on a swivel, anyway, subject to tracking everything passing within view. Restrict the view, he had learned somewhere back in Mississippi or on the Mekong or maybe it was here in Memphis sometime during the last fourteen years on the force. Restrict the view, narrow the sight, and improve the depth of what you're focusing on.

"Why ain't you looking at these fine young people, J.W.?" Tyrone Walker said. "Folks are going to start thinking you some kind of a misfit the way you're sitting there."

"I bet J.W.'s the kind of tourist when he gets to Destin he turns his back to the water and watches the pelicans flying over," Nova Hebert said. "A contrarian's what they call that. Marches to a different drummer."

"I call it perversity," Tyrone said. "Man trying so hard not to play the game he makes everybody think he is the game. He gets attention by acting like he hates and despises it."

"Y'all leave J.W. alone," Marvella Walker said. "I expect he's trying to rest his nerves after that busy Sunday afternoon y'all had yesterday."

"That, and get his head full of gin," Tyrone said. "See how much he can hammer down while they got that price per drink down where it belongs as these evening shadows are a falling."

"Tyrone wasn't all that busy," J.W. said, "yesterday in that big old house in the Nathan B. Forrest Estates. He wasn't doing nothing but talking to that little bitty cowboy brother while I was doing all the heavy lifting."

"Him and Ricky Nelson, you mean," Tyrone said. "Don't forget about the traveling man. I was with him, too."

"Poor little fool," Nova Hebert said.

"I was a fool, oh yeah," Marvella sang. "Uh huh, I was a fool, I was a fool, oh yeah."

"I thought any sister worth her salt wouldn't have paid no attention to Ricky Nelson," J.W. said. "You don't find a boy nowhere whiter than he was."

"That's what I'm talking about," Marvella said, stirring her red-colored drink with a swizzle stick bearing an image of the globe mounted with a large M. "Don't get me started now, J.W., thinking about the way Ricky Nelson looked."

"Speaking of which," Tyrone said, "there he goes now, ain't he?"

"Where?" J.W. said, twisting around in his chair. "Is he wearing that pink sport coat, with that flared up collar on the shirt underneath it?"

"He's over yonder walking along with Buddy Holly," Tyrone said. "See them holding hands?"

"Jesus Christ," J. W. said. "Why do they have to mess it up like that? Neither one of them boys was gay, was they?"

"Rock and roll began as an androgynous statement, Mississippi Boy," Nova Hebert said. "Everybody knows that now."

"Elvis," J.W. said. "He wasn't one, that's for shit sure."

"What you call a man wears eyeshadow?" Marvella said. "Tarzan?"

"I've heard that before," J.W. said. "I don't believe a word of it. Where would an old boy from Mississippi buy eyeshadow?"

"Any drugstore," Nova said. "Maybelline brand. That was the eye shade of choice back then."

"What time they going to start playing it?" J.W. said, thinking to change the subject before the women got well and truly wound up.

"Not until six o'clock That's when the Dewey Phillips Show used to come on. That's the witching hour." Nova looked down at her watch. "Nine more minutes."

"And then it'll be fifty years ago," Marvella said. "I of course wasn't born then."

"Shit, Marvella," J.W. said. "Neither me nor Tyrone was much more than babies then. How old do you think we are, anyway?"

"You as old as you act, J.W.," Marvella said. "That's how old."

"He's about sixty-five then," Tyrone said. "J.W. is. Where is that man with the drinks? Can't he tell I'm thirsty?"

"That little boy," Marvella said, "The rest of them I couldn't care less about. I can't help but keep thinking about him, though. His cowboy clothes and all. Boots. Everything all nice and new. His little hat."

"Do you suppose they'll let him wear his cowboy duds inside?" Nova said. "Looks like it wouldn't hurt anything to let him do that."

"If he's in Central State they won't care what he wears," Tyrone said. "You got to cater to psychos and nuts of every description to keep them calmed down some in that kind of institution. You get the right costume on one of them suckers, and lot of times he'll get just as gentle as a broke horse."

"Yeah," J.W. said. "Tyrone's right. See, a criminally insane crazy man, he just lives in his head. So anything you can do to accommodate that helps to keep him quiet."

"My," Marvella said. "Aren't you just impressed and amazed about how much these two Memphis detectives know about psychology, Nova? All these terms and everything. Goodness sakes."

"I don't know much about it from books," J.W. said, swung back around to face the building again, the crowd of paraders swelling behind him. "But I know what makes a nut tick. I seen enough of them."

"You say if they put him in Central State, Tyrone," Nova Hebert said. "They wouldn't do anything else with him, would they? He's obviously deeply disturbed and going to stay that way."

"There's disturbed, and there's disturbed," Tyrone Walker said. "See, if you don't act on your desires to eat your fellow man or consort with chickens or act like a cowboy just come to town with his sixguns a blazing, the law in Tennessee don't give a damn what you do. But if you start acting out your fantasies, killing old ladies and shooting people through the aorta and stuff like that, the State of Tennessee won't cut you much slack for being nuts. They'll slap your ass in a real prison where you ain't allowed to go western in your wardrobe."

"I predict Brushy Mountain and a nice set of matching gray pants and shirts for Randall Eugene McNeill," J.W. said. "It's a whole lot simpler to put him there than worrying about whether he meets the entrance requirements for Central State over yonder in Nashville. He'll have company wherever he ends up, though. The traveling man ain't about to desert Randall Eugene."

"I think I'm going to call him Colorado," Nova said. "Not Randall Eugene McNeill. No matter what school he gets into. That's the name he wants and the one he's earned."

"Look out yonder," Marvella said, "talking about earning a name. If that ain't Elvis Presley, I'll ride a motorcycle down this sidewalk backwards."

Everybody turned to look at where Marvella was pointing, J.W. rotating his chair all the way around to see. It was worth the trouble, he decided as soon as he saw the King surrounded by four attendants dressed all in black as they moved in step down Madison. The man at the center was an older Elvis, not yet gone completely to flesh, his eyes not covered by shades, no more than two rings per hand, and no sequins on the jumpsuit. In J.W.'s estimation, the Elvis moving before them was fixed in time just the wrong side of the date when the King had done the Singer Special attired in black leather and a deep tan, still alive from the neck down and unable to conceal that fact from the world.

"Who is that one?" Nova said. "Hot damn, he looks just like him. Y'all ever seen him before?"

"Yes, I have," J.W. said. "That there is Lance Lee, the best impersonator there ever was. I'm glad to see he's still around."

"Long as there's virtue in hair dye and girdles, I expect we'll keep on seeing him," Tyrone said.

"Naw," J.W. said. "He's a legend, Lance Lee is. He'll drop out of sight for two or three years at a time and then show up at something like this thing in Memphis today. Nobody knows where he's been staying in between. It's like he's been in a time capsule, Lance Lee has."

Gerald Duff

"A Global Moment in Time," Marvella said. "That's what we're witnessing, officers."

"You got that right," J.W. said, and then holding his hand up as though to quiet the multitudes, "Listen. It's starting up."

From every loud speaker on Madison Avenue in Midtown Memphis, from every radio and TV station in Memphis and the MidSouth, from every sound system in every car on every street, from the fringes of each crowd of parading impersonators of rock and roll singers to the middle of the space where they lived, truly and surely in their heads, came the first note of the tune that started it. All worshippers fell silent and all listened, and the nineteen-year-old truckdriver sang it in Memphis again, the way he did fifty years ago, from beginning to end, from the inside out, and the outside in.

"Damn," J.W. Ragsdale said as he sat in Memphis, Tennessee, whiskey working in him like a blessing on July the fifth, 2004, a global moment in time. "That's all right, mama, y'all. Let's have a drink."